P9-CJJ-315

Praise for E. J. Copperman's
Haunted Guesthouse Mysteries

Chance of a Ghost

"An enjoyable escape for any reader wanting to laugh and sympathize with a woman who succeeds by working with unreliable ghosts."   —*Lesa's Book Critiques*

"The writing is excellent with nonstop humor and clever and witty dialogue. . . . This is one of the best books in this delightfully charming series."   —*Dru's Book Musings*

"With an outstanding cast of characters, a well-plotted mystery and some sentimental reunions, this is a standout series."   —*The Mystery Reader*

"[An] entertaining mystery full of humor with absolutely charming and likable characters and a plot that flies at full speed. Copperman writes dialogue that bites with sharp wit but never sacrifices its heart."   —*Kings River Life Magazine*

Old Haunts

"Great fun with a tinge of salt air."   —*The Mystery Reader*

"An entertaining and spellbinding tale."
                                          —*The Mystery Gazette*

"I knew *Old Haunts* was gold before I finished reading the first page. . . . Not only is Alison's dry sense of humor and hilarious commentary on other characters enough to give the book ten stars, but even the ghosts and their former lives are written to perfection."   —*Fresh Fiction*

"An entertaining read that never disappoints . . . *Old Haunts* is like an old friend (or your snuggy blanket)—dependable, solid and just what you need it to be."   —*Night Owl Reviews*

continued . . .

An Uninvited Ghost

"A triumph . . . The humor is delightful . . . If you like ghost stories mixed with your mystery, try this Jersey Shore mystery." —*Lesa's Book Critiques*

"Funny and charming, with a mystery which has a satisfying resolution, and an engaging protagonist who is not easily daunted . . . Highly recommended."
—*Spinetingler Magazine*

"Each page brings a new surprise . . . This series is one to follow. Craftily written and enjoyable."
—*The Romance Readers Connection*

"There are several series out now featuring protagonists who can interact with ghosts. Some are good, but this one is the best I've read. . . . I look forward to Alison's next spooky adventure." —*Over My Dead Body*

"If you love a great mystery like I do, I highly recommend getting this book." —*Once Upon a Romance*

"A fun and entertaining read that I could not put down. It was that good . . . [A] charming and fabulous series."
—*Cozy Chicks*

Night of the Living Deed

"Witty, charming and magical." —*The Mystery Gazette*

"A fast-paced, enjoyable mystery with a wisecracking but no-nonsense, sensible heroine . . . Readers can expect good fun from start to finish." —*The Mystery Reader*

"A delightful ride . . . The plot is well developed, as are the characters, and the whole [story] is funny, charming and thoroughly enjoyable." —*Spinetingler Magazine*

The Thrill of
the Haunt

E. J. COPPERMAN

BERKLEY PRIME CRIME, NEW YORK

THE BERKLEY PUBLISHING GROUP
Published by the Penguin Group
Penguin Group (USA) LLC
375 Hudson Street, New York, New York 10014

USA • Canada • UK • Ireland • Australia • New Zealand • India • South Africa • China

penguin.com

A Penguin Random House Company

THE THRILL OF THE HAUNT

A Berkley Prime Crime Book / published by arrangement with the author

Berkley Prime Crime Books are published by The Berkley Publishing Group.
BERKLEY® PRIME CRIME and the PRIME CRIME logo are trademarks of
Penguin Group (USA) LLC.

For information, address: The Berkley Publishing Group,
a division of Penguin Group (USA) LLC,
375 Hudson Street, New York, New York 10014.

ISBN: 978-0-425-25239-0

PUBLISHING HISTORY
Berkley Prime Crime mass-market edition / November 2013

PRINTED IN THE UNITED STATES OF AMERICA

10 9 8 7 6 5 4 3 2 1

Cover illustration by Dominick Finelle.
Cover photos: *Flock of Birds* © Alexusss; *Painted Background* © iStockphoto/Thinkstock.
Cover design by Judith Lagerman.
Interior text design by Kristin del Rosario.

To Copper, who gave me a name.
Rest well. Good boy.

ACKNOWLEDGMENTS

The longer this series goes on, the more grateful I am to the cast of characters—off the page—who make it go. First and foremost among these is Shannon Jamieson Vazquez, whose editing and refusal to let me get away with *anything* is absolutely essential to each book. How she can catch my every indulgence and laziness and get me to fix them without making me resent her is a work of magic. Never let it be said that an author doesn't need an editor—it just isn't true.

As essential to the process is my long-suffering agent Josh Getzler and all at HSG Agency, as well as Christina Hogrebe of Jane Rotrosen Agency, who started this process back in the Stone Age. My hat would be off to you, if I wore a hat.

Special thanks to Cathy Genna, who lent me her name, and all booksellers everywhere; to Anna Boffice, who lent me her last name only; and to Tom and Libby Hill, who lent me their names without knowing it. Surprise!

Thank you as ever to Dominick Finelle, who makes the incredible covers for the Haunted Guesthouse books and probably got you to pick this volume up just because of how good it looked. I'm in awe, Dominick.

Most of all, for now and always, my love and thanks to Jessica, Josh and Eve, who make every moment of every day worthwhile.

One

"Are you the ghost lady?"

I've heard the question many times, but I'm not crazy about it, frankly. Living in a large Victorian with my eleven-year-old daughter and two dead people who never took the hint—while trying to make a go of the place as a guesthouse—is difficult enough. But since Harbor Haven, New Jersey, is a small shore town, and everybody knows all about everybody else, the question does come up.

Usually, to be honest, I try to summon up an icy stare that makes the asker back down, but in this case, I did my best to force a small, knowing smile and nod. You had to be nice to Everett.

Everett, as far as I knew, was the only homeless man in Harbor Haven. He was in his mid-fifties now and never bothered anybody. It was rumored that he was a veteran of one war or another, and post-military life had clearly not been kind to him. Even on this fine spring day, he was bundled up with clothing because he couldn't afford to jettison anything that he wouldn't be able to replace before winter.

Everett was an oddly beloved figure around town. In a community that liked to flaunt its concern for its own, Everett gave everyone an opportunity to show how understanding we could be; we out-kinded each other when dealing with him. There was a great deal of hypocrisy, of course, as no one really ever tried to know him or tried to help in any substantial way, but that was almost beside the point.

Everett had taken up residence, more or less, outside Stud Muffin, our local pastry shop, which showed a good deal of intelligence on his part. People grabbing a quick snack or a coffee would provide him with spare change, and Jenny Webb, owner of the establishment, might occasionally sneak him a day-old product or two. Even now, with the Stud Muffin still a little shabbier than usual, since what we call "the storm" and the media calls Hurricane Sandy, it wasn't unusual to see Everett in his Mount Vesuvius of clothing, with shoe soles worn through, eating a raspberry-filled croissant on any given morning.

I'd just been leaving the shop with my best friend, Jeannie, when Everett had stopped me with his question. Jeannie had recently returned to work at Accurate Insurance (although why accuracy is the first quality one would look for in an insurance company eludes me) after maternity leave, and her son Oliver was now spending time with a nanny named Louise, whom Jeannie had hired after an exhaustive search that made the vetting process of a Supreme Court justice seem like answering an ad on Craigslist. Jeannie is, let's say, a hands-on kind of mom.

"I guess so," I told him. I gave Jeannie a glance and reached into my overstuffed tote bag for my wallet, then took out a five-dollar bill to give to Everett. Jeannie did the same.

But Everett held up a hand like Diana Ross singing "Stop in the Name of Love."

"Thanks, Ghost Lady," he said, "but I don't need money. I need other help."

"What kind of help?" I asked. I held on to the money in case Everett changed his mind.

"Ghost help," he insisted. Jeannie, to my left, stifled a snicker. She doesn't believe in ghosts, especially not the ones in my house. Jeannie has seen objects fly by her face, holes inexplicably open in walls, watched her best friend (me), my mother, daughter and Jeannie's own husband, Tony, all hold conversations with the local spirits (in Tony's case, one-sided conversations), and still she refuses to acknowledge their reality. Her complete denial is a talent I sometimes wish I could cultivate in myself. It would make life so much simpler.

Jeannie is very persistent. Some would say stubborn, but not me.

"What do you mean, ghost help?" she asked Everett, clearly amused by the whole conversation.

Everett, who never used the bench outside Stud Muffin ("That's for paying customers"), gestured toward it, beckoning us to sit down. But we were on a tight schedule. Jeannie had to get back to her job after this quick lunch break, and I had to get back to the guesthouse to greet newcomers this afternoon, so we chose to remain standing.

"I'm being haunted," Everett said. "I've got ghosts after me."

I've been able to see some—not all—ghosts ever since I suffered a head injury after I bought the guesthouse, so I immediately looked around to scout the area. There *were* some ghosts nearby on Ocean Avenue, but that's not unusual. Nothing looked threatening. I could see an elderly couple hovering over a bench half a block down, a policeman from about 1950, judging from his uniform, who appeared to be patrolling his beat a foot above the pavement, and a small tabby cat that was just lying around, albeit with nothing holding him up. He stretched and looked bored.

"How do you know there are ghosts after you?" I asked Everett. "I don't see anyone following you now."

Jeannie gave me a look that indicated she thought I was patronizing the unfortunate mentally ill man, but I curled my lip and sneered at her—a talent I'd been practicing for exactly this purpose—and turned my attention back to Everett.

"Been getting vibes," he said. "Been hearing people say things." That was it?

"What do you want me to do?" I asked him. "How can I help?"

Everett looked surprised, as if I should have known. "Make them stop," he said. Simple.

"If I could do that . . ." I started to say. It was a knee-jerk reaction. Sometimes having ghosts in the house is not as much fun as you might think.

Perhaps I should explain.

I'd bought the Victorian at 123 Seafront Avenue specifically to turn it into a guesthouse (and no, it's *not* a bed and breakfast, although I'd started providing coffee and tea in the mornings lately and had been thinking about asking my mother for cooking lessons) less than two years earlier. While I was doing the necessary repairs and renovations, I got hit in the head with a bucket of wall compound, and when I recovered, I could see there were two ghosts on the property I'd just bought.

Paul Harrison had been a fledgling private detective in his thirties when he died. He'd been hired to protect Maxie Malone, a twenty-eight-year-old newly minted interior designer. The protection hadn't worked out that well, though, as both Paul and Maxie were poisoned the day after he was hired, and they both died in what, almost a year later, became my house.

They were both stuck on the property—that is, they were unable to leave it—at that time, and if I wanted to keep the building into which I'd just sunk my entire life savings, my divorce settlement and the receipts from a law-suit I'd settled (never mind), I was stuck with them.

Paul wasn't bad company; he's a thoughtful, considerate man who might have appealed to me in other ways if he'd been, you know, alive. But Maxie . . . well, my mother says she has "good intentions." Perhaps. Maxie also likes to drive me insane, and ever since she's gained the ability to move around outside my property (which Paul still can't do; the rules seem to change from ghost to ghost), she's almost inescapable.

Paul compensates by being able to contact other ghosts through some sort of telepathy I call the Ghosternet because I don't have a better name for it. He goes off to some remote corner of the property and manages to send and receive messages from other dead people. I try not to think about it too much, to tell you the truth. Except when it can be useful. Other times, Paul likes to put forth on the Ghosternet that he (meaning we) can investigate for the deceased, which has historically led us (meaning me) into trouble.

All in all, I can't say I was always crazy about having ghosts in the house. My mother and my daughter, Melissa, however, were very pleased; it turned out that they'd had the ability to see and hear ghosts all their lives but had never mentioned that little detail for fear of "upsetting" me (to be fair, it probably would have sent me into therapy). They still see more ghosts than I do, and there are days I wished they were still the only ones in the family with the "skill" to do so. That sentiment has changed somewhat since my father, who passed away a few years ago, started dropping by regularly to visit with me and his granddaugh-ter. On those days, I'm more than glad to be able to com-municate with the dead.

"I don't know how to make your ghosts go away," I told Everett. "But if you take this five dollars, you can go inside and Jenny will give you some soup." I extended the money again.

Everett gave me a disdainful look. "I don't think soup is going to keep the ghosts away," he said. He took the money, though, and shuffled off, mumbling to himself that even the ghost lady wasn't going to help.

I didn't have time to explain, though, because once he moved, I noticed that Kerin Murphy had been standing behind him, no doubt listening in on our conversation. I'd heard Kerin, who had once been a queen bee in the Harbor Haven PTSO (Parent Teacher Student Organization, and no, it's not the PTA), had returned to town after an absence of more than a year, following a separation from her husband. It was rumored she'd fled Harbor Haven for South Florida and a waitress job at an IHOP, but this was the first time I'd laid eyes on her since her resurfacing. She gave me a hollow smile and approached.

"The sharks are circling," Jeannie muttered under her breath.

We probably should have tried to leave, but Kerin was too quick. "Why, Alison Kerby," she said. "It's been much too long."

"Compared to what?" Jeannie was still close enough to me that I could hear her murmur, but Kerin was out of range.

"I know!" I pretended to be enthusiastic. If Kerin could, I could. "How have you been?"

Kerin twisted her face into an expression she must have thought looked contemplative but came across sort of constipated. "It's been a trial," she answered. "But I think we're through the rough spots now." The "rough spots" presumably included Kerin's husband and all of Harbor Haven finding out about her affair with a real estate mogul. For this, I was fairly sure, Kerin blamed me. I'd been the one who'd discovered the truth while investigating Paul's and Maxie's murders, but it wasn't *my* fault that everyone else in town had found out. *I* don't run the local newspaper.

I just have a good friend who does.

"I'm so glad to hear it," I lied. "You remember Jeannie, don't you?"

"Yes," Kerin said flatly. She didn't need to be nice to Jeannie, because Jeannie lived in storm-torn Lavallette (although her home was intact), not Harbor Haven, and her son, Oliver, still less than a year old, would probably never attend Harbor Haven schools. Therefore, Jeannie, in Kerin's world, didn't exist.

"I feel exactly the same way," Jeannie said, taking Kerin's hand in hers.

I flashed a look at Jeannie in the sort of language only very close friends can exchange without fear of retribution, and she let go of Kerin's hand. "Well, we should be moving on," I said pleasantly. Sort of pleasantly. I'm pretty sure I didn't actually gnash my teeth.

"Oh, I don't want to hold you up," Kerin said. "But I'm wondering. Why didn't you help Everett with his problem?"

Huh? "I'm sorry?" I said. That's the polite version of *huh?*

"Everett," Kerin repeated, as if it were the identity of the homeless man that was the confusing part of the question. "He wanted you to help him with a ghost problem. Why didn't you?"

Jeannie's face hardened, but she knows I don't let her off her leash unless I think I can't handle the situation myself.

"You were listening to our conversation?" I asked, just to buy a little time and try to figure out Kerin's motives.

"Well, I didn't mean to *eavesdrop*," she said, affronted at the very notion. Clearly, this was my fault. "But I was right there." She pointed to where she had stood, perhaps in an attempt to prove she'd been there.

"Must have been hard to ignore," Jeannie said. "What with us speaking at normal volume and everything."

I'd say the situation was threatening to turn ugly, but it hadn't been that gorgeous when it had started. "I didn't help Everett because I *can't* help him," I said. "I'm not a social worker, and I'm not a psychiatrist."

"No," Kerin agreed. "You're the ghost lady."

Jeannie made a sound like *pfwah*, which indicated that she considered Kerin's comment something other than brilliant.

"I'm aware that's what people around town call me," I said, through what I hoped were not clenched teeth. "But you should know better, Kerin."

"Oh no," she said. "I know better than to know better."

Kerin had witnessed actual ghostly behavior at my house and had gone around telling many people in town what she'd seen. Rumors had always circulated about my house being haunted, but everybody sort of believed them in the abstract, not the concrete. Kerin's assertions had been dismissed as the lunatic ravings of a vengeful mind. Because that was more fun.

"You don't really buy all that stuff, do you?" Jeannie asked.

"It doesn't matter what people say," I attempted. "I couldn't help Everett, or I would have. But his problem isn't something I can fix."

Kerin narrowed her eyes. "Of course," she said. "Well, I'll see you around town, Alison." She turned and walked away without acknowledging Jeannie again.

Jeannie shook her head as she watched Kerin turn the corner and disappear. "People in this town are awfully protective of that homeless guy," she said.

"We are," I agreed as we headed back to where Jeannie's car was parked. "He's a local institution."

"Your pal there is the one who belongs in an institution," she said, gesturing toward Kerin's last known location. "The ghost lady. Really."

Really.

No. Really.

I had to admit, the ghost-lady thing was more than just

a rumor about the house being haunted. See, the ghosts are sort of an asset to my business, in a strange way. (As if they could be an asset in anything *but* a strange way.) Just before I opened for guests, I was contacted by a company called Senior Plus Tours, which provides vacation experiences with a little something extra to people over a certain age. Someone at the tour company had heard tales of spooky happenings at 123 Seafront—in part because word had gotten to them of the shenanigans the night Kerin was there—and offered me a deal: Senior Plus Tours would guarantee a certain number of guests per season as long as I could assure them there would be ghostly "interactions" at least twice a day.

So I took the proposal to Paul, easily the more approachable of the two dead people in my house, and he'd agreed that he and Maxie—who took some persuading—would put on "spook shows" twice a day and cooperate at other times with the guests so I could start my business with a boost.

But Paul wanted something in return. He'd been just getting started as an investigator when his life had been cut short, and he had loved the work. He wanted to "keep a hand in," and in order to take on the occasional investigation, he needed a partner (or as Paul put it, an "operative") who had the advantage of still being able to breathe. He also needed someone who could leave the house and its surrounding property since Paul was unable to do so. And he needed someone who could talk to living people and be heard.

In other words, he needed me.

I had agreed, probably without thinking about it hard enough, to train for and receive a private investigator license, which I kept in my wallet mainly to impress the supermarket checkout "yenta" who loves to ask about everyone's business. I had never intended to actually put the license to use, but Paul had other ideas. So once in a while, when Paul conjures up what is usually an already dead client, I do the legwork on an investigation and let Paul do the thinking. I know that seems backward—I should be the one out of harm's way because nothing more can happen to Paul—but circumstances force us into illogical situations.

"People will just believe anything they hear, won't they?" Jeannie asked, bringing me out of my reverie. Oh, yeah. Walking back to Jeannie's car. Right.

"Anything they think is fun," I agreed.

"I have to admit, you've done a great job of selling that ghost thing, got you a lot of business," she said. We stopped, having reached her minivan. I've learned not to belabor the whole ghost subject with her. "You go get back to work," I said. "I've got to get some cleaning done before I pick up Melissa, and then I have a new crew of guests on the way."

Jeannie chuckled. "It sounded like you said you had a new crew of *ghosts* on the way," she said, getting into the van. I waved her off and turned to head back to my vintage (that is, falling-apart) Volvo.

A new crew of ghosts? Bite your tongue, Jeannie.

Two

"I don't like it," Maxie said.

That, in and of itself, was not unusual. Maxie was a decent bet to disapprove of anything I suggested within her earshot. She has a strong will, a contrary nature, and an ability to push my buttons that not even my daughter possesses. Sometimes I feel as if I'm raising an eleven-year-old girl and a twenty-eight-year-old ghost at the same time. I'm having better results with the eleven-year-old. Melissa has a higher level of maturity. So much so that she has it within her to be pals with Maxie. They're thick as thieves, assuming the thieves in question are fairly thick.

"What don't you like?" I asked.

We were standing—that is, I was standing, and Maxie was floating around—in what had once been my game room, where I'd kept a pool table and a padlocked cooler of wine and beer for those guests who were interested. The problem was, not so many guests were interested in the pool table. The wine and beer were a minor hit, but the large game room was using up too much space without providing enough return for the guests. So I was renovating, although I was still working out what it would become. It was going to be the first question I'd ask the two men in my life—Josh Kaplan, my sort-of boyfriend, who owns a paint store, and my dad, who was a handyman when he was alive and who, despite his death, still does some work around my house—when I next saw them.

Maxie moved into a vertical position and put her hand to her chin, looking almost like Paul when he strokes his goatee to indicate he's concentrating deeply. She glanced around the room. "I'm glad it's not so dark in here anymore, but the paneling is still ugly."

In an effort to lighten the room for whatever its new function would be, I had painted the 1970s-era walnut paneling white. You could still see some wood grain beneath the paint, which I thought was sort of a nice touch. But the only ghost in the room at the moment—Paul was off brooding about something; he'd been in a testy mood lately—was giving my decision the thumbs-down.

Because Maxie had been in the process of becoming an interior designer when she was alive, and especially because she'd briefly owned this Victorian before I did, she has definite opinions about how it should be renovated. This is especially infuriating since, one, it's my house now, which she refuses to acknowledge, and, two, she's usually right about the design choices.

"I didn't want to hang more drywall in this room," I explained. "The rest of the house has plaster walls, except for Melissa's room in the attic, which the guests don't get to see. It wouldn't look right to come in here and see wallboard."

"But white wood grain is okay?" Maxie countered. "It depends on what you're going to do with the room." She pulled a tape measure from her pocket. The ghosts have the ability to conceal physical items inside their clothing, and the items won't be tangible or visible until they take them out. It's weird, but true. Anyway, Maxie started to measure the space between two windows with, I noted, *my* tape measure, on which I'd written my initials—*AK*—in permanent marker.

Yeah, wall space was an issue and would dictate what I could do with the space. The former game room had a lot of large windows, but that left no space for bookshelves, so I couldn't move the library to that room. It was too large and the wrong shape to be another guest room, which would have been more profitable but wrong for the house. I knew I didn't want this to be a game room any longer, but the redesign was waiting for a purpose, and I didn't have one.

"It's going to be a dining room," I told Maxie, improvising. "I'm going to take cooking lessons from my mother and start serving breakfast in here."

She made a rude noise. "Yeah, you're gonna cook," she sneered. "Besides, this room is so far from the kitchen that the food would be cold by the time you got here."

I hate it when she makes sense.

Luckily, Paul chose that moment to rise up through the floor (he spends his "alone time" in the basement, while Maxie favors the attic) looking gloomy. "Alison," he intoned. "Is there any news?"

That was a stumper. "Yeah," I told him. "Congress still isn't doing anything. What are you talking about, news?"

"Cases," he said, reprising a theme he'd been singing for weeks. "I need a new case to investigate."

"Easy, Holmes," I told him. "Keep this up, and you'll be back on the seven-percent solution by the end of the week."

Paul stopped me with a stare. "You don't know what it's like to be dead and have nothing to do," he said.

That was a decent point. "I'm sorry, but we don't have any clients at the moment." That I was actively not looking for one might have had something to do with that. Okay, I'd gone as far as running an ad for the guesthouse in the *Harbor Haven Chronicle*, which mentioned under the phone number in small print, "Private Investigation" without explanation. I was being passive-aggressive with myself. But it had been so unobtrusive that I'd gotten no calls.

Paul looked defeated and sank back into the floor without another word.

"You have to do something for him," Maxie said, which was unusual. She doesn't often express sympathy for Paul, seeing as how she's pretty much in the same boat. At least she's stopped blaming Paul for not preventing their deaths. Still, this was new. "He's going to lose his mind if he doesn't have some problem to solve soon."

I didn't have an answer for that one either, but it was time for me to get back into the Volvo and pick Melissa up from school. After I pried her away from her friends, who tended to cluster together at the curb after school, she unburdened herself from her six-ton backpack and leaned back in the passenger seat. She sighed audibly.

"What new intrigue is this?" I asked her.

Liss's attention turned to me, which had been the point. "What?" she asked.

"What's going on?"

"Nothing special. Wendy's in love with this guy Jake." Melissa's BFF Wendy had a new crush every few days. Liss finds it amusing, for now.

"Let me ask you a question," I said. "Does the ghost thing come up a lot in school?" I get testy enough when people call me the ghost lady, but if Melissa was the ghost girl and it bothered her, we might have to think about moving.

She rolled her eyes; mothers are so exasperating sometimes. "Only Wendy and a few other people remember anything about that," she said. "It's not a *thing*."

"So it doesn't bother you?"

My daughter looked at me like I had grown a second head in the shape of an avocado. "No," she snorted.

It was possible I was more concerned than necessary. We didn't talk more on the short drive home.

Once there, we had about fifteen minutes before the Senior Plus van drove up to the front of the house. I like to greet the guests outside when the weather permits, which it was certainly doing today, so Melissa and I were on the front walk as the group made its way from the van to the front door.

The first to reach us were a married couple, Mr. and Mrs. Rosen, who told us they should be called Harry and Beth. They looked to be in their mid-seventies and very fit, and as always, when guests arrive (despite the paperwork I get from the tour group, which lists much of the information I need), I asked if there was anything special I could do to make their stay more enjoyable. I'm not a born innkeeper, but I've learned a lot in the past couple of years.

Harry looked at Beth with some embarrassment, I thought, and she leaned over to me to speak quietly. "We came for the *ghosts*," she said.

I get that a lot. Even though the Senior Plus guests are *all* here because they're curious about supernatural happenings, they often seem to feel that they're not supposed to mention it. I've learned to defuse such situations quickly. I took a step back and spoke loudly enough for everyone to hear. But I did check to be sure no locals were around—the ghost-lady stuff might not bother Melissa, but it was starting to chafe on me. Luckily, no one but guests were visible. "How many people came to see the ghosts?" I asked. Melissa smiled when all the hands in the group of five went up. "Great!" I said. "I'm sure you'll be seeing some evidence of them very soon!"

The usual afternoon spook show took place around four, but today we had pushed it back to five because the van had been a little late, and Maxie had a new effect in which she would "walk" a pair of my shoes through the air and up the back of a guest (one I'd point out to her, who I thought wouldn't faint or become upset). She was in the house somewhere, practicing.

I prefer Paul and Maxie not be outside when the guests arrive, although I've never explicitly mentioned it. My asking Maxie not to do something is tantamount to daring her to do it. But I'd rather not have the distraction. Learning new names, getting and making first impressions, and acting the perfect hostess (okay, adequate hostess) is as much as I can handle at one time.

The ice now broken, my arriving group seemed pleased to hear they'd soon be in contact with our resident spooks (before I began this grand adventure, I would have been terrified at the prospect, but hey, to each his own). I can accommodate as many as twelve guests at a time, now that Melissa has moved upstairs to a refinished attic room and her old bedroom is a guest room. But this week there would be only six—five from Senior Plus and one who'd booked separately at the last minute via my website and wasn't arriving until six o'clock. In addition to Harry and Beth Rosen, this group also had Cybill Hobsen, a single, and Libby and Tom Hill, a couple. Even adding in the still-missing sixth guest, only four rooms were in use. Previously, more fully booked tours had required some singles to pair up and room together. Since the storm, the number of guests per Senior Plus tour had declined. The shore was still rebuilding, and I had begun to wonder whether the number of people desiring to stay in a haunted house was beginning to exhaust itself. Perhaps, in the parlance of the marketing world, I was reaching market saturation. I'd have to start advertising more. I couldn't count on Senior Plus to fill the place anymore.

I welcomed the guests inside and told them to acquaint themselves with the place. Maxie descended through the ceiling while I was checking in with Libby Hill, whose husband, Tom, was still helping Mack, the van driver, bring in their bags. The Hills did not travel light.

I tried my best to ignore Maxie, who seemed to be in a serious mode, something she's never really able to pull off successfully. Her black T-shirt—a wardrobe staple—was plain, no clever or offensive logos, and she was wearing black jeans and glasses I knew she couldn't possibly need.

"Ghosts," Libby said, shaking her head. "I don't know how Tom talked me into this one."

"Are you afraid of ghosts?" I asked sympathetically. Even on ghost tours, you get some who are nervous.

Libby looked like she was going to laugh. "I would be if they were real," she said. I stole a glance at Maxie, but instead of scoffing, as I'd expected, she took a notepad out of her back pocket and a pencil from behind her ear and started to write something down. Luckily, she was behind our guest, who didn't see the flying objects.

"Doesn't believe in ghosts," Maxie said. "Significant."

"Well," I quickly said to Libby, "I'll leave you to get comfortable. We don't serve meals, but I can give you a list of some very good local restaurants."

"Thank you," Libby said. "And the first 'ghost experience' is . . . ?"

"Sooner than you think," Maxie intoned. I think she believed she was being amusing, not that Libby could hear her.

"In about half an hour," I answered and walked out into the hallway. Maxie followed me (as I'd expected), and I looked up at her and said, "What the heck are you doing?"

"You want me to interact with the guests more. I'm interacting." Maxie was many things, including a very poor liar.

I decided to let it go, realizing I'd get nowhere with her now. "I have one more guest to check in on," I said. "Go get Paul so we can have the spook show before the non-ghost guest arrives."

"What am I, your secretary?" she said, but vanished before I could answer.

"I think they prefer 'assistant,'" I said. So what if she was already gone. It made me feel better.

The last bedroom was occupied by Cybill Hobsen, a woman in her late fifties whom I had not been able to speak to at length when the guests were arriving. Cybill, who was a live-out-of-the-suitcase type rather than an unpacker (I'd noticed that tended to be more of a couple thing) was dressed less for a relaxing vacation on the Jersey Shore and more for a revival of *Godspell*, in a gauzy, flowing blue gown. She was sitting on the bed looking at her smartphone after she answered my knock, which was pretty standard behavior for people with smartphones—the heck with people standing right in front of you when you can communicate with those in other places. What was odd was that Paul was dropping down through her floor as I walked in. I assumed he must have been passing through on his way downstairs.

"Just wanted to see if everything was okay so far," I started to say.

Cybill looked at me with an intensity one usually sees only in vampire movies, and not the ones with romantic teenagers. "There are two spirits in this house," she said in a low voice.

Yeah. I was fairly aware of the two spirits and figured Cybill should be as well since they were actually mentioned in the brochure. "Yes, there are," I agreed with as sunny a tone as I could muster. "And you'll be meeting them in just a little while now."

"I'm not here to meet them," she replied. "I'm here to drive them back to their graves."

Three

I had to think hard about what my reply should be. Luckily, Maxie was not in the room, or there might actually have been crockery thrown through the air.

"Really?" was my imaginative response. I was taken off guard. Sue me.

"I am a recognized agent of cleansing," Cybill said, as matter-of-factly as if I'd told her that I had once actually baked brownies for one of Melissa's class sales (of course, two mothers later reported upset stomachs—their own—and I was asked not to contribute homemade pastry again). "I can rid your house of this infestation immediately, if you like. I will need only a few minutes to prepare." She opened her suitcase and rummaged through her belongings. "I just need to find my sea salt."

It occurred to me that the house was situated on a beach, so sea salt was not really in short supply, but instead, I told Cybill, "I really don't think that will be necessary."

She looked up from her task, puzzled. "You don't?" she asked.

"No. You see, I use the idea of ghosts in the house to build my business. If you were to appear to drive them out, I wouldn't be able to do that. The other people on the tour who came to see ghosts might feel cheated." I felt it best to plant a seed that perhaps Paul and Maxie were imaginary. If she thought I was playing a con to drive up business in my guesthouse, she might go along with the "gag" and give up the idea of an exorcism.

But what if she really could do what she said?

"I see," Cybill said, with a tone that didn't make it at all clear that she did. "So you prefer that I wait until the end of the week, when the guests will believe they've gotten their money's worth?"

Before I could answer, my father, who had recently resurfaced in my life as a ghost, "walked" in through the outside wall. Normally, Dad wouldn't enter a guest's room unless I asked him to, but he was good at sensing where I was at any given moment and then coming to that spot. "What's going on?" he asked, eyeing Cybill. "She get lost on the way home from an opera?"

Dad knew I wouldn't answer him in front of a guest, but it did occur to me in that moment that I should be very careful with Cybill. If she really was able to rid the house of ghosts, one of them might be Dad. I was not going to risk that.

"Well," I said, answering her question, "I have another tour coming next week, and for a good number of weeks after that. I think I'll have to decline your very generous offer, but thank you, anyway."

Cybill's eyes narrowed; this was clearly not the response she had anticipated. "You're going to let your child live in a house with dangerous spirits just so you can make money?" she demanded.

This was taking an ugly turn. "The fact is, there's no

danger. I wouldn't let her live with danger in any form," I responded.

"Damn right," Dad agreed.

Cybill pushed out her lips in a pout. "Really."

"Yes. Really." In the hospitality business, you have to do your very best not to tell your guests they're being inappropriate. Or let your deceased father hit them with a vase. So I sent him a warning glance just as he was looking at one.

"Very well, then," Cybill said.

"I do hope you'll want to continue your stay with us," I told her, thinking pretty much the exact opposite.

"I think I will," she answered, with a tone I wasn't crazy about. Then she went back to rummaging through her bag, which I saw as a gesture of dismissal, so I walked out, with Dad taking the direct route through the wall to the hallway.

"You do get an interesting crowd," he said, once we were out of earshot.

"They pay the bills. What's up? I wasn't expecting you today."

"Your mother kicked me out," he said, giving me an ironic look. "Not permanently. She wants to get some stuff done around the house, and you know how she is. Can't take a suggestion."

Dad, who'd been sort of a home-improvement jack-of-all-trades in life, can't resist telling Mom—or anyone else who can hear him—how things should be done. Mom probably just wanted to clean up without having a discussion about exactly which was the right mop to use on the kitchen floor. It was why they'd always gotten along best when Dad was working.

Now that Dad had reconnected with Melissa and me, he'd been dividing his time between my house (about a day or two a week, more when Melissa was on vacation), Mom's place, and Madison Paint, the store where he'd spent so many hours hanging out with the owner, Sy Kaplan, and other contractors and painters when he was alive.

"You might micromanage just a little too much for her taste," I agreed with Dad. "Listen, I want to talk to you about what I should do with my game room, but I have to go meet another guest arriving now. Can you stick around?"

"I've got nothing but time," he said.

I went downstairs as Dad disappeared up into the ceiling, and I heard, "Hi, Grampa!" from upstairs. I could see through the front hallway window that my last guest was pulling into the driveway. I hustled down to the front door and went outside.

Helen Boffice was in her mid-thirties, about my age, and much younger than most of my other guests. She was very small and petite, dressed in jeans and a plain pink top, and driving a very sensible Toyota Camry that was maybe five years old. She looked about as normal as a person can look outside of a commercial for life insurance.

But she did not look happy. I realize that guests are not required to be in a cheerful mood when they arrive at the guesthouse, but it does worry me a bit when one shows up looking like she'd just been sentenced to two years at Rikers Island.

"You must be Helen," I said, putting on my best warm-innkeeper demeanor. "I'm Alison Kerby. So glad to meet you." I extended my hand, and Helen took it in a very businesslike manner.

"Helen Boffice," she said, pronouncing it "BO-fi-chay." I half expected a business card to be her next form of communication. "Thank you for booking me last-minute like this."

"We're happy to have you," I said. "Can I help you with your bags?"

"Don't have any," Helen answered. "I'm not staying."

Wow! All I'd done was shake the woman's hand. "I don't understand," I said. "Is there something wrong with the guesthouse?" What I was really asking was, *Is there something wrong with me?* But you don't just come out and say things like that to a person you met six seconds ago.

Helen shook her head. "Not at all. I'm sure this is a fine place to stay, but I don't need it. That's not why I booked the room."

Enough Twenty Questions. "Why don't you come up on the porch and sit, and you can tell me what you have in mind," I said. Diplomacy, right? I'm good at diplomacy. I have a tween daughter.

Maxie appeared at my right as we walked to the porch. Helen sat on the glider I have there, looking as comfortable as Foghorn Leghorn at a KFC. "What's going on?" Maxie asked, despite knowing I wouldn't answer. Maxie saw the expression on Helen's face and added, "She taking out a hit on somebody?" Out came her notepad again, out of Helen's sight.

"What's the problem?" I asked Helen, trying to ignore the ghost hovering just over my shoulder. I started to wonder how selective Cybill could be in her eviction process.

"I didn't book the room for me to stay in," Helen said. Her left hand was tightly covering her right, almost white-knuckled, so there was clearly some stress in her; I'd have thought a vacation by the shore, even a depleted shore, would have been just the thing for her. She was speaking quickly, seeming to want to get the words out before she lost her nerve. "I booked the room because I wanted to make a down payment before I spoke to you."

"She's a nut," Maxie volunteered. Typically helpful Maxie.

"A down payment on what?" I asked.

But Helen didn't seem to have heard me. "I live not far from here, in Marlboro," she plowed on. "Originally, I *was* going to actually stay here for a few days, but I didn't want to explain that to my husband."

"I don't get it," I told her, trying to draw her eyes toward mine. "Why would you book a room at the guesthouse if you're not going to stay here? What are you paying me for?"

"I got your name from an ad in the *Harbor Haven Chronicle*, and when I did a Google search for you, I saw you run a guesthouse, too." That'd teach me to be passive-aggressive with myself.

Too? It took a second for my brain to say, "Uh-oh . . ."

"So I thought, *Well, that's killing two birds with one stone*," Helen continued, still not looking at me, watching her own shoes move back and forth as the glider swayed. "I'll pay for the guesthouse, and get the detective."

Yup. That's what I was afraid of. Now I had to pretend to be a professional private investigator again. I glanced at Maxie to send her urgent "GET PAUL" messages, but she was grinning and scribbling. "What is it you need investigated?" I asked.

Helen looked up from her feet, startled. "My husband, of course," she said. "I believe he's being unfaithful to me, and I want you to catch him at it so I can be sure."

I closed my eyes. This was exactly the last thing I wanted right now. "Are you absolutely certain you want that kind of evidence?" I asked Helen, although I was definitely hoping for a particular response. "Maybe you're misinterpreting signs or just being a little too suspicious. Do you want your husband to know you suspect him?"

"No," Helen said, shaking her head vehemently. "That's why I want to hire you. Because you can be discreet, and he won't know I think anything's going on until you can prove it."

I have never been a hundred-percent committed to the private-investigator thing, and this was sounding like one of the reasons why. "This sort of thing can be terribly upsetting," I tried. "Are you sure you want to face it head-on like that?"

Helen's eyes showed determination and a hint of anger, but her voice was pure business. "I'm sure," she said.

Her face was enough to convince me there was no escape. "If you're sure," I reiterated, and she nodded again, so hard and abruptly I feared for her neck muscles. "I'll have to go get a voice recorder I use for all client interviews. Will you excuse me?"

"Of course," Helen said.

I walked toward the front door, Maxie hot on my heels. "Voice recorder?" she asked. "You don't need a voice recorder—I'm taking notes."

Once inside the house—me through the door, Maxie through the wall—I turned to her. "Of course, you are," I said. "But I needed to get away from her so I could tell you something." I reached for my tote bag, which I keep on a hook by the door, and extracted the small voice-activated recorder I carry when doing interviews. I'd said I was going to get it, so now I had it.

Maxie looked eager, which is unusual for her. "What?" she asked.

"Go find Paul. Tell him I think we have a client." I pulled a pen and reporter's notebook from the tote as well. It had all been at my feet on the porch.

"It'll make his day," Maxie said as she dropped through the floor.

Four

Paul, indeed, arrived on the porch even before I could get back out there myself, and I found him floating next to Helen, stroking his goatee in his best Sherlock-Holmes-on-the-case manner. Rarely had I seen him look so happy. While he wasn't exactly letting glee rule his face—he had to appear professional, even if I were the only one who could see him—his body language had straightened up since I last saw him just a little while ago, and his eyes were absolutely gleaming with interest.

I waited a moment before Paul noticed me and moved back a little; technically, I could have just barreled through him, but that's just a little too creepy for me.

I made a show of taking out the recorder so Helen could see it, but I also had a pen and pad handy. Both were really just props, though, since the real purpose here was to get Helen to relate her story so Paul could hear it.

"Now," I said to Helen, trying to avoid looking back at Paul. "Tell me everything from the very beginning."

Helen did not seem upset; she didn't even appear to be especially stressed anymore. She was clearly dealing with whatever this situation might be by treating it as a business proposition. She was composed and her voice carried little expression. She was relating the facts.

"I've been married to Dave for six years," she began. "We're not an overly affectionate couple, but we love each other. At least, that was the way I'd always seen our marriage. We both work long hours—I'm a human resources manager at an auto-parts supply company, and Dave works as a sales rep for a wireless provider, selling to business clients. We see each other at dinner about three times a week, I'd guess, and one of us is often away on the weekend. We travel a lot for business."

This wasn't getting us to why she thought her husband was cheating on her, but I know Paul is very devoted to the idea of letting clients talk at their own pace, so I did my best not to hurry her along.

"Was that the kind of marriage you expected?" I asked. "One that was mostly devoted to both your careers?"

Helen nodded. "We were both very honest with each other from the beginning. Neither of us wanted children, not even a dog. We loved each other, and we loved our work. We were both ambitious—Dave invests our money so that he can eventually own some technology franchises, and I'm hoping to work in the New York corporate office soon."

Paul was watching Helen's face for expressions, which were subtle at best, and listening for inflection that might betray emotion. Again, these were few and far between, which I was sure Paul would say made them that much more significant.

"Ask her how she met her husband," Paul said when Helen stopped speaking for a moment, seeming to regroup and arrange her thoughts.

I passed the question along, and Helen answered, "We

met at a singles bar; can you believe it?" She chuckled absently. "I don't think I know anyone else, any other couple, who met that way. We did. Things were going along really quite well until this happened." Her voice caught, just for a second, and Paul watched intently. I tried my best not to look at him, and if I did, Helen didn't seem to notice.

"What happened, exactly?" I asked, without being prompted.

Helen seemed to steel herself to begin the more painful part of her story. "It's the usual thing, I guess. You must have heard this a thousand times." This was actually my first case involving a straying spouse (aside from my own straying spouse, but The Swine was long gone now). However, I saw no reason to tell our client that. "The two or three nights a week we had dinner together? That became one night a week. Maybe. Then Dave had to be away every weekend, not just some. And often, he said he slept at his office. It's a cell-phone service provider; *nobody* sleeps in the office, ever. But he said he was working on a deal with a company in Japan, and the time difference was forcing him to stay there until three and four in the morning."

Paul looked over at me, willing himself not to watch our client for a moment, which was clearly an effort on his part. "Ask this next question exactly as I tell you," he said.

I listened, and asked Helen, "Is it possible your husband is doing something other than seeing someone else? Perhaps a gambling problem or a drug habit?" I wouldn't have used the word *perhaps*, but I was basically taking dictation. With forced practice, I've gotten good at passing on Paul's words almost as he says them. There are times I feel like an instrument, an amplifier between the living and the dead. Except my amplitude is low or something.

Helen's mouth twitched, and for a tiny moment she actually seemed amused. "Dave had a drug problem when he was younger," she said. "He went through rehab. I've never seen him so much as take a sip of wine."

"People relapse," I said.

"Not Dave. He's exactly the same as he was the day I met him. Except he's being unfaithful. And yes, I know who she is, if that was your next question." Paul nodded, as if he were having the conversation with Helen himself.

"Who is she, and how do you know?" I asked. Paul gave me an approving glance—he says I've been getting better at anticipating the questions he wants me to ask—then focused on Helen again.

"Her name is Joyce Kinsler," Helen said without hesitation, her unemotional armor back on. "I've seen e-mails he didn't delete from his laptop and watched him field phone calls from her—the name appears on his iPhone before he picks up—when we're together. She's one of his clients. She works for a payroll management company in Freehold, Human Solutions." She chuckled without amusement. "I think I might have sent them a résumé at one time or another."

"Push her a little," Paul said. Just then, Maxie, who apparently had been watching, maybe from the roof, descended onto the lawn next to us, wearing her traditional sprayed-on blue jeans and a black T-shirt with the legend "It Wasn't Me" across her chest.

"Couldn't your husband have been e-mailing and talking business with Ms. Kinsler?" I asked.

Helen shook her head. "My husband is an excellent businessman, Ms. Kerby, but he's a terrible flirt, and I mean that literally. He's bad at it. The texts, the cell calls, the e-mails—he could barely keep from giggling when he sent them. This was definitely *not* business. I saw one of the e-mails he sent, and believe me, they weren't talking business." She stared off for a moment. "She's older than him, too. Maybe ten years." She shook her head.

"Why—" Paul began, but I had my own question, and I asked it before he could finish his sentence.

"Why do you need me to confirm this for you if you

know what he's doing and with whom he's doing it?" I asked, noting my excellent syntax. "New Jersey has no-fault divorce. You don't need evidence."

Paul pointed at me and said, "Excellent. Just what I was going to ask."

Helen looked startled. She hadn't heard Paul, of course, but it turned out that my question had taken her by surprise. "Oh, I don't intend to divorce Dave, Ms. Kerby," she said.

Paul and I exchanged a glance, which may have looked odd to Helen, but she said nothing. I was choosing not to relate Maxie's reaction; suffice it to say it was the spelled-out version of initials frequently seen on the Internet when something surprising happens. I'll leave it at that.

"You don't want a divorce?" I said when I regained the use of my vocal cords.

Helen stuck out her lower lip in an expression that I usually see from Melissa, accompanied by "Duh . . ." But instead, Helen said, "Certainly not. I'm perfectly happy with the life we had before he started seeing this *woman*, and I intend to get that life back."

Have you ever felt as if you were the slow-witted cousin at the Mensa family reunion? "How are you going to do that?" I asked. "And what do my services have to do with it?"

Helen might have been mentally considering alternatives to my services (which would have actually been okay with me), but she simply said, "You catch him in the act, and I let him know I have evidence of his indiscretion. He'll fall back in line."

"You're going to use whatever I find to blackmail your husband into giving up his mistress?" Okay, so *mistress* wasn't a word I use often, but this conversation was going in directions I hadn't expected, and I was winging it.

"I don't think I'd characterize it as blackmail, but that's essentially what I had in mind, yes," Helen told me.

I stole another glance at Paul, who was looking a little stunned, but when he saw me looking at him, he held out his hands and changed his expression to a pleading one. "I know it's not what we usually do, but I could really use a case," he said.

"Besides, this one sounds like a hoot," Maxie added, and Paul's look in return indicated she should go back to spelling out Internet expressions.

"If you wouldn't call it blackmail, what would you call it?" I asked Helen.

She thought for a moment and answered, "Leverage."

It was all I could do not to glare at Paul again, but a repeat of that motion would no doubt draw a question from the woman who, against my better judgment, was about to become our latest client.

I sighed. "Okay. Fill out our intake form, and write down all the details you can think of. Give me your address and your husband's work address," I said.

"Ask her to also include an approximation of her husband's daily schedule, where he goes for lunch, whether he often stops for a drink on his way home, that sort of thing," Paul added.

"So you'll take the case?" Helen said.

"You've already paid for it," I admitted. "It doesn't seem like I have a choice." And that time, I *did* risk a glance in Paul's direction.

He looked thrilled.

Five

"So let me get this straight," Josh Kaplan said. "This woman wants you to catch her husband cheating so he *won't* divorce her?"

"That's about the size of it," I answered.

Josh and I have known each other since we were kids, but we'd only recently reconnected. We'd lost touch around the time we both graduated high school. That, for me, was two colleges, one marriage, three jobs and a daughter ago. For him, it was one college, one graduate program and then a decision to become his grandfather's partner in the paint business. A move that had no doubt thrilled his parents, whom I still had not met, because they lived in Arizona.

We began dating in January, and now it was May. We were taking things very, *very* slowly, partly because I have an eleven-year-old daughter, partly because he works absurdly long hours most days and weekends as well, as do I. If I were being honest, I'd been keeping things . . . slow . . . because it felt weird to have a real relationship with someone without telling him about the two sort-of-dead spirits inhabiting my guesthouse.

He knows about the Senior Plus tours and the rumors around town. I've never exactly lied to him about the whole ghost thing, but I might have implied that it's a marketing tool—largely by mentioning the value of a reputation for something different in the house as a business plan, whenever the subject came up.

Dating is complicated when you have dead people in your house.

He also knows I'm a private investigator and finds that part of my work fascinating, although this was the first case I'd taken on in a while.

Josh had been good-natured about my seemingly glacial approach to dating and hadn't pushed the matter. I hadn't even been to his apartment, which I was told was on the third floor of a building in Asbury Park and had escaped storm damage. Many others were not as lucky.

We were standing at the entrance to my former game room, looking at the white paneling and the numerous windows. The pool table, not yet discarded (I just didn't have the heart, and Mom and Liss liked to play occasionally), was covered with a drop cloth from the painting process.

Most of the guests—in fact, all of them except Cybill—were out scouting the town and finding themselves some dinner, in the restaurants I had recommended, I hoped. Cybill was up in her room; I knew because I had asked Maxie to keep an eye on her. That whole exorcist routine had gotten me nervous, so I hadn't mentioned it to the ghosts, but I made it a point to know when Cybill was nearby. Just to be sure I didn't act too "ghosty" with people who, to the naked eye, weren't there.

In fact, my father was hovering near the ceiling right now, tilting his head from side to side to get different perspectives on the room. I half expected him to hold up his hands as a frame, like the directors in old movies used to do. Dad knew his way around a renovation, and he was weighing my options. But it was still weird to see him like this; I'd never known Paul and Maxie when they were alive, so watching them hover around like loose Mylar balloons wasn't nearly as strange as seeing my dad behave that way. Even after a few months, I wasn't comfortable with the sight.

"You don't want a bar," he said mostly to himself. "It's too big a room, and besides, you have no liquor license." All of which was true.

"It would be way too expensive to put in a bowling alley," Dad said, and then waved a hand at his own thought. "A bowling alley," he scoffed at himself.

"That's odd," Josh said.

Dad looked down at the sound of his voice. Had Josh sensed someone else was in the room? But Dad smiled; he liked Josh. He'd known him from Madison Paint since both Josh and I were in grade school. Our new arrangement was . . . somewhat different. Then again, maybe not that much.

"What's odd?" I asked.

Josh looked at me funny. Not ha-ha funny. "That she doesn't want a divorce, but she wants you to track down her husband and the girlfriend." Oh, yeah.

"Clients want things they want; it's not my job to make moral judgments." That was something Paul had told me once, and he had sounded roughly as unconvincing as I did saying it to Josh.

"I'm not making a moral judgment," he said. "I'm trying to figure out the motivation. He's having an affair, yet she wants to stay married? Is their marriage really that competitive? That she'd want to have something to hang over his head just so she could control him?"

"True loves takes many different forms," my father said. Dad thinks of Josh as family and wants me to marry him. Dad is a million wonderful things, but subtle is not one of them. The fact that neither Josh nor I had come within driving distance of the subject was, apparently, irrelevant.

"I won't know until I start investigating," I said. "If I have free time tomorrow, I'll try to follow Dave Boffice on his lunch hour to see if there's anything fishy."

"His lunch hour?" Josh asked.

"Helen was very specific. Dave is a creature of habit, and she is convinced that he's meeting Joyce Kinsler during his lunch hour. So I'll get in the car and follow him."

"Ooh," Josh said. "A stakeout."

"I hope not," I said. "They're really boring, and you have to make sure you don't need a bathroom." I read that in a detective novel once.

"Next time you need to be on a stakeout, you should call me," Josh suggested. "I could watch while you find a ladies' room."

"Man, are you romantic," I said.

He snuggled up a little behind me and kissed my neck. "In my own way."

I'm not sure if it was weirder that my father was watching or that he seemed pleased. Either way, I was relieved when the doorbell rang. "Gotta go see who that is," I said. "Probably one of the guests forgot their key." I headed for the front door, despite Maxie's hovering around the ceiling and Melissa's (who has never missed a doorbell ring in her life) getting there ahead of me. Once I saw who it was, though, I wished I had stayed in the game room and let Dad watch Josh kiss my neck. Well, maybe not, but I wasn't happy.

Kerin Murphy was standing on my doorstep looking less perky than I'd ever seen her. Under normal circumstances, that wouldn't have bothered me so much—Kerin could use a few less pounds of perky per square inch—but she appeared to have brought half the members of the Harbor Haven PTSO with her. They were all looking just as non-perky as Kerin, and all the anti-perk seemed to be directed at me.

"Mrs. Murphy is here," Melissa told me.

"No kidding." It was out before I could stop it.

"Alison." Apparently Kerin was showing off that she remembered my name. The posse behind her—honestly, they really looked like they should be carrying torches and pitchforks—just glowered.

"Hello, Kerin," I said as Josh walked in behind me. I saw Paul arrive from the basement, as well. Thank goodness, most of the guests were out; I was starting to feel crowded. "Can I help you ladies with something? Would you like to come in?"

One of the women behind Kerin, whom I recognized as Anabel's mom, looked positively petrified at the very thought. "I'm not going in," she muttered. A couple of the others nodded in agreement.

"What's going on?" Josh said quietly in my right ear.

"It's the ghost-lady thing," I groaned back. I took a deep breath and looked at the mob—which to be fair was only about six women—on my front porch. "I'll come out there, then," I said and stepped forward. I gave Liss a look indicating that she should stay inside, and she gave me one that indicated she would no doubt hear everything through the window anyway. Plus, Maxie, who was half in/half out of the house, could pass on the action like a play-by-play announcer.

Paul came all the way out with me, as did Josh, who leaned against a porch post, one foot crossed in front of the other, looking casual. I was sure he'd help out if there was trouble, but by his appearance, you'd think he was completely unconcerned and probably not even listening.

Kerin looked at Josh but didn't ask who he was, and I didn't volunteer. I knew girls like her in high school, and they were the ones who tended to steal the good boy-friends.

"Is something wrong?" I asked her. The idea was to get

the conversation started so it could be over sooner. It's always best to see the silver lining.

"Yes," Kerin said. "Something is definitely wrong."

I waited, but she didn't elaborate. I guessed that she had planned this conversation in advance, and I was stuck in the role of straight woman, so I supplied her with the appropriate setup, again in the service of getting Kerin and her posse off my porch before the guests started returning. "What's the problem?" I asked.

"You could have helped him, and you didn't," she said. "He asked you for help. I heard him."

I thought back over the day. I had seen Kerin outside the Stud Muffin with . . . "Everett?" I asked. "You mean when Everett said he had a ghost following him?" That didn't seem logical, but it was all I could think of; there wasn't anyone else who had asked me for help around Kerin Murphy recently. Unless she'd been following me around and hiding in the shadows. I wouldn't put it past her.

"Yes, of course, Everett," said Anabel's mom, who appeared to be serving in the capacity of Kerin's sidekick in this particular melodrama. "You knew who she meant." That sounded like an accusation, and the tone was starting to irritate me.

"You want me to throw some mud at her?" Maxie asked. "It's no trouble." I shook my head in the negative. After a second.

"Okay," I said, trying to keep the edge off my voice. "I get it that Everett calls me the ghost lady. I know there are rumors around town about my house. I'll take it from Everett because he has some problems. But I don't think you ladies should listen to silly rumors. I'd like to think more of you than that."

Kerin took another step forward, and for a moment, I actually thought she was going to take a swing at me. But what she said was more devastating than a punch (especially from Kerin, whom I seriously thought I could take in a fair fight).

"Everett is dead," she said. "He was stabbed to death in the men's room at the Fuel Pit gas station."

I staggered back a step or two, and for a second I thought Josh was going to have to catch me, but I steadied myself. Paul's eyes widened—I wasn't sure if it was in surprise or interest in the crime. I felt the breath push its way out of me, and had to remind myself to inhale.

"That's awful," I said when I got my bearings again. "Poor Everett!"

"Sure, now it's 'poor Everett,'" said one of the women in the back of the group, which was starting to look more like a mob again. "Where were you when he needed you?"

"Me?"

Josh took a step in my direction. The great protector was going to put himself in harm's way in the face of a marauding band of . . . soccer moms? It was a nice gesture, anyway.

"Maybe you need something stronger than mud," Maxie said and ducked into the house before I could stop her.

"Of course, you," Kerin answered. "You were the only one who could have saved him."

"How do you figure that?" I asked. "I was nowhere near the men's room at the Fuel Pit." It occurred to me to say that I'd never been inside any men's room, anywhere, but that wasn't going to make me sound any more noble.

"Neither was anyone else," Kerin said, and I think she was hiding a little smile at my expense. "He was alone in there."

Maybe it was me, but I didn't see how that made me culpable. "What has that got to do with Alison?" Josh asked. He'd clearly had enough of this kangaroo court.

"I said, no one was in the men's room except Everett," Kerin said, her tone insinuating that Josh must clearly have an IQ similar to that of shredded wheat. "He didn't stab himself."

"So?" I was glad Josh said it; I couldn't figure the line of logic being pursued either.

"So, it's obvious to you, isn't it? A ghost killed him, right?"

Six

That stunned pretty much everybody except Kerin and her posse. Paul's brow knit to the point that I thought he might not be able to smooth it out without a hot iron. Josh let out something similar to a laugh. I felt my mouth drop open and quickly closed it again, trying desperately to think of the proper withering response, while all my brain could come up with was "Wha?"

Naturally, that was the moment Maxie decided to zoom out of the house, through the front window, wearing a trench coat. The idea that she needed a trench coat to hide whatever she'd brought was not a pleasant one; for all I knew, Maxie had a submachine gun.

"A ghost?" I said, loudly enough to stop Maxie in her path. "You think a ghost killed Everett in the gas station men's room?"

Maxie looked surprised and stopped her forward motion. "Whoa!" she said.

Paul's eyes flickered back to what he approximates as

life. "Get her to explain," he said. "Find out why Everett couldn't have stabbed himself."

I bit my tongue for a second, just because what I really wanted to say to Kerin would not have helped the situation at all. Then I said, "That's a real stretch. A homeless man dies of a stab wound, and you go straight to ghosts? You seriously believe there's no human explanation for this? That it's not possible Everett stabbed himself?"

"No," Kerin answered without a mote of hesitation. "*I* don't think it was a ghost, but we want answers. Everett was found with knife wounds in the men's room, which was locked from the inside. But there was no knife. No trace of one."

I waited, but there was nothing more. "So the only logical assumption based on that was a dead spirit took out some insane vendetta on Everett?"

"Do you have an explanation that makes more sense?" Anabel's mom challenged me. "You're the ghost lady." And there it was.

"No. I am *not* the ghost lady," I snapped. "I am the victim of vicious rumors around this town by people"—and here I'm afraid I chose to stare directly at Kerin—"who have decided that I'm responsible for their problems. It's not true." I searched the area for Senior Plus guests and found none, so I could go on. "There are no ghosts in my house."

Technically, that was only a little false; while Dad was presumably still inside puzzling over my game room, Maxie and Paul were technically both *outside* the house. Paul frowned, but I couldn't tell if it was because of what I'd said or because he was concentrating. Paul can be inscrutable. *I* can't scrute him, anyway.

Josh, perhaps sensing the mood without understanding it, drew a little closer to me but didn't say anything.

Maxie, however, glared at me. "Oh, own up to it," she said with an edge in her voice. She stopped, like a thought had suddenly occurred to her. "Are you ashamed of us?" I couldn't answer.

"Isn't this the basis of your business?" Paul asked. "Don't you *want* people to know there are people like us here?" I had no answer for him, either.

Melissa opened the front door and tried to look casual walking out of the house. She knew I'd instructed her to stay inside, but I had no doubt she'd been listening to the conversation. She looked concerned.

I bit my lower lip and gave Maxie a quick glance.

"What's going on?" Melissa asked, as if she didn't know.

"It seems that poor Everett passed away today," I told my daughter, using a tone that she knew was not my natural cadence. I sounded like I was talking to a little kid, not a tween who was, in fact, smarter than me. "These ladies are here to collect for his burial arrangements. Can you bring me my checkbook, please?" Let's see you squirm out of that one, Liss.

She didn't get to answer immediately, because Kerin stepped a little closer. Josh stood up straighter but didn't move. I knew Kerin wasn't a physical threat so much as an annoyance, so my demeanor kept him from going all macho. I saw Maxie slip back inside the house with an irritated expression.

"We're not here *just* to ask for money," Kerin said. Her voice indicated she was playing along "for the sake of the child," but "the child" wasn't buying a word of it. People underestimate children all the time; being young doesn't mean being stupid. "We're here to ask your mommy for help." I rest my case on the word *mommy*.

Maxie burst back through the door and floated behind Melissa. The two of them working together was rarely a good thing. "My help?" I asked Kerin. "I honestly don't see how there's much I can do beyond a contribution." I turned back to my daughter. "Go inside and get my checkbook, won't you?" I asked her again.

But Melissa brought a hand from behind her back and held out the item in question. "I brought your checkbook with me," she said. "I thought they were collecting for a PTSO bake sale or something." Nice move, Maxie. Keeping Melissa out here just because you knew I wanted her inside.

I took the checkbook but didn't open it. Kerin smiled her chilly smile—the one everyone else thinks is ingratiating—and put a hand on her hip. "Before you write a check, Alison, we should come to an agreement. We're here because we want you to find out who killed Everett."

If I were a cartoon character, my jaw would have hit the porch floor, and Josh would have had to pick it up and hand it to me. As it was, I just stood there gaping for a moment, and he picked up the thread of conversation. "You want Alison to investigate this man's death?" he asked. "Why?"

Kerin didn't take her gaze off me. "Well, she's a *private investigator*, isn't she?" she hissed. Sarcasm dripped off her voice and formed a puddle on the floor. "Isn't that what you're supposed to ask an investigator to do?"

The others rattled their pitchforks—okay, so they fanned themselves; it was a warm night and they were in close quarters—while I regained the power of speech. "We have a very efficient police department in Harbor Haven," I told Kerin. "You don't need a private investigation. The public one will be very thorough, I'm sure."

Kerin scoffed. "The police? An investigation into the death of a homeless man? I doubt they'll spend ten minutes on it before they decide he died of exposure on a warm spring night, despite the loss of blood." I flinched at the gory detail—Kerin had apparently lost sight of the fact that "the child" was here. Or more likely, she'd never actually cared. I knew Liss could handle it, but I took the opportunity to resent Kerin for not being more sensitive anyway. I was making a bid for a plaque in the Resentment Hall of Fame.

My daughter, I'm proud to say, did not flinch. Anabel's mom, however, put her hand to her mouth as if to suppress the gag reflex.

Paul was looking interested. That was bad.

"Why do you really care?" I said, loud enough for the entire gathering to hear. "Who among you even knows Everett's last name?"

They exchanged some confused looks, but Kerin didn't move her eyes from mine. "Why?" she asked innocently. "Did *you* know it?"

Josh took a step closer to Melissa and me with a sly expression on his face. "If you want Alison to investigate professionally, you shouldn't be asking her for a contribution," he told Kerin. "You should be negotiating the fee she's going to charge you." I've liked Josh since the day I met him, when we had a very vigorous discussion on the merits of *Saved by the Bell* versus *The New Mickey Mouse Club.*

Surely the suggestion that the gathered minivan lynch mob pay me for my services would be enough to get them off my back. This group was tight with a buck, as I'd found out back when I'd petitioned the PTSO to subsidize a trip for our fourth-graders to visit the Newark Museum, where I happened to know that a land lease signed by George Washington himself would be on display. You'd have thought I'd asked them to donate all their blood to some Communist vampires (which would be a great band name, by the way). Don't even get me started on attempts to procure Sandy relief contributions from this crowd—none of *their* homes had been seriously damaged, so they'd assumed the storm was "overhyped." That's a direct quote, but I don't remember from which woman.

Indeed, Kerin looked positively blindsided by the idea. She stopped in mid-gesture, blinked, and opened her mouth without saying anything, which was probably a first since she'd graduated grade school.

During the resulting interim, Paul looked over at me

and said, "We're taking the case, aren't we?" I practically caused myself a neck spasm not looking toward him. I was already looking into Helen Boffice's marriage, basically as a favor to Paul. I did not feel obligated to relieve his boredom with a murder case as well, especially not one that would require me to have contact with Kerin Murphy.

So I was somewhat unprepared when Kerin, after looking back at her posse, said, "We'll give you a thousand dollars."

Well, that settled . . . *what*? Paul smiled from ear to ear. Josh looked a little confused, worried that he had somehow precipitated this unfortunate turn of events and probably wondering if this would put a complete halt to our glacially moving relationship. Maxie, of course, said, "You should definitely take it," knowing it meant doing something I didn't want to do.

Before I could even form a reply, Melissa, standing behind me, said, "Five thousand."

I looked at her, then back at Kerin, whose eyes narrowed as her ingratiating smile evaporated. "Fifteen hundred," she said.

From behind me: "Forty-five hundred." I looked at my daughter again. It was like watching a really well-played tennis match, except I was playing the part of the net.

Kerin realized now that she was competing with a formidable opponent. "Two thousand," she said. "Final offer."

"Three thousand," my daughter countered. "You need us."

"Two thousand," Kerin repeated. "Your mother"— *Mommy* now appeared to be a thing of the past—"is not the only investigator in the area."

I was still watching Melissa, and she shrugged. "Fine," she said. "Go get yourself one of the other ones. You said a ghost killed Everett. How many private detectives are going to go along with that theory?" Aha, so she *had* been listening from inside!

"I did not say that," Kerin said. "I said your mother would believe it."

Melissa didn't blink. "So go elsewhere," she said.

Kerin, remembering now that this whole charade was about forcing me into a position that I would find uncomfortable, growled a little in the back of her throat. "Twenty-five hundred," she rasped.

Melissa, cool as a cucumber. Or any other refrigerated food material. "Three. Thousand."

Kerin did not consult her coconspirators but made a noise like *uch* before she said, "Fine. Three thousand. But only when we see *proof*."

"Proof?" I asked. "I'm going on the record saying I'm *not* the ghost lady, there *are* no ghosts, and a ghost *didn't* kill Everett. What kind of proof is it you want? Do *you* believe in ghosts, Kerin?"

Her attitude couldn't have been more imperious if she were on the set of *Downton Abbey*. "Of course not," she said.

"Then what are we talking about?"

"We're talking about you and your house," Kerin answered, her voice three decibels short of a hiss. "Weird things happen here, and since you deny you're housing anything unusual, that must mean you're doing them yourself. People think there are ghosts in your house. You investigate crimes. I'm betting you'll come back and say a ghost killed Everett. And if you do, you have to admit you're the ghost lady."

A few in the posse actually applauded.

Paul snorted, kind of. "Just because a ghost didn't kill this man, doesn't mean there are no such things as ghosts," he said. I didn't repeat his words, and he looked confused. "Tell them."

But I didn't—couldn't, especially not with Josh there looking torn between pride in me and bewilderment at the situation. "I'm *not* the ghost lady," I said slowly. "And I'll take your case to prove it. For three thousand dollars. Half in advance."

"No."

I was looking for the way out of the deal and so was prepared to turn and walk into my house. But my daughter, who knows what college is going to cost, would not be denied. "A third in advance," she said. "The rest when the case is solved."

Kerin looked at Melissa, then at me, then back at Liss. "Oh, fine," she said, reaching into her purse for her checkbook.

Melissa was about to make a large, exaggerated nod to signal her jubilant victory, but Josh caught my eye with a look of desperation. I didn't want to make him feel worse—after all, I didn't see a way out of this job, either—and said, "Hang on a moment."

"Breach of contract," Kerin said before I could continue. She stopped writing.

"There *is* no contract yet," I told her. "And there won't be if you insist that I only get paid if a ghost is discovered to be the killer. I won't prejudice the investigation that way." Paul gave me a nod of approval, but I wasn't in the mood to be nice to him, so I didn't return it. "You don't want to pay me until the job is done? Fine. Keep the advance. And you don't have to pay me if—as I expect— the police wrap up the investigation before I can. But if I investigate and find that a living, breathing person killed Everett, you still have to pony up the three large. Are we clear on that?"

"And you have to tell them that the ghosts in your house are real," Maxie offered, apparently under the mistaken impression that she was a part of this negotiation. I didn't respond to her, either.

I spotted Harry and Beth Rosen heading up the walk toward the porch. "I'm not discussing this any further in front of my guests," I said quietly to Kerin. "It's yes or no, and it's right now. So what'll it be?"

For a moment, I thought she was going to call it all off, but she said, "It's yes," turned on her heel, and walked back toward the street, with the Several Mom March in step behind her.

I made a quick turn and looked at my daughter. "Where did you learn to negotiate?" I asked.

Liss shrugged. *"Pawn Stars."*

Seven

"Everett Sandheim?" Detective Lieutenant Anita McElone (rhymes with *macaroni*) sat at her desk and regarded me up and down. "Who hired you to investigate a guy's death when you don't even know his whole name?"

"Believe me, it wasn't my idea," I assured her. "I'm just glad *you* knew it. Now if you can also tell me that the police department has the whole thing all sewn up, I'll let the people who hired me know that they don't need my services, and everybody walks away happy. So go ahead."

McElone just sat there.

"Tell me," I urged.

McElone did not even so much as blink.

"Please?" Maybe the magic word would help.

Nothing.

I sighed. "Okay. Since they hired me, I'm obligated to investigate, so—anything you can tell me?"

McElone sighed louder. "Many, many things," she said. "But that doesn't mean there's much that I *will* tell you.

Except that asking the police to do your job is sort of cheating your client. Who *is* your client?"

"You wouldn't believe me," I said.

She started a little, then caught herself. "This isn't one of your ghosty things, is it?" she asked.

McElone and I have been around the block together more than once since this whole ghost-and-private-detective thing began. She is a very good detective who might or might not have a grudging respect for me but will never show it either way. But she is spooked (pun intended) beyond all reason by my house and a few things she's seen happen there that she can't explain. I truly believe she wouldn't set foot in the place without a 911 call forcing her to do so.

I'd come here straight from the ten a.m. spook show, at which Paul had strummed a guitar I'd found at a local antique shop, and Maxie had flown a small rug runner I had in the hallway around the house and then folded it into the shape of a canoe, all the while complaining to me that she was "not a trained chimp." She'd vanished right after the performance, which was a plus, because now that she has figured out how to appear in the passenger seat of my car, whenever I'm going somewhere, she pops up. This trip had been Maxie-free.

"As a matter of fact, no," I said. "It's about a group of hysterical women who are trying to get me to say a ghost killed Everett so they can run me out of town on a rail or something."

McElone looked at me as if I were speaking a language other than English, and she had nothing but a very thin phrase book to help her. "And how is that *not* a ghosty thing?" she asked.

"Well, technically, it's not one of *my* ghosts," I explained, although hearing it aloud didn't help much. There are a few people I've told that I live with ghosts because it's easier than always pretending I don't; McElone is one of them.

"Believe me, I think this is just as ridiculous as you do, and I'd like to prove that an actual living human stabbed the poor man."

McElone is freakishly neat—which in my opinion signals a serious psychological problem—so she had no papers to shuffle, but she did the best she could with the one sheet of paper she had on her desk. "So, why are you here, exactly?" she asked.

I glanced around the room and noticed that McElone's cubicle looked the same as it always had, except that the pictures of her children had been replaced with pictures of bigger children. I thought about what I could ask her that might have a fighting chance of being answered.

"I'd like to get up to speed," I said. "Can you at least confirm to me that the knife wound was the cause of Everett's death?"

"M.E.'s report isn't out yet," McElone answered, sounding every bit the straitlaced police functionary. "But it seems like a good bet. And it's not a knife wound—it's multiple knife wounds. Blood loss will likely be listed as the actual cause of death unless there's some surprise I'm unaware of yet. It just happened yesterday. Could be a while before it's confirmed."

That wasn't much of a help, but then, what had I expected? "Can you tell me what background you have on Everett? I heard he was in the Army or something about twenty years ago. Is that right, or is it just a rumor?"

McElone looked at me for a few moments, presumably deciding whether to give me her usual speech about doing my own research (actually, Maxie does most of the online research for my investigations, since she's good at it and has plenty of time on her hands). She probably realized that things pretty much always end up with her sharing information anyway, so she gestured futilely with her hands and punched some keys on her desktop computer.

"Everett Martin Sandheim was fifty years old at the

time of his death," she said, reading from her screen. "He was born in Atlanta, Georgia; went to Fairleigh Dickinson University in Madison, New Jersey, ROTC. Then he got out of college and immediately went into the Army. Participated in the Grenada invasion in 1983. No injuries as far as I can tell, but two commendations for bravery. Came home a lieutenant just about thirty years ago."

"How did he end up homeless?" I asked.

McElone gave me a withering look. "All I have is official records," she answered, her tone indicating that I should have known better than to ask the question. "It doesn't list everything about the guy's life. He was first cited for loitering seven years ago, a couple of times against municipal ordinances for disorderly conduct, which probably means they wanted to get him off the street on cold winter nights. Occasionally some tourist who didn't know better would complain, but it never led to an arrest. Hasn't been cited for two years, because nobody ever complained about the guy during that time."

"So there's nothing in his record to indicate why someone might be really mad at him," I said, thinking aloud. I looked up at McElone. "Did he have any family?"

She punched a few more keys, probably just to scroll down the page. "He has a sister in Montana, and his father is currently residing in South Carolina. We've contacted the sister, haven't gotten through to the father yet."

"I thought all older people from New Jersey went to Florida," I said.

"Get with the times. South Carolina is the new Florida. Closer to the grandkids and still no snow in the winter."

"More hurricanes though." We exchanged a look.

McElone looked over the page, turning the screen toward herself so I couldn't crane my neck and look at it, then took her hands off the keyboard. "That's about it," she said.

"What are you guys doing about it?" I asked. Then,

realizing that it sounded like I thought the police were not investigating, I added, "I don't want to step on your toes if I start asking around."

McElone's eyes indicated either irritation or amusement; with her it's hard to tell. "We're investigating," she said with an edge. "When we get the M.E.'s report, we'll know more. I talked to Marv Winderbrook, who owns the gas station where Everett was found. He says he didn't see anything."

"They don't have security cameras?" I said. I thought it made me sound professional.

"Not in the *bathrooms*." McElone was indicating that my intention had not been realized. "But they do have some outside, and we're checking to see if anyone went in or out while Everett was in there. So far it doesn't look like anybody did."

"And the door was locked from the inside," I said, chiefly to myself.

"That's right. Now. Is there anything else I can do to make sure you continue to be employed, or can I get on with *my* actual job now?"

I stood up. "You know," I said to McElone, "there are times when I think you don't consider me with a good deal of respect."

Not even a flicker of amusement. "Run with that thought," she said.

Well, if she was going to be *that* way about it . . . I picked up my tote bag and took two steps toward the squad room entrance. Then I turned back and looked at McElone again. "Is anybody looking into Everett's estate?" I asked.

She took off her reading glasses and considered me. "The guy was homeless. What estate are you talking about?"

"That's what I thought," I said and continued toward the door. I had no idea what I'd meant when I said that, but somehow I felt a little better.

* * *

My mother was waiting for me on a bench outside the police station. Mom doesn't really have anything against cops, and she will go inside if it's necessary. But she's leery of what she insists on calling precinct houses. Mom watches a little too much television.

We had arranged to meet because Mom was going to give Melissa and me (mostly Melissa) a cooking lesson by way of making dinner while we were there. To road test said dinner, Jeannie, Tony (and their son Oliver) and Josh were coming to the house tonight to eat. Also, Tony is a contractor and a good one, so he could offer more ideas on my soon-to-be-not-a-game room.

"There was a very nice man here just a minute ago," she said after I'd filled her in on my consultation (which is what I'd decided I'd call it) with Detective McElone. "He thought it was possible that poor Everett was killed by a thrown knife, rather than one the killer held."

"Multiple times? Even so, that wouldn't explain what happened to it after Everett died. There was no knife found in the men's room." We started toward my pathetic old Volvo, which was parked around the corner. "What are you doing asking strange men in the street about the murder of a homeless man anyway? Do you think that's the best way to solve a crime?"

Mom sniffed a bit at what she perceived as my rudeness. But she'd never say anything because she believes I'm perfect (which is not as great as it sounds, believe me). "He was just hovering over my head," she said pointedly. "It would have been impolite to ignore him. You were in there awhile, and we couldn't just stand out here and talk about the weather."

Mom is probably the best ghost spotter in the family, although Melissa is getting better the older she gets. Guess who that leaves as the least talented in the line? I'll give you a minute.

"Well, I don't think your ghost buddy's theory is very plausible," I said. "And I'd appreciate it if you didn't start random conversations in the streets of my hometown with people no one else can see. They already call me the ghost lady. Do you want to be the ghost lady's even crazier mother?" Mom has gotten more brazen about her ghost not-so-whispering since I joined the club.

"People shouldn't be so quick to judge," Mom said. "Anyway, I don't see why I had to come with you here; I thought you wanted cooking lessons. Why couldn't I have just come to your house after you were done with the lieutenant?"

I opened the passenger door of the geriatric Volvo for Mom, and she looked at me questioningly. "We have somewhere else to go first, and I wanted you with me for it," I said. She got in and reached over to unlock the driver's door for me.

"Where are we going?" Mom asked as I started the car.

"To watch a man go to lunch," I told her.

I'd followed Helen Boffice's presumably wayward husband, Dave, from their nice-but-not-fancy home on Surf Road to his office in Red Bank this morning at eight and watched him go inside, and then I drove back to my house in time for the morning show. That was just to get the lay of the land; Helen had been clear that I only had to follow Dave at lunch. Luckily, the guests—even Cybill—all left for the day after the show. One of the advantages of not providing meals is that guests have to leave the house to eat, which frees up some time during the day for me. I give all my guests the number of a cell phone I keep specifically for them to call me on if there are any issues, but so far, no one ever had.

I filled Mom in on my non-ghost case during the twenty-minute drive to Lakewood. You might think a woman in her late sixties would be appalled at the idea of being hijacked to stake out a suspected adulterer, but Mom was quite pleased. She reached around to the backseat to get her backpack, which she uses in lieu of a purse, and which was no doubt full of food and cooking supplies. She pulled out a pair of dark sunglasses. "These will be good to hide my face," she said.

"We're not supposed to be seen at all. Besides, he's never seen you in his life," I reminded her.

"How do you know?" Go argue with that.

Fortunately, we were pulling up to the office building, a three-story mostly glass structure whose second floor was completely rented by ClearServe Industries, Dave's employer. I'd discovered that by walking up to the building directory. Buildings largely made from glass are excellent for stake-outs because you can often see people even when they're inside.

"What makes you think he'll be coming out now?" Mom asked, now pulling on a baseball cap she'd also retrieved from the backpack.

"Helen gave me his daily schedule," I told her, doing absolutely nothing to conceal any part of my face. "She said he pretty much never varies from it at all; he's a real creature of habit."

Of course, once I had said that, it was inevitable that we would sit there checking a picture of Dave that Helen had given me for about twenty minutes before Dave, of medium height, medium weight and medium attractiveness—in short, the most average man in history—walked out of the building.

"I was afraid we'd missed him," Mom said, re-buckling her shoulder harness. Once snapped in, she put a hand up to her face in a really awkward attempt to obscure it from view.

I started up the Volvo, which I'd parked far enough away that the inevitable coughing, sputtering and grinding it does wouldn't attract any attention. "I showed you his car when we drove in," I reminded her. "Unless he'd decided to walk to his mistress's place, there was no way we were going to miss him."

"Do you have to say 'mistress'?" Mom asked.

I didn't answer and instead just drove behind Dave as he pulled out of the parking lot, hoping I was being discreet. If Helen's outline of his daily routine was accurate, we had a ten-minute drive to Joyce Kinsler's garden apartment in Eatontown.

We took Route 35 south into Eatontown, but we didn't make the turn at Broad Street that would have been the logical one to get to Joyce's, according to the British woman who gives directions on my portable GPS box.

"She sounds a little annoyed," Mom pointed out about the mechanical guide. "Maybe she doesn't approve of where Dave is going."

"I don't think she makes that kind of value judgment."

Luckily, there was no opportunity to continue our assessment of a person who didn't exist, because Dave began signaling a right turn.

"He's pulling into the mall," Mom said, just in case I hadn't figured that one out on my own.

The Monmouth Mall is not one of New Jersey's most prominent (those are all in Bergen County), but it's pretty big, and if this was indeed where Dave was planning to meet his girlfriend for an afternoon quickie, it was not only an indication that he had some really kinky ideas but also a problem for me, because there would be people everywhere and plenty of places for Dave to elude a tail.

He pulled into a parking space near the movie theater entrance, and since it was a midweek afternoon, it wasn't difficult for me to find another one fairly nearby. I didn't have much time to give Mom instructions, because he had just gotten out of his car and started toward the mall.

"I'm going in after him," I said and didn't allow her to answer. "You stay here. If I lose him, I'll call you. You have your cell phone, don't you?"

"Always. I—"

"If you see anything suspicious, text, don't call me," I said, noting that Dave was already starting toward the entrance. She looked a little startled. "And use vowels!" I warned as I opened my car door, leaving the key in the ignition so Mom could listen to the radio if she wanted. Mom's version of text shorthand consisted of using all consonants, therefore making everything look as if it were written in Cyrillic, which doesn't make it easier to understand.

It was a warm day but not humid; that wouldn't come for another month or so if we were lucky. When this kind of day hits us, New Jersey can be a lovely place, particularly down the shore, where a sea breeze can remind you of your childhood, and the sun shows you the deep blue of the sky and the rich green leaves on the trees.

Which is why I couldn't believe I had to spend it in a shopping mall.

I typically avoid malls like the plague (which I'm pretty sure first gestated in a mall). I'd rather shop at neighborhood stores, certainly in individual stores, than be trapped in an environment where the very air seems manufactured and the population is glassy-eyed and intoxicated with consumption of things I don't want or can't afford.

I made sure Dave was far enough ahead of me that I wouldn't be noticeable, but I couldn't get too far behind or he'd get lost in the throng. People on the hunt for whatever passes for bargains at a mall, where a pretzel is four dollars, are determined beings and will not yield for a woman simply trying to take pictures of a man cheating on his wife. What has this country come to?

Dave seemed to be on an urgent mission, and I had to really hustle to keep up with him. He sliced his way through the crowd until he reached a bank of escalators and hopped—gingerly, I noticed—onto one. I followed as well as I could without actually gasping for breath.

Once at the top of the escalator, though, I panicked—Dave was nowhere to be seen.

I scanned the area while disgruntled mall patrons (there are no other kind) treated me like the impediment to their progress that I was. Already I was rationalizing: So I didn't catch Dave *today*. Surely his wife could wait another twenty-four hours before she got the details of the extramarital affair she wasn't planning to use as grounds for a divorce? She could just hang on for one more rotation of the globe before holding his infidelity over him like the Sword of Damocles, constantly present and usable should he fall out of line again, right?

There are marriages, and there are marriages. Theirs didn't sound like either one, but who was I to judge?

Wait! I spotted Dave behind a woman with a stroller being pushed by her older child with a younger one sitting inside. He headed away from me again, and I took up the chase once more. I reached into my pocket to ensure that my cell phone, which would double as my camera in this case, was ready. I pulled it out.

Only one bar of power was left. I'd have to make sure I got the shot on the first try.

To be honest, I still wasn't really sure what I thought I'd be photographing. Clearly Dave and Joyce, if she showed up, were not going to be doing anything scandalous while surrounded by countless mall patrons. But Dave was obviously in a very big hurry, and Helen Boffice had been absolutely sure he was going to be seeing his girlfriend today at lunch. Of course, Helen believed that he saw his girlfriend *every* day at lunch, but my experience has been that men are generally neither that consistent nor that dependable.

Perhaps being married to The Swine hadn't given me the best basis for comparison.

Doubling my speed, I reached the corner Dave had turned; I took a moment to build up my reserve of non-

chalance. Then I let out a breath and casually turned right
to look for him.

Dave was in the food court. Which appeared to be his
intended destination.

Okay . . . maybe his affair with Joyce consisted of buying food that was bad for them and eating it together?
Hardly grounds for divorce, but since Helen didn't want
one anyway, maybe it was a win-win for everybody. I
scanned the area for possible Joyce candidates, but I'd left
her photograph with my mother, and it was hard to remember her face. Not that it seemed to matter, because no one
was approaching Dave, male or female.

He walked past the Salad Works and the Burger King,
but stopped at Master Wok and . . . yes! A small blonde
woman, somewhat obscured by larger New Jerseyans hus-
tling by her with trays and shopping bags, walked over to
him and smiled broadly. Dave reached toward her. If this
was going to be a passionate embrace, I was much too far
away to photograph it. I started to trot toward them.

But Dave's hand, which had appeared to be making
scandalous advances a moment before, turned out to be
merely reaching for a sample on the tray the woman was
carrying. The tray bore small cups that no doubt held sam-
ples of Master Wok's most flavorful menu items. Dave tried
whatever it was, nodded in appreciation, dropped his tooth-
pick on the young woman's tray, then turned to move on.

Good: I hadn't missed the picture. Bad: *Still* no sign of
Joyce.

Dave walked to the far end of the court and stopped at
Nathan's Hot Dogs. He walked to the counter and ordered
something, and in very little time was eating the first of
two franks he'd gotten with a side of fries and a (somewhat
ironic) diet soda. He sat—by himself—at a table and
wolfed down the whole trayful of food with absolutely no
sign of contact with anyone who could be named Joyce, or
for that matter anyone who could be named anything.

Not only had I not gotten any incriminating photographs, now I was really hungry. And I couldn't even buy anything to eat, because Dave, no doubt in a hurry to get back before his lunch hour was over, was already done and practically sprinting out of the mall. I hadn't eaten, he had, and there had been no sign of an affair with anybody for me to immortalize in pixels. All in all, Dave was easily getting the better end of the deal this afternoon.

I kept him in sight as best I could until we were back out in the parking lot, Dave heading to his sensible Nissan and me to my prehistoric Volvo. Mom started talking even before I'd restarted the car to follow Dave back to his office. "Why didn't you answer my texts?" she asked.

"My battery was low. What's the problem?"

"Dad texted me. He says to come home now."

Eight

It transpired on the ride home that Mom had kept Dad's cell-phone plan active, despite his having died almost six years before. Ghosts can't be heard across phone lines, but some of them (apparently like my dad) can text. It had never occurred to me to give him my cell number, but in my family, death is not always an impediment to communication. Anyway, Mom hadn't asked questions when she'd gotten the text. Dad said to get home; we were on our way.

As I parked the Volvo at home, Dad was already outside, waving his arms at us as if we weren't going to notice him floating around near the kitchen door. Mom practically leaped out of the car, and although there was nothing on earth that could possibly hurt my father anymore, I understood the impulse. He looked panicked.

"There's some woman inside threatening to drive all of us out of the house!" he shouted. "She says the house needs to be cleaned, and she doesn't mean vacuuming the rugs."

Cybill.

I moaned a tiny bit, involuntarily. "I'll deal with it, Dad," I said as I walked past him into the kitchen. I saw Mom out of the corner of my eye, carrying her backpack and looking confused at my lack of concern.

Cybill was indeed setting up what appeared to be incense sticks in a vase I leave on the table in the den, and she was wearing an outfit directly out of 1966. Her long, gauzy dress matched her long, flowing gray hair, and she appeared to be trying to revive Flower Power by sheer force of will. Cybill also seemed to be humming to herself.

Harry and Beth Rosen were nowhere to be seen, but Tom and Libby Hill were watching Cybill from the opposite side of the room with looks of incredulity, mixed with anticipation: Was this part of the planned ghost shows? The Hills were seemingly unwilling to get too close to the crazy lady; Libby was actually standing in the far doorway, looking as if she was gauging the time it would take her to get to the front door if the place caught on fire or was under attack by evil spirits.

"Cybill?" I asked in my most pleasant innkeeper voice. "What's going on?"

She turned and looked mildly surprised to see me in my own guesthouse. Perhaps I needed to spend more time with the guests. "Why, I'm cleansing the house of spirits," she said, as if that explained everything. Then she went back to arranging the incense in the vase.

I could vaguely hear Mom and Dad talking in the kitchen, and the fact that only my mother's voice would be audible to the other living people in the room wasn't helping my blood pressure much.

"But I said that would be a bad idea right now," I reminded Cybill. "Remember?" The sugarcoating was starting to rub off my voice.

I saw Maxie appear, headfirst, through the den's ceiling, possibly attracted by the conversation. It was unusual for her to pay attention to anything going on with the guests.

Even if the incense had been lit, she wouldn't have smelled it, and the next spook show wasn't scheduled for at least two hours. She only came down if she thought there would be something amusing going on, which usually meant something that would cause me embarrassment.

Again, Cybill looked back over her shoulder. "But you have a small child living here," she argued. "It's not safe for her to be existing with these specters." I saw Libby's eyes widen at the prospect that the ghosts in the house they'd come specifically to see might be dangerous. (They're not.)

Now, you can tell me that I'm not a good hostess, and I'll be a little miffed. You can tell me I don't know anything about being a detective, and the likelihood is that I'll agree with you. But nobody on this planet can ever look me in the eye (or over the shoulder) and inform me that I'm a bad mother, particularly when it's related to Melissa's safety.

Besides, Maxie let out a *whoooo* and said to me, "I'll show *her* how dangerous the *specters* are." And she started toward the fireplace, where there are cast-iron pokers. She was grinning. Paul rose up through the basement and saw what Maxie was doing, flew to her side and started an unnecessarily sotto voce conversation with her about what was and was not all right to do when trying to prove the house was truly haunted.

I wanted to shout out to Maxie to forget the poker, but that would have probably been a move in the wrong direction, given that Cybill had questioned the security of my establishment in front of two other guests. My teeth felt fused together.

Still, I think you'd be proud of the way I pulled in my breath, took a second or two, and said, "It's really quite safe for Melissa and *everyone in the house*. I can assure you of that."

Mind you, things probably would have been fine after that if I'd simply stopped talking at that moment. I can see that now. Instead, trying to convince Cybill and the Hills that there was no danger, I said loudly, "You needn't worry. The ghosts *don't actually stay here in the house.* They come by to entertain you."

Maxie, who had barely raised the fireplace poker three inches from its stand, dropped it with a loud clatter, causing everyone in the room to look her way. "We're here for *what*?" she hissed.

I saw Dad zip in through the kitchen door—and when I say "through the kitchen door," I mean *through*—with Mom hot on his trail. To the other living people in the room, I'm sure the place looked wide open. To me, it was starting to get overcrowded. "What's going on?" Dad asked. It seemed to be the question of the day.

"Your daughter seems to think we're the circus clowns around here," Maxie huffed. Then she vanished completely, which is something she does when she gets really peeved.

Cybill, who for all her purported abilities with ghosts, appeared not to have seen or heard anything and still looked incredulous. "You *want* there to be deceased spirits in your house?" she asked.

"Absolutely," I said, giving Paul a reassuring look. "I can control them." His expression indicated that *control* wasn't his favorite word, but he didn't say anything.

"Well," Cybill said. "If you're certain . . ."

"Completely certain," I assured her.

She didn't answer but nodded slightly and began putting her exorcism equipment back into a canvas bag emblazoned with a five-pointed star, which she had dropped on the floor. Tom Hill looked relieved, and Libby practically collapsed into one of the armchairs. I shuddered to think of what Cybill might have told them in the ramp-up to her attempted act of kindness. I'd have to talk to all the guests later and reassure them of their safety.

I retreated to the kitchen with Mom in tow, to think.

Dad and Paul followed. I'm always happy to see my father, but right now, I was sort of ghosted out and really just wanted to regroup.

"I looked that woman in the eye and told her I didn't want her to 'cleanse' my house," I said, mostly to myself. "Maybe I'm not communicating as well as I should."

Dad didn't help matters by telling me, "You might want to work on your people skills," as we entered the kitchen, and I put on a kettle of water to boil. I wasn't sure what I wanted, but it was definitely a hot drink.

I looked at him. When Mom's around, Dad doesn't hover up near the ceiling or do much that's especially supernatural. He was right next to her, at the same level, although an inch or so of his feet fell below the plane of the floor. Being a ghost, I've observed, is an inexact science. But he does his best, and since he was always a few inches taller than Mom, the sinkage was insignificant.

"My people skills?" I asked. "I just handled a woman who was performing some odd ritual in my house, despite my specifically telling her not to, and without asking me ahead of time, all the while reassuring my other guests of their safety, and you think I need to work on my people skills?"

"In the process, you insulted Maxie and Paul, baby girl." Dad has always called me that, and I've always loved it, except between the ages of fourteen and twenty-five.

"He's right," Mom chimed in. They have presented a united front for as long as I can remember, and Dad's being dead was not changing the rules at all, I'd noticed. "You can't treat Maxine and Paul like the unpaid help around here."

Coffee. With extra caffeine. That was what I needed. I turned off the burner with the kettle on it and started getting the coffeemaker prepared. After taking a few seconds to clear my head—which wasn't really all that clear even now—I looked at Paul. "Did I really hurt your feelings?" I asked him.

Paul didn't make eye contact. "I knew what you meant," he said.

"But you didn't like the way I said it."

He looked at me sideways and a half-smile forced its way through. "It might not have been my choice of words," he admitted. "The problem really is Maxie."

As usual. "I'll apologize to her when I see her because she won't show up if I call her now, and I really don't want the guests to hear me just screaming her name," I said. "But I apologize to you now, Paul. I really didn't intend to make you feel bad. I was just trying to keep the guests feeling comfortable here. That's important."

Paul nodded. "Yes, it is. And I accept the apology. But keep in mind that Maxie . . ."

"I know."

"No, you don't. She was already miffed at you about last night," Dad said. "She was talking about it before."

Last night? What happened last night? "Miffed about what?" I asked.

"She said some woman was saying you were the ghost lady and you said there were no ghosts in the house," Dad reported. "She said you were ashamed of . . . us, I guess."

Coffee was going to take too long. Did hot chocolate have caffeine? I went to check the box. Why wasn't there a Dunkin' Donuts in my kitchen?

"You know that's not true," I told Dad. "I spent years hoping you'd come here."

"That's me," he answered. "Maxie thinks you don't like her."

I thought we'd settled that some months before. "Maxie isn't always easy to like," I told him.

Just then, there was a knock on my back door. While I

would have expected Maxie to materialize in the kitchen to show off my bad timing, it was even worse news: Kerin Murphy, looking perky.

I hate perky.

"Here comes a real test of my people skills," I told Dad.

I walked to the door, considered looking Kerin directly in the face and telling her I wasn't home, and then decided she wouldn't get it, so I opened the door. "Kerin," I said, unable to put the exclamation point she probably expected after her name. "What brings you here?"

Mom, the only other person in the room Kerin could see, exchanged nods with her. But Mom's eyelids were a little lower than usual. She knew I didn't like Kerin, knew why and was on my side.

"How are you, Alison?" Kerin said, and then didn't wait for a reply, indicating that she really didn't care. "I'm here for a progress report."

"A progress report? I've only had eighteen hours to begin an investigation, Kerin. I'm also working for another client, and I have a house full of guests. Believe me, I'll let you know when there's progress to be reported."

I saw Dad wince at my tone. He was a contractor in life and always exceedingly polite to his customers.

"How are the children, Kerin?" Mom asked, in her usual subtle style of changing the subject.

Kerin nearly rolled her eyes, but she knew better than to diss Mom. "They're just fine, Loretta," she said. The expression on Dad's face indicated he thought "Mrs. Kerby" would have been a more appropriate form of address. "But what I'm really here to do is get a sense of where the investigation into Everett's murder is going," she continued, looking back at me with a challenging expression. One-track mind, that woman.

"Well, Kerin, so far I've checked in with Lieutenant McElone at the police station," I said. "Everett's autopsy report is not available yet. I intend to get over to talk to Marv Winderbrook at the Fuel Pit as soon as I have a chance. Other than that, the case hasn't progressed much in less than a day. I apologize if you thought these things happened more quickly, but they don't."

My attitude probably wasn't good for business, but then I wasn't really a PI, so that wasn't a very high priority for me. I was an innkeeper and would be happy to never have another investigation client as long as I lived.

"This is not what we expected when we agreed to your exorbitant salary demand," Kerin said.

I shrugged. "So fire me," I said. Dad shook his head, but he didn't understand that my business plan was to get out of business as quickly as possible. "Feel free to find yourself another investigator, or as *I* would advise, let the police handle it. Why are you so hot and bothered over Everett's death anyway? I agree it's very sad that the poor guy was killed, but I didn't know him very well. Did you?"

Kerin sniffed. "My estimation of a person's worth isn't based on how well I know them," she said. I considered asking whether she estimated a person's worth in dollars or negotiable bonds, but instead I noted Maxie floating in from the backyard, looking bored. She perked up when she saw Kerin, though, no doubt recognizing that her presence meant conflict, something Maxie enjoys no matter what her mood. "Everett was a part of this community, he was valued, he was worth caring about."

"I agree," I said. "What was his last name?"

Kerin's head came close to the land speed record for snapping up. "His last name?" she asked.

"Yes. Everett's last name. Surely you know it, since you cared *so* deeply about him that you would pay three thousand dollars to find out who killed him." I couldn't figure out why Kerin was pretending—and I was sure she was pretending—to be so upset about Everett's death. I wanted to push her into a situation where she would have to drop the mask and have an actual human moment.

But I had underestimated her. "Sandheim," she said after a moment. "Everett's last name was Sandheim."

Damn it!

Nine

Kerin stayed until the very moment I had to leave to pick up Melissa from school. In fact, she walked me to the door of my Volvo before taking off herself, although she said nothing more that was the least bit interesting or helpful. Which figured. There was clearly something very, very odd going on with that woman.

"I think your pal Kerin is up to something. What do you think it is?" Maxie said, pulling out her notepad and a pencil. I hadn't been quick enough pulling the car out of the driveway, and she'd hopped in and was now sitting backward in the passenger seat, arms behind her head and legs extended into the rear seat. I half expected her to start doing the backstroke.

"She's trying to get her revenge on me by making me 'come out' as the ghost lady," I explained. "She wants to humiliate me in the circles of Harbor Haven."

"Being the ghost lady isn't humiliating," Maxie said, licking the pencil point because she thought it made her look more professional. "You should own it. Tell everybody how awesome we are."

As I mulled that one over, we pulled up in front of the school and Maxie put down the notepad and pencil to spot Melissa. What did she mean, own being the ghost lady? Shout it from the rooftops? I'd never be able to talk to any of the "normal" people in town again.

Melissa was ensconced among her bevy of friends and didn't notice me for a moment, which was not atypical. I touched the horn gently and indicated to Maxie that she should move into the backseat. She chose instead to fly out of the car and over to Melissa, who was hugging all her friends in turn, as if she were leaving on a raft expedition down the Amazon, rather than a ten-minute drive to her home, only to see them all again tomorrow. Eleven-year-olds live in drama. It would be so much better if they lived in musical comedy.

Maxie whispered into Liss's ear as she walked to the car, and I saw my daughter's head snap up to catch her eye. I guessed Maxie had passed along the news of Kerin Murphy's mysterious visit, and that was confirmed the second Melissa opened the passenger's door.

"What's the deal with Mrs. Murphy?" she demanded.

"It's nice to see you too, honey," I cooed at her. Once her seat belt was in place, I started out of the circular drive around the front door of the school and headed back onto the street. Maxie took up a position in—and I do mean *in*—the backseat, a smug expression on her face.

"Mom," Melissa insisted. "What's going on? Are you going to admit to being the ghost lady?"

Something dislodged itself from the back of my throat. "I can't imagine where Maxie got that idea," I said honestly. "I'm not going to do that."

Maxie, never one to leave well enough alone, volunteered, "You're just insulting us, you know. It's like you don't want to admit you see us, because we're not good enough to talk to."

"I never thought that."

"But you won't tell people otherwise," Maxie said. Maxie has to have the last word.

Accordingly, nobody said anything for a while. Paul Melançon played uninterrupted in the CD player as we all tried to figure out what the heck the latest developments could have meant.

Now I *really* wanted some alone time to talk to Paul and would have to hustle it up because Josh, Jeannie and Tony were coming for dinner tonight. "What's really important," I said to no one in particular, "is that we figure out who would have a reason to want Everett dead. Paul always says the only two reasons people kill someone is for love"— well, he actually says sex—"or money."

"Did Everett have someone who would be jealous of him?" Melissa asked. "I never saw him with anybody—he would just ask for money or a blanket or something."

"I only saw the guy once or twice," Maxie said. "And it was when I was alive. But he didn't seem the type."

"Well, he certainly didn't seem the type to have money," I noted.

Melissa ran her teeth over her bottom lip, a habit she calls scratching, which indicates she's thinking. "Maybe he was one of those homeless people who really has a lot of money but is just, like, eclectic or something."

"Eccentric, you mean," I suggested.

"Yeah. That."

We were just passing the office of the *Harbor Haven Chronicle*, and Melissa pointed out Phyllis Coates, the paper's editor/publisher/owner/entire staff locking the front door on her way out. I stopped at the curb and called to Phyllis, whom I've known since I delivered copies of the *Chronicle* on my bike when I was thirteen.

"Alison!" Phyllis said. She walked to the car and leaned in the window. "Hey, Melissa. You ready to come deliver papers for me yet?"

Melissa looked eagerly at me, but before she could say anything, I answered, "No, she's not. But I'm glad we ran into you. What do you know about Everett Sandheim?"

Phyllis shrugged. "He's dead," she said. "What do you want to know?"

"Come on. A murder in Harbor Haven, and you're saying you're not looking into it? I don't believe you."

Maxie looked Phyllis up and down. "What good is she going to do?"

Liss knew better than to look back reprovingly at her, but her eyebrows lowered. She'd talk to Maxie later. And Melissa was one of the few people to whom Maxie might actually listen.

"I didn't say I'm not looking into it," Phyllis corrected me, a sly smile trying to disguise itself on her lips. "I asked what you wanted to know. You have a client?" Phyllis is one of the few people who treats my PI license seriously, not like a funny little hobby I picked up along the way.

"I have a gaggle of clients," I said, the irritation sneaking into my voice. All right, invading my voice frontally. "Kerin Murphy and the assembled membership of her odd fan club have taken an unexplained interest in Everett's death, and they think—you'll love this—that a ghost killed him, so I'm the person to investigate."

Of course, Phyllis has heard all the ghost-lady talk around town, and she even knows about my arrangement with Senior Plus. She has chosen not to ask me about it, because she is a journalist (Phyllis spent twenty years with the *New York Daily News*) and doesn't believe anything she can't definitively prove. I love Phyllis. "Well, I guess that makes sense, if your brain is as twisted as Kerin Murphy's," she said. "That woman is a walking high colonic."

"What's a high colonic?" Melissa asked.

"You don't want to know," I said. She let that go, which is one of the many reasons I also adore my daughter.

"What can you tell me about the murder that the cops won't?" I asked Phyllis.

Phyllis thought about it. She has a "friend" in the county medical examiner's office, and the less said about how she gets her information from him, the better. "I hear the stab wound wasn't a stab wound," she said. Before I could react, she added, "It was a lot of very small stab wounds."

"Very small?" I wasn't expecting that. "How small?"

"Well, not like a nail file or something. It was a knife, but either not a big one or the person using it wasn't especially strong."

That got the wheels turning in my head. "So it's possible he was stabbed somewhere else and went to the Fuel Pit to recover but bled out instead," I suggested. As always when discussing such things, I quickly looked at Melissa to see if she was freaked out by the conversation, but she's a veteran now and was merely concentrating.

Phyllis tipped her head to the side a bit to indicate "maybe." "There was no blood found leading into the restroom," she said. "I think it's really unlikely that whoever it was cleaned up after themselves on the way out."

Okay, so I'm not Sherlock Holmes. "Anything else I ought to know?" I asked. When in doubt, put the burden of the conversation on the other person. In other words, punt.

"I don't know what you've been told," Phyllis said. "Lieutenant McElone probably gave you the same plain vanilla report she gave me when I called her for a quote yesterday. But there is something I found out while writing Everett's obituary."

"An obituary for a homeless guy?" Maxie asked. "Who does that?"

"Phyllis," Melissa said. Phyllis turned her head to look at Liss, who remembered that Maxie was not in Phyllis's conversation, and covered by asking, "What did you find out?"

"Well, you know about Everett's family, right?" Phyllis,

like many reporters, got into the news business with one purpose in mind—getting to find out stuff before everybody else and then telling them about it to show off how smart she is. Phyllis is *very* smart, so she gets to do that a lot, and it's obvious the thrill of it has never left her.

"Yeah," I said, just to show I was smart, too. "He had a father in South Carolina and a sister in Montana, right?" I looked at her.

"And an ex-wife. He was married to a woman who was stationed with him in the Army."

"When did they get divorced?" I asked.

"Six years after they both got out," she answered. "His sister said Everett was trying to find work and failing, and his wife wasn't interested in sticking around to watch him become, well, what we all knew him as."

"Don't tell me, let me guess," I said. "It was an acrimonious divorce."

"I have no way of knowing yet," Phyllis told me. "But how many divorces have you heard of that were sweet and adorable?"

"Not yours," Maxie said, despite not having been around for my divorce. I wanted to give her a look that reminded her the daughter of that marriage was in the car with us, but Maxie caught herself and said, "Your divorce was probably just civil, right?"

"Not many," I answered Phyllis, hoping as usual that Maxie would just go away. She didn't, but she kept quiet this time.

"It's not much of anything yet, but you never know," Phyllis said. She looked at Melissa. "You sure you're not ready for a route yet?"

"She's sure," I jumped in. I had been thirteen when I had the route, and Melissa would be, too, assuming the *Chronicle* wasn't entirely an online publication by then. "What's the ex-wife's name?"

"Brenda Leskanik," Phyllis said without hesitation or notes. "Formerly Specialist Brenda Leskanik."

"I'll do some Internet research," I said, looking at Maxie, who would actually do it. "I'll see what I can find out."

"So will I," Phyllis assured me.

Ten

"This is a lovely town," Libby Hill said. "But it's not quite a real shore town, is it?"

That was puzzling, since Harbor Haven is right on the beach and more than two-thirds of our economy is centered around the tourist trade, so I asked, "What do you mean, Libby?"

I was spending a little time with the non-Cybill guests—Tom and Libby Hill, Harry and Beth Rosen—in the den following the late-afternoon spook show. Soon the guests would be heading out in search of dinner while I took remedial cooking classes from my mother in anticipation of three dinner guests, at least one of whom was a really good kisser. And if you think it was odd that I was kicking people out of my house to eat while my mother showed Melissa and me how to cook dinner for three other people, well, you haven't spent that much time around my house.

Melissa was upstairs getting her homework out of the way (after complaining that she could be of more use helping in the investigation, although she didn't specify how or which one), and Maxie had been tasked with finding out what she could about any of Everett Sandheim's surviving family members, including Brenda Leskanik, the ex.

"What do you mean it's not a real shore town, Libby?" I asked again.

"Well, there's no boardwalk or rides or anything like that," she answered. Libby didn't sound disappointed so much as mildly surprised.

"Things have changed here since the storm," I told her. "We're still very much in the rebuilding phase." It's hard to describe what the Jersey Shore looks like now, and worse, it's getting harder to remember what it used to look like. The storm ripped through this area with a malicious vengeance, destroying people's homes, their businesses, their lives. The storm pushed sand two feet deep on city streets, and water levels reached the second floor of some buildings. The Seaside Heights roller coaster, a staple for decades, had been entirely washed out to sea. We're still trying to figure out how to bring the tourist trade back beyond the curiosity factor—some people have to see the state of the devastation.

People are weird.

"That's not really what I was getting at, dear," Libby said. "It's not that I'm desperate for an amusement pier. This is a darling town, and I like it, don't get me wrong. But," she leaned over and said confidentially, "if it wasn't for the ghosts, it would be just like home." She winked. "I told someone in town today where I was staying, and she referred to you as the ghost lady." Libby made a little chuckle. "I thought that was adorable, don't you?"

"Adorable isn't the word," I said, doing my best to maintain a smile. "Thanks for passing that along." I resisted—with some difficulty—the impulse to find out who had been bandying the ghost-lady stuff around in Harbor

Haven, but quickly came to the conclusion that it didn't matter. It could have been anyone. Except Phyllis.

"You're not really going to let Cybill get rid of them, are you?" Libby asked. "The ghosts?"

Oh, brother. "Is she saying that again?" I asked. "I've told her specifically it's not something I want to happen here." Note to self: Lock Cybill in her room. Too drastic?

"She muttered something about you not understanding the danger," Libby told me. "There isn't any *real* danger, is there?"

"Absolutely not," I said, watching Maxie float from the library into the former game room without so much as a glance at me; she was irritated, which is her natural state. "Will you excuse me, please?" The number of people annoyed with me was growing, and I didn't want to add Libby to the list.

I walked past the as-yet-to-be-determined-purpose room, where I'd earlier conferred with Paul, albeit briefly, before he'd had to go rattle window dressings and "fly" Melissa around the room, which was harrowing for Melissa's mother (that's me) to watch every time he did it.

"It sounds like the Sandheim case has a lot of possibilities," Paul had said, pacing a couple of feet off the floor.

"Possibilities?" I asked. "You want to turn it into a musical? What do you mean, possibilities?"

"I mean there are a lot of different ways the investigation can go, a number of avenues we can pursue. That's very promising."

"What avenues? The only thing I can think to do is get Maxie to find out about Everett's family," I admitted.

Paul stopped pacing and hovered in the center of the room, which looked disturbingly empty. I hoped Tony would have some encouraging suggestions on a use for the place. This whole just-gut-it-and-see-what-happens strategy was now seeming quite ill-advised.

"Take out your notepad," Paul said, so I retrieved it

from my tote bag. When he saw that I had, he continued, "First, you're going to have to go to the scene of the crime."

"You want me to go to the men's room at a gas station?" I asked.

"There's no substitute for on-site experience," Paul said, repeating an axiom he'd beaten me over the head with before.

"What am I looking for?" I didn't want to think about what I'd find, even if there was no evidence of Everett's murder in the restroom.

"You'll know when you find it," Paul said.

"You never wrote fortune cookies professionally, did you?"

He ignored that remark, something he's become extremely good at doing since we met, particularly when Maxie and I were conversing (arguing) or when Josh was around. Paul's more tolerant of Josh than he's been of some other men I've known (such as my ex, but he had a point there) since I moved into the Victorian, but if you ask me—and even if you don't—Paul has some jealousy issues where my dating life is concerned. He doesn't say anything, but his silences can be deafening. On the other hand, Maxie tends to either get a crush on guys I date or pull pranks on them to encourage them to leave. She had already mentioned that she thought Josh was cute, but she hadn't made things fly by his face or tried to pull his shirt up from behind him.

And you wonder why I don't tell Josh about the ghosts in the house.

"There's no way I can tell you what to look for, because I can't know what the scene looks like," Paul explained. "Take your phone or a real camera, and get pictures that I can look at when you get back. But look for anything that seems unusual or incongruous."

"You might be surprised, but I've spent very little time in men's restrooms," I told him. "I might miss something 'incongruous.'"

Paul smiled. "Aside from the odd piece of equipment, I don't think you'll find it all that different from what you're used to," he said. "But I'll look at the pictures in case there's some secret thing only men will understand." He has a sly wit. That wasn't an example, but he does.

"Okay, M," I said. "What else am I assigned to do?"

Paul's face got serious (its usual state) again, and he thought. "Find out if there was a will." He held up a hand. "I know, Everett was homeless and not exactly wealthy, but he still might have filed something before he got that way. See if his old Army records include anything."

"His life was different in those years," I reminded Paul. "He had a wife, for one thing."

He nodded. "Yes. That will be an interesting thread to explore. Once Maxie gives us some results, we'll know which direction to take it. In any event, we certainly want to know where Everett's ex-wife is living now and whether they were in contact."

I saluted. "Okay, boss," I said. "Now, do I need the cyanide pills for this one, or will the service revolver to the temple do the trick if I'm captured?"

"You're hilarious," he said without smiling and vanished into the floor.

It always makes me feel better to talk to Paul about these things. Most of what he tells me would probably occur to me independently but not until much later. And hearing it from someone who at least acts like he knows what he's doing is very reassuring.

I continued on to the kitchen, where my mother was already setting her stage. Mom has a real theatrical streak, and given that she was about to show off in front of her granddaughter, she was indulging it to unprecedented extremes. She had cleaned every countertop in the kitchen to a positive gleam (despite the fact that my complete lack of desire to cook meant they were virtually never made dirty). She had spread out ingredients for the massive

lasagna she intended to make—pasta, ground beef, toma-
toes, parmesan cheese for grating, ricotta cheese not for
grating, and I couldn't tell what else—in the exact order
she would use them, and I'm pretty sure lined up perfectly
as well. I didn't have a level handy to check.

Mom was, honest to goodness, sharpening a knife when
I walked in, and Melissa, who apparently had finished her
homework to the point that she could tell me so with a
straight face, was watching her raptly.

"Put some salt in the water when you cook pasta," she
was telling Liss. "Most people don't because they think it's
bad for them, and their pasta doesn't cook evenly." *Most
people* I assumed, included all the people in the room who
were me.

"What's with the knife sharpening, Mom?" I asked as I
walked in. "What part of lasagna needs to be chopped?"

Mom, her spotlight slightly dimmed when Melissa
appeared to be considering my questions, shook her head
slightly at my ignorance and reclaimed center stage. "You
can't just serve everyone a lasagna, Alison," she instructed.
Any moment and her voice would enter a Julia Child–like
upper register. "We will be having a roast chicken, as well."

I hadn't seen any such chicken in any stage of prepara-
tion, but I kept my mouth shut, reminding myself that I
had, literally, asked for this. "Sorry," I said. "What'd I miss
that might be on the final?"

Mom proceeded to hit the rewind button and start from
the beginning, and to my surprise, Melissa did not look the
least bit annoyed at me for causing the reiteration. I pulled
over a barstool from the center island, where we usually eat
the dinner I've "prepared" (by way of calling for its deliv-
ery) and folded my hands in my lap. I'd be the best little girl
in class, not counting my daughter.

For the next twenty minutes, I went through basic training on lasagna (it turned out that the roast chicken—which
had been prepared with lemon and parsley, in case anyone

ever asks—had just gone into the oven). There were, in fact, questions along the way, but I was so attentive that I didn't even have to take notes. Of course, I'd also turned on the voice recorder in my tote bag so I could refer back to Mom's lecture if I was ever foolish enough to try doing this myself.

"Cooking isn't really that hard at all," Mom concluded eventually, placing the lasagna in the oven and letting out the aroma of the roast chicken. "Even if you're not inclined to try things on your own, you can always just follow the instructions in a good cookbook, and if you do exactly what you're told, you can come up with a very good result."

I'm not sure how much of this was intended to be a life lesson rather than a cooking symposium, but I was mostly getting hungry. Luckily, the back door opened then and Jeannie trundled herself, her husband and their eight-month-old son, Oliver, into my kitchen, sniffed the air and said, "Mrs. Kerby, you've outdone yourself!"

My best friend, ladies and gentlemen.

Melissa immediately got up to try and pry Oliver from Jeannie's arms, but the car seat into which he was still buckled was an impediment, as was Jeannie's reluctance ever to let anybody—including Tony—other than herself see to her son's needs. Things had loosened up a little since Jeannie had gone back to work, but when she was "on duty," it would take a crowbar and a pretty strong back to get Oliver away. Still, Liss is determined and resourceful. Shortly thereafter, Josh arrived. He gets to the house later than everyone else because he has to close the store, then go home and change into what he calls paint-free clothing before heading out.

Over the past few months we had become a congenial group, but one that was still in the process of defining itself (in part because one half of the group didn't know that the other half existed). It didn't get any easier when I took Tony and Josh to the game room—which Josh had pondered with me a few times before—where Maxie and Dad were already discussing possibilities. To my horror, Dad seemed to be taking Maxie seriously. Had I no confederates in this house anymore?

"It's the right size and configuration," my father was saying, pushing his hat—a sharp Frank Sinatra style that Brooklyn hipsters think is their own—back on his head. "It's a possibility."

The worst part was I couldn't say anything to Dad or Maxie, because Josh was there. Tony would have understood, Jeannie would have ignored me, and everyone else was in on the ghost thing.

Clearly, that meant I wasn't being fair to Josh. But I realized as I thought about it that my stomach was clenching, and I'd have to take the time to think about that later when I was alone.

As if you could ever be alone in this house.

"It's not like I haven't been here before," Tony said to me. "I've been in this room a hundred times."

"I'm telling you, I've got it!" Maxie insisted to me, but again, I did not respond. And I started getting annoyed; it's not as if this was the first time I'd played it straight in front of Josh, let alone the "civilian" guests.

"I know," I told Tony. "But you haven't seen it since I painted the paneling and cleared stuff out. Tell me what you think about the space. What's the best thing to do with it?"

"Home theater!" Maxie yelled. "It's perfect. A few couches, a big-screen TV at that end." She pointed. "Then you put in fill speakers and a kick-ass Blu-ray player, and you could have movie nights!"

That wasn't even close to the experience I wanted to offer my guests. I was trafficking in a quiet, relaxing experience at the beach, not a *Die Hard* film festival with extra oomph to the explosions. Besides, all that equipment sounded expensive. I shook my head slightly, and Maxie looked positively stupefied.

"No?" she said, drawing the two letters out to a few hundred (mostly *o*'s). "Why not?"

"Well," said Josh, having heard none of this, "what are you hoping you can offer to the people who stay here?" A perfect softball question that could enable me to talk directly to Maxie without giving myself away; the man was a gem.

"I want it to be a place for *relaxation* and *quiet*," I stressed, maybe a little too vehemently, because Tony and Josh both gave me odd looks. "I'm looking for something that can give the guests a place to go to take it easy and enjoy the time away from their normal lives of noise and constant demands." Okay, so that might have been aimed a little too squarely at Maxie.

She made a sputtering sound, shook her head like she was dealing with a crazy person and swept herself up through the ceiling. Dad looked at her, then at me, and said, "*I* thought it was a good idea."

"In that case," Tony said, walking in a large circle around the room, "I think you're going about it the wrong way."

What else was I doing wrong? "How so?" I managed to get out.

"Because it's redundant. The rest of the house is quiet and relaxing. You've got a library where people can sit quietly. The den is homey and a refuge from the outside world, and the beach is pretty much right outside the French doors there. What you had in this room was for fun, like with the pool table. It was recreation."

"But nobody was using it," I pointed out. "The only people who ever played pool in here were Mom and Melissa."

"Your mother can really break a rack," Dad interjected, still looking up to see if Maxie was coming back. I love the man dearly.

Tony nodded. "Maybe something a little different. A movie room? A place where the guests can get together and socialize a little?"

Josh pointed at Tony. "That's really good," he said. Great. Now I had a grand total of no allies.

I shook my head. "Not what I'm looking for. Besides, there are seven windows in this room. Getting it dark enough for a movie would be pretty near impossible, especially during the summer when it doesn't get dark until after nine."

"Room-darkening shades," Tony said. "Use paint remover and stain the walls back to a darker wood tone."

"You could use that karaoke machine you have in here, too, and host events on the nights you're not doing 'ghost' things," Josh suggested. "It's like a common room."

There was just no point. "If you two aren't going to take this seriously, I'll have to figure it out on my own," I said, and headed back to the kitchen, taking in their incredulous stares as I went.

Men.

Back in the kitchen, I gave Jeannie (I still wasn't sure I wanted to talk to Tony or Josh) a rundown on what I'd done so far on my PI cases. There's nothing that generates conversation more than a good murder and an alleged marital indiscretion, so my latest cases were excellent ice-breakers. Jeannie has a sharp strategic mind and can be very helpful in thinking deviously, something at which I'm just a novice.

"So you followed this guy to the Monmouth Mall," Jeannie recapped, "and he went to Nathan's. Doesn't really seem to justify hiring a detective to tail him, does it?"

"It was just one lunch hour," I said. "Maybe he'll do something dirty and disgusting tomorrow." Mom gave Melissa a look, but there was no reaction from my daughter. I believe that not talking down to children makes them expect people to tell them things straight and encourages them to be straight with people in return. So far, Melissa is bearing me out; she is the very epitome of honesty and doesn't tolerate anything less in others.

"It's okay, Grandma," she told Mom. "I know about sex and everything."

Mom's head vibrated a little, but she didn't say anything. Dad, hovering near the stove, let out an involuntary laugh. And that got Mom to chuckle, too. "You're such a good mother," she said to me.

"So you think he's cheating on his wife?" I asked Jeannie, as if there'd been no side exchange.

She waved a hand. "Of course. If the wife has noticed something, you can bet your money the guy's got something on the side. Men are so easy to read."

"Good to know," Tony said through a bite of lasagna. "This is delicious, Loretta."

"All I saw was a guy buying a hot dog," I insisted to Jeannie.

"So keep watching," she said lightly.

"Exactly," Paul added to those of us who could hear him. He'd wandered into the kitchen when we started discussing the investigations. Ghosts are quiet travelers, and frankly, it gets a little creepy when you realize they're already in the room. "You can't give up on the stakeout after one attempt. You should be back there tomorrow."

I nodded slightly. "What about Everett?" I asked the room at large.

"Follow the money," Dad suggested. "Even if there isn't any. A guy doesn't get knifed just for entertainment."

"I dunno," Melissa said after she'd finished chewing a bit of lasagna. "Everett didn't have a house or a place to stay. He always wore the same clothes. He didn't have a car or anything. I don't think anybody killed him for his money."

Dad pointed to his temple and then to Melissa. "That's a smart girl." Liss smiled.

"Well, nobody said they did, but you're right, Melissa. I'd look for the ex-wife," Jeannie said. "People get awful mad at each other in a divorce." She looked at me and said, "Sorry." I waved a hand to assure her I wasn't at all offended.

"It was years ago," I said. "We're fine now." Well, that was a little fiction for Melissa's sake, but mostly The Swine and I *are* fine, as long as he stays three thousand miles away.

"We had a homeless man outside the store for months," Josh said. "He just used to sit there on a cardboard box he'd flattened out. Didn't write anything on it or ask for money. He just sat. The most defeated guy I've ever seen. Sy and I tried to help, called Social Services, offered him hot meals and stuff like that. It was really hard to watch during the winter, but we only got him to come inside the store to warm himself a few times. Then one especially cold day I went out to insist he come in, and the poor guy was gone. We never saw him again; I never even found out his name. He wouldn't tell me. It was just . . . I realize he might have had a substance-abuse problem or a mental illness or something, but what I remember more than anything else is how completely without hope that poor guy was." He shook his head a little.

The story clearly touched Mom. "Eat something, Joshua," she urged.

"So, what are you saying?" I asked. "That if Everett felt the same way as the homeless man in front of the paint store, he didn't have any hope either?"

"I don't know," Josh answered. "I never met this Everett guy, and it's not like all people living on the street are the same; there are some I never would have invited into the store. But I think after a while living like that, it just doesn't seem possible that your life can get any better, and that's a terrible thing to think."

"I'm not sure I get it," Melissa said, and for once, I felt a little regret about letting her in on the adult conversation. "Do you think Everett killed himself?"

There was a little pang in my heart as my daughter seemed to be feeling Everett's mental anguish for herself. "Oh, honey," I began.

Josh, ever trying to come to my rescue, jumped in. "I don't really know, Liss," he said. "I'm just saying he might have given up on himself, and maybe he decided he wasn't strong enough to go on."

"But you think he *could* have killed himself," Melissa said, apparently letting it sink in. Then she looked at Josh and shook her head. "With a tiny little knife? In a gas station men's room? I don't think so."

Josh looked at her and blinked a couple of times without speaking. It was my mother who finally broke the silence.

"She's a genius," she said. "There's apple pie for dessert. I didn't make it, but it's still good."

Eleven

🔑

"I can't believe you talked me into this," Maxie said.

We were sitting outside the Fuel Pit in my Volvo. Okay, *I* was sitting in the Volvo. Maxie was lying down—her favorite pose—with her legs extending into the engine block, not that she seemed to even notice. Which made sense, in a weird way.

"I didn't talk you into it," I reminded her. "Paul and Melissa talked you into it. I just watched."

"And grinned the whole time," the ghost noted.

That part was true. But how many times had Maxie conspicuously enjoyed my discomfort when Paul had "persuaded" me to take on an investigation I found scary or inconvenient? Taking a little pleasure at seeing the worm turn was hardly an actionable offense. Particularly when the aggrieved party was, you know, deceased.

Paul had been adamant about getting pictures of the room in which Everett Sandheim had died. It made sense from Paul's investigator point of view; he couldn't go to the scene of the crime, so seeing it from a number of angles would be especially helpful for him in determining whether there were any clues the police had left behind or over-looked. But I got Maxie's point—it wasn't the kind of place I'd want to enter either.

"I'm sorry about that," I said, mostly sincerely.

"I don't want to go in there," Maxie said without acknowl-edging the apology. "I don't see why it has to be me."

"It makes perfect sense," I told her. We were parked across the street from the Fuel Pit, watching the door to the men's room. Marv Winderbrook, who owned the station, was in the enclosure/convenience store near the gas pumps. There were no cars at the pumps. Marv appeared to be napping behind the counter. "You won't be seen. I would be. It'd be a lot harder to explain what I was doing in there."

"I still don't see why," Maxie insisted. She offered no rationale. "Why don't you just ask the gas station guy if you can go in and take pictures?"

"What if he says no?" I countered.

Maxie was silent.

"Come on. The sooner you go in and look around and take a couple of pictures, the sooner you can come out and it'll be over," I told her. I held out my camera. "Put this in your pocket."

She gave me the same look Melissa does when she wants to prove me wrong. "I don't have any pockets," she said. It was true; neither the black T-shirt (with the legend "More Than You Think") nor the running shorts she was wearing had pockets.

"You can have pockets anytime you want, and you know it," I countered. "Move."

"Suppose there's somebody *in there*," she said with what appeared to be a shudder.

"We've been watching the door for fifteen minutes," I said. "If there's someone in there, he's got bigger problems than you."

"Ugh!" Maxie said, but suddenly she was wearing a New York Jets warm-up jacket, snatched the camera out of my hand and stuck it in her pocket. "You owe me!" she said and was out of the car and moving across the street before I could answer her. She stole a look back at me and stuck out her tongue, but I decided to let that go because I had no alternative.

I listened to the radio while I waited. There were very few cars going by and fewer pedestrians, so no one was going to question why a woman in a dilapidated Volvo was sitting across the street from a gas station listening to Marvin Gaye.

The wait gave me time to mull over my relationship with Josh. We'd been seeing each other—if you didn't count impromptu playdates at the paint store when we were tweens—for about four months now. That's not an insignificant amount of time. And I had never had a reason to think Josh was anything but a caring, intelligent, funny guy who seemed to like me quite a bit. You don't find those all that often, especially when you're a single mother. Would I be risking losing it all by telling him the truth? I felt like it was somehow holding us back that I couldn't tell him about Paul and Maxie—and Dad for that matter—but I didn't know how to impart the information about them without making myself sound like a first-class lunatic. Yes, he'd heard the whispers around town about me being the ghost lady, and he knew all about the Senior Plus tours, but I'd let him assume that I was using those things as marketing to further my guesthouse's business. Which, technically, I was.

"Floor it!" Suddenly, Maxie was back in the passenger seat, looking positively terrified and shrieking at the top of what had once been her lungs. "Get me out of here!"

I put the Volvo in gear immediately and pulled out onto the street. "What's wrong?" I asked. "Was someone in there?"

"No!" she yelled. "Keep going!"

"Did you see something? Was there a ghost in the men's room?"

No longer hyperventilating, Maxie looked at me with what appeared to be pity for my deplorable stupidity. "Do you think I'm afraid of ghosts?" she asked, her voice easily an octave lower.

"Well then, what? What are we speeding away from?" I turned a corner so the gas station would be out of view, even in the mirrors.

"It was *disgusting*!" she wailed. "Men are pigs!"

My heart slowed down to the same rate it beats when I exercise, and I brought the car to the speed limit and left it there. "We're peeling away and burning rubber because it wasn't nice in the gas station men's room?" I asked.

Maxie looked at me sheepishly. "It was really bad," she said in a small voice.

"Honestly," I said. "A grown woman. Sort of."

"What does that crack mean?"

I ignored her and started driving up Shore Drive toward Route 35. "Did you see anything *helpful* in there?" I asked.

"I don't know. I took pictures. Paul can decide if they're helpful." Calmer now, Maxie stretched her feet down like Fred Flintstone and put her hands behind her neck like she was relaxing. "Don't I get a thank-you?"

"Absolutely. Thank you for acting like a six-year-old."

She sat up and pouted. "For going in there all by myself, something *you* didn't want to do."

"You're right, actually. Thank you."

"Hey, this isn't the way home," Maxie said as we got on the highway. "Where are we going?"

"To follow a guy who's supposed to be cheating on his wife," I answered.

"Now that's more my style!" She was suddenly wearing sunglasses and a trench coat. Maxie seems to have a vision of the world formed by watching old Warner Brothers cartoons.

"Keep the camera ready," I told her.

We made it from the Fuel Pit to Dave Boffice's office in about twenty minutes, then sat and watched the building, which was doing remarkably little. Maxie asked what kind of snacks I'd brought, which was an odd question on her part, considering she couldn't eat them, and I told her I hadn't brought any, which wasn't odd at all, considering I shouldn't. She wanted to blast the radio, and I reminded her that we were attempting *not* to draw attention to ourselves, a concept she seemed to find difficult to process.

I checked my wristwatch and then looked up. "There he is," I said, relieved for an excuse to end this inane conversation. I'd kept the car running, despite being down to a quarter tank of gas because I didn't want the sound of it starting up to attract attention. The fact that Dave was fifty feet away and unlikely to have heard it hadn't occurred to me.

"Let's roll," Maxie said.

"Nobody says that." That I knew of.

Much as I had the day before, but with a more talkative passenger in the car, I followed Dave Boffice for a number of miles before he decided to stop. It was clear that Dave was not heading for the Monmouth Mall this time; the route went east rather than south, and the drive was much shorter, only a little over five minutes.

Dave stopped in front of a little house in Fair Haven that had suffered storm damage. We had passed a number of Colonials and some newer McMansions, none of which were as cozy-looking as this less expensive one. But this one had blue tarps on the roof, indicating work being done, and the stump of what must have once been a very impressive tree in front. I backed the car into a driveway three doors down, with no sign of an inhabitant at the home. If someone were to open the front door, however, I figured I'd be able to pull out in a hurry.

"This must be it," Maxie said. "The girlfriend's house."

I looked through the file I had on the back seat. "Not

according to the information Helen gave me," I told her. "Joyce Kinsler lives in Eatontown."

"*Ooh,*" Maxie said. "Maybe he's got *two*!"

"Will you take it easy?" I went through some more forms and the notes I'd made on Joyce's interview.

"I'm going to go take a look," Maxie said. It was unusual for her to volunteer for . . . anything, but she seemed to really be relishing this stakeout. I guess after the men's room, anything was an improvement.

Maxie got out of the car and walked, or hovered or whatever it is she does, over to where Dave's car was parked. He was already at the front door, ringing the bell. I pulled a pair of binoculars out of the glove compartment—real ones, not one of Melissa's toys—and watched to see who would open the door.

But the storm door in front was solid and opened out, blocking my view. I couldn't see the person behind the door, but I saw Dave smile, lean over as if to kiss someone and then vanish inside the house.

Maxie came wandering back to the car a few minutes later and walked directly through the hood and the windshield to sit with her back to the dashboard and look at me. "The name on the mailbox is O'Toole," she said. "Does that ring a bell?"

I decided not to speculate. "Did you see who opened the door?"

"No," Maxie said. "I didn't get there fast enough, and I didn't want to go inside in case something dirty was going on. Did you find the Fair Haven stuff in your notes?"

"I haven't been looking. I was watching you."

I looked through the documents again, including the intake form I had given Helen to fill out when we met.

"Look!" Maxie said. "The door's opening again."

Maxie might be annoying and juvenile, but she is accurate. The door opened, and Dave Boffice walked out, his shoulders slumping just a little bit.

"He's really quick, too," Maxie scoffed. "This guy's a loser."

Dave turned, and I very faintly heard a voice calling to him from the door, which was still impossible to see through. But I held up the binoculars anyway. "Go look—" I started to tell Maxie.

There was no need. The door opened wider, and a woman walked out onto the front steps as Dave turned back to talk to her. She was definitely not Joyce Kinsler. She was, in fact, a small, gray-haired woman in a housecoat and slippers who—honest to goodness—had her hair in curlers.

"She's old," Maxie said with her usual suave mixture of nuance and compassion.

I couldn't get a really good look at the woman's face. "She's not *that* old," I said. "I don't think." I went back to looking through the file. Finally I found the line I was looking for on Helen's intake form. "Fair Haven is the town where Helen grew up," I told Maxie, "and O'Toole is her maiden name. I bet that's Helen's mother, Margaret O'Toole," I said aloud, mostly to myself.

"Omigod!" Maxie screamed. "That's horrible!"

I looked her down and exhaled. "Visiting his mother-in-law on his lunch hour?" I said. "I really don't think that's such an awful thing."

"Oh. Yeah. That's what I meant."

Dave and probably-Margaret talked very briefly, then she shook her head and kissed him on the cheek. He turned back to his car, and she headed up the stairs to her front door. On his way, Dave wiped a little lipstick off his cheek. She hadn't gotten dressed or taken the curlers out of her hair, but Margaret O'Toole had still put on lipstick.

"Maybe Helen thinks he's cheating on her because of the lipstick, when he's actually just going to visit her mom," Maxie suggested.

I'd been thinking the same thing. "But why wouldn't Dave want his wife to know?"

"Maybe they don't get along," Maxie said. "My mom never liked my husband."

It was true but irrelevant. "You were married for four days," I reminded her.

"Three of them were good days," Maxie noted.

We didn't talk much on the way home.

Twelve

"It looks like a men's room," Paul said.

He was making a very big show of carefully examining each photo Maxie had downloaded from my camera onto my several-generations-ago MacBook, searching for the one anomaly that would surely solve Everett's murder and get the ghost-lady posse off my back. In theory, anyway.

"Isn't it supposed to look like a men's room?" I noted. We were holding an impromptu meeting in my bedroom, which is never my first choice, but I was hiding from Cybill, who seemed bound and determined not to leave the house during her *vacation* (and I use the term loosely). It was already everything I could do to keep her from donning that robe and troubling my other guests again. "What did you expect?"

"I didn't expect anything," Paul said, using his college professor voice. "I have to look at the scene with no expectations in order to see what I need to see."

This was a lecture I'd heard more than once, but I

managed to curtail the groan trying to organize in the back of my throat. Instead, I asked, "So what do you think?"

Paul frowned. "These aren't great pictures."

Maxie, perched near the top of my dresser, looked down with wide eyes. "I've never used that camera before," she defended herself. "And it was a men's room. I didn't want to look too closely."

There was no response to that from Paul. He kept staring at the picture on the screen and stroking his goatee. The game was no doubt afoot.

"What?" I asked.

"According to the police report you got from Lieutenant McElone," Paul said, "Everett was found sitting in the men's room with blood pooled around his feet. But there were no footprints in the blood. Whoever killed him either got out before he had bled very much or . . ." His voice trailed off.

"Or what?" Maxie wanted to know.

"Or they didn't leave footprints."

"Don't you start," I warned him. "I get enough of that from the Kerin Murphy Brigade. I'm not going to listen to it from you."

"You don't think it's possible a ghost murdered Everett?" Maxie said. "It's not like we haven't come across that kind of thing before." She loves it when she can puncture my argument. Maxie still holds a little resentment because she owned the Victorian before me, but being alive is ten-tenths of the law, so it was a moot point.

"I'm just saying it doesn't seem like a real likely occurrence," I said.

"But we can't definitively rule it out yet," Paul said, clearly thinking he had closed the book on the issue. Maxie's smug smile bugged me, but I decided to be an adult about it. For now.

Of course, it was possible that thinking about Josh and the two cases and my guests all at the same time was making me a touch irritable. Mostly the part about Josh.

"Okay, but aside from the lack of bloody footprints and other horror movie clichés, what do the pictures tell us?" I asked Paul. He likes it when I use words like *us* and *we* because he thinks that means I accept the idea of our having an actual detective agency. He's wrong, but why make a big deal of it?

He studied another shot that Maxie had taken from the ceiling looking down. One major benefit of having ghosts take pictures is their ability to get an angle like that.

"I see the window is open," Paul said. I waited, but that was all he said.

"So? It's a bathroom that I'm willing to bet doesn't have an exhaust fan. I'm *hoping* the window is open."

Paul shook his head just a little but didn't take his eyes off the photograph. Then he reached down and tapped the button to get to the next photo. His fine motor skills and ability to interact with physical objects have really progressed since I first met him.

"It's open, and there's no shade or screen on it," Paul said. "The window is probably there to stay up to code and provide a little more light than the single fluorescent fixture in the ceiling."

Maxie floated down and admired her handiwork. "It still creeps me out to look at that place," she said.

"I don't get what's so important about the window being open," I said to Paul, so as not to respond to Maxie. "Maybe Everett wanted a little air."

"While he was bleeding to death?" Paul countered. "No. What's important is that it might explain how the killer got in and out."

Maxie looked more carefully. "That's a pretty small window," she noted.

"But not impossibly small. It's something to test out, anyway."

"How do we do that?" I asked, despite not really wanting to know.

Paul actually took his gaze off the picture and looked directly at me. "One of us is going to have to try it to see if it's possible," he said.

"Easy," I tried. "Maxie can just . . ."

He shook his head. "Maxie's body isn't material. It wouldn't provide the kind of data we'd need to prove conclusively that a person could squeeze through that window."

Something moved around in my stomach. "Well, all people aren't the same size," I said. "Even if . . . someone . . . were to try it, there's no guarantee a smaller or larger person would have the same results."

"No," Paul agreed. "What we need is more in the area of a base reading. Something we can use as a referent."

"Yeah," Maxie said. "A referent."

It was lucky for her at that moment that her body was not material.

"You have to climb through a bathroom window?" Josh asked.

After I'd seen to the late-afternoon spook show—at which Maxie had done little more than juggle some fruit because she just "wasn't into it today"—cleaned up a little, and addressed all my guests' needs (which were pretty skimpy—even Cybill had given in to the need for food and left the house), I'd showered and changed. Mom arrived about five and was watching Melissa tonight. Josh had said something about a cause for celebration, something special, so we were going out to dinner.

The restaurant in Asbury Park was a little trendier than the ones we usually frequented (I'm a cheap date), done up in neon and no TV screens, which has become something of a rarity. It was only a block down Ocean Avenue from the Stone Pony, famous for being where Bruce Springsteen used to gig. He was not performing for the 13,735th consecutive evening, however. At least the Pony was still standing.

Josh had been almost giddy with anticipation when he'd arrived, but insisted he wasn't telling me his news until he could get a bottle of champagne, which was on its way. Instead, he made the mistake of asking how my investigations were going. "I suppose I have to," I said, making the revolting excursion through the men's room window sound like it was my own idea. "It's the only way I"—I'd almost said *we* out of habit—"can get an accurate idea of whether the killer could have gotten in or out that way."

Josh was a great listener; he could listen you into a stupor if you weren't careful. He was leaning on his right hand, all the fingers curled under his mouth except the index finger, which pointed up toward his temple. He took in what I'd had to say, seemed to consider it, then asked, "Why can't you just measure the window?"

"Oh, that wouldn't work," I said, all the while wondering why the hell I couldn't just measure the window.

"Oh." He nodded.

"How would I be able to tell if a person could fit through it?" I was going to prove to him that the thing that would make a trip into a gross bathroom *through a window* unnecessary was in fact wrong.

"Well, all you'd have to do is measure the width and height of the window when it was open, and then you could measure it against yourself, and you'd know if you could fit through the window. You could get exactly the same information as you would if you squeezed through, but without all the trouble. Besides, how are you going to get the gas station guy to let you climb through his men's room window? I bet he'd have insurance issues with that."

Boy, was I going to let Paul have it when I got back home. Maxie would claim I was being a wuss, but I'd seen how she looked—and heard how she sounded—when she'd left the scene of the crime, so I had leverage.

Just then the waiter brought over the champagne, so I wisely didn't take the bathroom conversation any further and watched as the cork was removed expertly and two flutes of champagne poured. Josh thanked the waiter, and then gave me his full attention again. I love it when he gives me his full attention; his eyes absolutely sparkled more than what we were about to drink.

"I'd like to make a toast," Josh said, clearly having rehearsed this moment for some time. We held up our glasses. "First, to you, for making the past few months the best I've had in a very, very long time."

I did my best to look modest, but I'm sure I was grinning hideously. What was this about? My mind raced. As it was, I didn't have long to ponder, because Josh went on.

"But I'd also like to toast my grandfather, Sy Kaplan, who has informed me that he is retiring, and that as of the first of next month, I will be the full owner of Madison Paints!" He smiled broadly.

I joined him without hesitation. It was no surprise Sy was retiring. He was ninety-one years old and couldn't really carry a gallon of paint anymore. For the past few years since Josh had been a partner, Sy's function had largely been decorative, sitting in the back of the store with the regulars, painting contractors who frequented the place and used it as a hangout when there was no work. He could still kibitz with the best of them, and his presence was a draw for many of the steadiest customers Madison Paints had.

"That's terrific," I said, clinking glasses with Josh. We each took a sip. Champagne, to be honest, has never really been a huge favorite of mine—I like a nice white wine or a beer, myself—but as sparkling things went, this was a good one. "Congratulations to you. I'll have to stop by and see Sy before he stops coming to the store every day."

"Oh, you have plenty of time," Josh said with a mischievous grin. "He's not going to stop coming into the store every day."

I squinted in confusion. "Didn't you just say he was retiring?" I asked.

"Oh, yeah." Josh's tone was amused. "His idea of retiring is that he's giving up his half-ownership, selling it to me for a fraction of what the store is worth, and then still coming in every day to hang around with me and the regulars. He says that's his retirement resort because we're the only people who'd put up with him." What wasn't being said was that since Sy's wife, Rose, had passed away a few years before, he didn't have much of a life outside the store and was probably terrified of having to spend his time somewhere else.

"Well, I still think it's great," I said. "You've worked hard on that store, it's what you like doing, and now you're going to own it outright. You are a very impressive man."

Josh cleared his throat nervously, and that was the moment I did queasily wonder if he was going to propose something I wasn't prepared to consider. And in a way, he did. "Well, thanks for that," he said. "Because I think you're pretty impressive, too. And that's why I want to talk to you about something."

When people want to talk to you about something fun or exciting or delightful, they never tell you they want to talk to you; they just talk to you. It's when they have to announce it in advance that you need to be on your toes. I felt my neck muscles tighten up.

"Since we met—I mean, since we met again—I've been doing my very best to be open and honest with you," Josh began. I could tell that he'd rehearsed this part, too, but he was more nervous now. "I don't hold anything back, and I always tell you what I'm thinking. Well, most of the time, anyway." I even think that part was scripted. "But I'm not sure that you've been as straightforward with me."

That took a second to sink in. "What do you mean?" I asked. I knew exactly what he meant, but it was a way to buy time, if not much time.

"I mean, I've been feeling, especially lately, that you're holding stuff back," Josh answered, not angrily but sounding almost a little offended. "Like there's something you're not telling me, and it's having an effect on our relationship." I'm pretty sure that was the first time either of us had used the word *relationship* to describe what we had.

I glossed over that. "What kind of effect?" I asked. I figured if I kept asking questions, I wouldn't have to address the issue, which was that Josh knew something was up with me, that I wasn't telling him about it, and that he was now calling me on it.

"Well, not a good effect," he said.

That was not what I wanted to hear. I had *not* rehearsed for this moment, had not created a speech in which I explained about the ghosts and tried to convince him I wasn't a terrifying lunatic he should never see again. And I don't do well on the fly. I needed time.

"What do you think I'm keeping from you?" I asked.

Too late. He was on to me. "Stop stalling by asking me questions," he said. "You know exactly what I mean, and I'm asking you directly: What is it that you don't want to tell me?"

"There's nothing," I said. "Really." *I have ghosts in my house, including sometimes my dad, and one of them is a former PI. And that's why I make believe I'm a detective sometimes. Happy now?* It didn't seem the best strategy.

"Fine," Josh said, when it was clear all was not fine. "Let's have dinner." He picked up his menu.

"Josh," I tried. I really didn't want to ruin this celebratory evening for him. "I promise you, there's nothing to say." Nothing that wouldn't scare him away, anyhow.

"Absolutely," came the reply from behind the bill of fare. Swell.

"Come on. Let's celebrate your news. I'm so happy for you!"

"Thanks." Imagine a pouting seven-year-old, but with a deeper voice.

It was like that all through dinner. Josh answered everything I said in one syllable or less. I was watching the best guy I'd been involved with since I divorced The Swine—which meant the best guy I'd been involved with since before I met The Swine—slip away because of the secret that would undoubtedly break us up, but which I was obviously incapable of sharing.

Josh drove me back to Harbor Haven mostly in silence because I was too miserable to keep up the pretense of pleasant conversation. He walked me to my door, said something vague about having to open the store early in the morning, and left without so much as a peck on the cheek.

That wasn't good.

Suffice it to say, I was not in a genial mood when I entered the house. And it didn't get much better when Mom informed me that after Melissa had talked her into a trip to the local ice cream parlor, Ice Queen, she'd gone to bed with an upset stomach.

"You *know* she gets that way when she has too much ice cream at night," I scolded Mom. Let's be clear—on a normal evening, I would probably have caved and taken Liss to Ice Queen myself, but I was not in a forgiving state of mind and needed to let out my frustration on somebody. Who better than Mom?

"Don't scold your mother," Dad's voice came from behind me. "Grandmothers are supposed to spoil little girls, or have you forgotten that?" I hadn't even known he was in the house tonight, but then, of course, he would follow Mom here on a night she was watching Liss.

"Sure, take her side," I snarled at him as Paul ascended from the basement. "If Grandma had gotten *me* sick when I was eleven, you'd have been all over her in a heartbeat."

"She's right, Jack," my mother chipped in. She'll defend me even when I'm attacking her. Why did it make me angrier?

"Alison, Maxie has found something," Paul began, but I wasn't listening.

I didn't answer Mom, mostly because Tom and Libby Hill walked in asking about any all-night diners available in the area. The Hills thanked me and went out to search for a late-night omelet. And Paul once again began, "Alison, there's something you need to see."

Mom and Dad looked at me, expecting a response.

"You handle it," I told Paul. "You're the brains of the outfit. You take on cases when I don't want to get involved. You get me in danger when all I want is to run a quiet little guesthouse. So I'm handing all responsibility for the investigation back to you. If there's something that needs to be done outside the house, you'd better make a really strong case, because otherwise I'll be assuming the investigator at 123 Seafront is handling it, and that's not me."

Mom's mouth was open in shock, and Dad seemed to be trying to figure out what I *really* meant because clearly, it couldn't be what I'd just said.

Paul did not move a facial muscle, then vanished.

"Was that really necessary?" Dad asked finally.

"Yes," I said, without any confidence that it was.

But truthfully, I felt better—at least I did until Melissa called from upstairs, saying she'd thrown up in her room. Mom looked sheepish and offered to help, but I waved her off and headed upstairs myself.

That was my job—being a mother.

Not investigating crimes.

Thirteen

The rest of the night was spent trying to get my daughter to take an Alka-Seltzer, something she was inexplicably reluctant to do, and then simply sitting with her and holding a cold cloth to her forehead until she fell asleep. Four times.

By the time I got to bed, it was almost time to wake up. I usually straighten up the house before the guests awaken, so my mornings begin early. And despite my desperate desire to get some rest, last night's dinner with Josh weighed on my mind and kept me from falling asleep.

Melissa woke at her regular time for school and said she was feeling better. I considered suggesting she stay home and rest up, but she seemed eager to see her friends, and she had a vocabulary test that morning. So after determining that she could in fact hold down cereal, I drove her to school. Personally, I'd have liked to get in twelve or thirteen uninterrupted hours myself, but responsibilities called, like making sure my guests were having the vacation they had paid someone else (who was paying me a percentage) to have.

So you can imagine how great I felt when the time for the morning spook show arrived and Paul did not.

"He's pissed at you," Maxie reported after she had done a decent job of simulating two ghosts for the price of one by kicking pictures on the wall with her feet while shaking the chandelier in the hallway with her hands. She also took a comb out of Cybill's hair and honked a claxon horn she'd found in my basement. It was a game attempt, but we were lucky to have had only three audience members—Harry, Beth and Cybill—to astound this particular morning; the Hills, having sampled the fabled shore cuisine late last night, were still asleep. And Cybill, rather than seeming entertained, appeared quite annoyed with the comb-grabbing (something I would have warned Maxie about if I had been fully awake), grumbling that it was "unnatural" to allow such a creature unfettered access to my home.

Because I'm a good innkeeper, I didn't respond with the fact that I wouldn't have known how to fetter Maxie if I'd wanted to (which sometimes I did).

"I get that he's upset," I told Maxie in the game room, which I was assessing for the nine billionth time and achieving the same unhelpful result. "He thinks I was rude to him last night, and he's upset. But missing a show—"

"He didn't miss the show because he's upset," she informed me. "He missed the show because he says you told him that the deal's off. If you don't want to be a detective, he doesn't want to put on spook shows." How dare he actually expect me to keep my word!

"What do you think would get him back?" I asked Maxie. Asking Maxie for advice—just goes to show how completely at sea my mind was at that moment. Fatigue is a funny thing, except when you have it.

"Get back on the cases," she suggested. She looked around the room. "You're sure you don't want a home theater in here? It would be really cool."

"Yes, I'm sure. This is a quiet guesthouse, not a drive-in movie," I snapped.

"Somebody didn't get enough sleep last night," she singsonged.

"Paul said you'd found something last night," I said, ignoring both the game-room question and my lack of sleep. "Was it about the Boffice marriage thing?"

Maxie was looking at the walls like they were bacon and she was a hungry basset hound. She'd come up with a better idea for the room than me if it . . . well, that ship had sailed. "No, it was the homeless-guy-murder thing," she answered.

"Well?"

Maxie put on a very unconvincing surprised expression. "I thought you were off that case," she said.

"I was. Am. That doesn't mean I'm not curious. What'd you find?"

Maxie, despite her protestations that she hates the work, loves being recognized for her research skills. She practically beamed at me. "There was something in the homeless guy's ex-wife's military records," she said.

"Brenda Leskanik?" I asked. "Everett's ex-wife? What was in her . . . wait, you can hack military records?"

"Not the classified ones or anything. These ones were more or less a matter of public record, but you have to know where to look." Maxie allowed herself a moment to bask in her brilliance, and I allowed her a moment during which I did not groan melodramatically at her egotism. It was a good moment for both of us.

"So what was there?" I reminded her.

"Her discharge from the Army was a little odd," Maxie answered.

"Dishonorable?"

She shook her head. "Medical."

That was interesting. "Was Brenda wounded in action?" I asked.

Again Maxie shook her head. "No record of an incident."

"Was she ill? She's still alive, so it couldn't have been too bad."

"Oh, she recovered all right," Maxie said, playing the moment for all it was worth. "She requested an honorable discharge rather than waiting it out and left the Army a little more than three years before her husband. And she got better all of a sudden about seven and a half months later."

Seven and a half . . . "Whoa. Brenda was pregnant?"

Maxie waved her eyebrows up and down. "Give the woman a cigar," she said. "She gave birth to a healthy eight-pound, two-ounce baby boy."

"Who would now be—"

"Thirty-four years old," Maxie said.

"Wait, then he'd have been listed among Everett's next of kin, wouldn't he?" I'd prove her wrong, even if there was no reason to.

"The son, Randall, disowned Everett," Maxie answered. "Took his mother's last name."

"Did you find an address for him? For Brenda?"

"Brenda's living in Old Bridge," Maxie reported. Old Bridge was a town about forty minutes away. "There's something screwy about Randall's records, but I haven't figured it out yet."

"We can't follow Dave *and* go to Old Bridge the same day," I mused aloud. "I have to be able to see to the guests. I'll call Brenda today, if you can find a phone number, and try to arrange to see her tomorrow."

"I thought you were off the case," Maxie teased again.

"Shut up," I said. I was in a witty mood.

* * *

David Boffice did not leave his office for lunch as he had the two previous days. For a guy whose wife insisted he was as predictable as Big Ben's chimes, Dave was being insistently uncooperative with the woman trying to follow him to his mistress's house.

"Maybe he's brown-bagging it today," Maxie suggested from somewhere in the backseat. I didn't turn around to see what she was doing.

"That doesn't help," I pointed out.

"You invited me," she pointed right back.

It was true; I'd asked Maxie to come with me. Maybe it was the idea that Paul was so upset he wasn't talking to me, which was new. Maybe it was my thinking that we might go back to the Fuel Pit after this, and I'd rather have Maxie measure the bathroom window than do it myself. Maybe, truth be known, I just didn't want to be by myself on a stakeout.

I had a Carly Simon CD on the stereo, not turned up very high, and she was singing about how she and a lover (pick one) had "no secrets." I started looking through the console between the seats for another CD.

"Get something more rockin'," Maxie suggested, which made me immediately start looking for James Taylor or Jim Croce, just to irritate her. I found neither and instead inserted a compilation Melissa had made for me so "you'll have something that was recorded after color TV was invented," which was not only insulting but also historically inaccurate.

Guster started playing a song, and while it wasn't exactly what I was looking for, I had to be impressed with the maturity of my daughter's taste, or what she suspected was mine. Even Maxie stopped, considered saying something derogatory, realized it was from Melissa, and smiled at the music.

"You have a great kid," she said out of nowhere.

"I like to think so."

"I mean it," the ghost continued. "If I'd had a daughter . . ." Maxie doesn't often talk about what might have been if she'd been allowed to live. She sees her mother, Kitty, about once a week, and they communicate via text message and computer screen, but they never discuss what didn't get to happen.

"She's a special girl," I said. "I'm very lucky."

"Do you want to have more kids?" Maxie asked. Maxie and subtlety have met, but they don't speak the same language. She barges through conversational walls the way she flies through the material ones: without thought for consequences and always assuming she's right.

"I don't know," I answered. "I haven't thought about it." Well, maybe I had, but it really wasn't something I felt like discussing with Maxie.

"Sure you have," she said, clucking. "You might not talk about it, but I guarantee you've thought about it. Especially now that this *guy* is around."

"His name is Josh. Use it." I didn't want to mention that I had no idea if he'd be "around" anymore. I intended to call him later today, if I was ever alone. What I'd tell him would be . . . an excellent question. I'd have to give that some thought.

"Fine. Since Josh is around. You like him more than you've liked anybody else I've seen you with, even your ex."

"Especially my ex. Can we stop talking about this now?"

"Why?" Good Lord, she meant it.

"Because we're here to watch a guy go visit his mistress, not to discuss my personal life."

"I don't see why we can't do both. Do you want to marry Josh?" I'd like to point out here that Melissa, who was eleven years old, did not ever ask me questions like this. And I would have answered *her.*

Luckily, Dave bailed me out by emerging from the glass building and heading for his car. "We're off," I said, putting the Volvo into gear.

"Some more than others," Maxie muttered.

The third time appeared to be the charm: This time we actually headed in the direction of Joyce Kinsler's home, a town house in a development in Eatontown. And Dave did not diverge from the route the British GPS lady had set for that very destination.

"I think we've hit pay dirt this time," I said.

"I've heard that before," Maxie answered.

The town house development, Seaside Manors, was not grand, but it was serviceable. There were clearly spots where trees had been before the storm, still indentations in the ground. A woman like Joyce, with a decent job but not a wildly lucrative career, could probably afford a place like this without feeling as if she were living beyond her means. And maybe it was because of Maxie's recent interrogation, but I also noted that it was very much the kind of place where single people and childless couples would live; there was no sign of a playground, no minivans parked in driveways, no strollers left folded by front doors.

Dave drove directly to Joyce's address, which was handy since it looked just like every other address in the complex, and I'd never have been able to find it alone, British lady or no British lady. I drove past Joyce's unit, turned the next corner, and then parked the car with maximum view of her front door.

"He's going in," I said to myself.

"No kidding," Maxie said. I'd forgotten she was there; she'd been silent during the drive, which was uncharacteristic of her.

Dave rang the doorbell and waited. But the door did not open. So Dave waited some more. Apparently he didn't have a key, which I found surprising.

"Maybe it's the wrong day," Maxie suggested. "Maybe he was supposed to come the day he went for hot dogs instead."

I was looking through the binoculars and seeing Dave stand there not doing anything. "I don't know. It's weird that he doesn't have a key if they really have this long-term relationship, and it's weirder still that she's not answering the door if she's expecting him."

"Maybe they don't, and she's not." Maxie likes the simple solutions.

"Go up there and see if you can see anything," I told her.

"No, you go up there. I went up there for the mom."

"You can be more surreptitious than I can," I explained.

"I can't be anything if I don't know the word."

"Sneaky. You can be sneaky."

Dave checked his watch.

"Uh-uh," Maxie insisted. "You want to take a picture of him gettin' busy with the girlfriend, you do it. I'm not the PI." Maxie wasn't making it easy.

The bickering might have gone on for months with neither of us leaving the car, but Dave took matters into his own hands. Having waited long enough, he had the presence of mind to try the doorknob, which must have turned because the door opened and Dave walked into the unit.

"Are you going over there or what?" Maxie said after a second. "Helen wants pictures to blackmail her husband with."

"And how am I supposed to get them?" I asked defensively, knowing Maxie was right. "I'm not going inside, and there are no windows except in the front; it's an attached row house. If they're not doing . . . whatever they're doing . . . in the front room, I have no view."

"Fine. You go back and tell Helen that you can't actually prove her husband's cheating on her because you're too much of a wimp to do what she's paying you to do." Maxie stretched her legs into the engine.

My teeth were grinding. I hate it when Maxie is right. "Fine," I squeezed out between my jaws. "I'm going." I grabbed the camera from my tote bag and got out of the car. I shot Maxie a glance. "I'm not leaving the keys, so you can't listen to the radio." That told her.

I was still left with the question of how to photograph people who were not within my line of sight. Maxie, of course, could have slipped into the house with the camera in any number of possible pockets, taken the necessary pictures, and been back in the car in a minute, but convincing her to do so would have taken so much time, Helen and Dave would be celebrating their fortieth wedding anniversary before she'd get the photos, and what fun would there be in that?

Once again, Dave saved my bacon, but not in the way one would expect. He burst out the door of Joyce's town house, leaving the door wide open, with an expression of pure and absolute panic on his face. I was about halfway to the front door when he ran out, and I was briefly worried that he might notice me, but he tore to his car so quickly, he didn't even have time to glance in my direction. He had started the car and pulled out of the driveway, doing everything but burning rubber, before I could even react.

I stood there watching his car drive up the road and out of sight. It never so much as occurred to me to get back to the Volvo to follow him.

"That was quick." Maxie said, appearing at my side. She misses nothing that is shoved directly into her face.

"Too quick," I answered. "He looked like he'd seen . . ."

"Me?" Maxie asked.

"Not you specifically."

We stood—okay, I stood and Maxie hovered—there for a long moment before she said what both of us were thinking. "I guess you should go in and see what's going on, huh?"

Well, a variation on what we were both thinking, anyway. "I was thinking maybe *you* should go in and see what's going on because Joyce wouldn't be able to see you."

"Uh-huh." Maxie made no sign of moving. "I'm still thinking it should be you."

"And I'm fairly stuck in my idea that you're the girl for the job," I said.

One of the neighbors across the street opened her front door and looked out. She was wearing jeans and a sweatshirt bearing the legend "Marist College," but she didn't walk all the way out of her house. She'd obviously noticed something going on at Joyce's—probably heard the sound of Dave's car screeching away—and now was watching the stranger across the street talk to herself in the middle of the sidewalk.

Going on a stakeout with a ghost can be awkward. Usually I carry a Bluetooth headset for such times to make people think I'm having a power conversation, but I'd left it in the car.

"Let's go in together," I suggested to Maxie, moving my lips as little as possible.

"Okay," Maxie responded. "You go first."

I wanted to glare at her, but Marist College was watching, and that would make me look even more crazy, if such a thing was possible. I used my favorite motivational technique for difficult tasks—imagining my ex-husband telling me I couldn't do it—and started walking toward Joyce's place without so much as turning my head to look at Maxie.

Funny, it hadn't seemed this far away when we were driving by. Now every step seemed to move the door back just a little bit. Not that I was complaining; getting there, in this case, would probably be *all* the fun.

The door was still wide open. I walked up the three brick steps to the threshold and drew a breath. Then I knocked loudly on the door frame and called inside. "Ms. Kinsler? We saw a man run out. Is everything okay?"

The sad fact was, I knew before I walked inside that everything definitely was *not* okay. Call it ESP or whatever you like; maybe now I can sense when things are wrong (not that I'd exhibited such a talent in the past, but things develop. After all, I hadn't always been able to see ghosts).

I called out one more time with the same message, then saw Maxie go past me into the house. I followed her immediately. Call me juvenile, but the idea that Maxie would be able to say she'd gone in first was now a motivation.

Once inside, I saw Maxie head up into the ceiling to the second floor, and I decided I'd search this level.

It was fairly clear that Joyce hadn't been living here long—there was very little furniture in the living room, just a coffee table and a small love seat, but a huge brand-new flat-screen TV was mounted on the wall. There were still some boxes marked "books" and "linens" in one corner of the room. She hadn't moved all the way in yet.

Dave hadn't stayed inside very long, so whatever had alarmed him to the point of panicked flight probably wasn't far from where I was standing, if it were down here. Against my better judgment, which was to run outside as fast as Dave had and drive the Volvo back home, leaving Maxie to hoof it from Eatontown to Harbor Haven, I decided to head for the kitchen.

It wasn't a large room. It held a small breakfast table a little to the right of center, and a stove/oven and refrigerator at the far side. And there were more cartons, marked "dishes" and just "kitchen," stacked next to the fridge. The room had been designed by its previous owner to look like an old family kitchen done in modern materials, with laminate wood flooring, granite countertops (of course), and a ceiling fan with one lightbulb burned out and the other two shining. There were exposed beams in the ceiling.

From the main crossbeam hung a long, thick extension cord that had been slung over the center of the beam. And hanging from the cord by the neck was a woman whom I

assumed to be Joyce Kinsler. I gasped, tried very hard to
hold down the lunch I hadn't eaten yet, and realized in a
split second that there was no longer a reason to worry about
someone hearing me talk.

"MAXIE!!!"

Fourteen

Detective Michael Sprayne of the Eatontown Police Department, who looked to be in his mid-forties and was refreshingly unrumpled, walked out of Joyce Kinsler's town house and sat down next to me on the stoop.

"What made you walk into the house?" he asked, without any kind of social niceties.

To be fair, Sprayne had allowed me to leave the house after making me go back in—I'd called 911 from the stoop after hightailing it out as soon as Maxie had swooped through the ceiling (and coincidentally through Joyce's feet). We'd both been fairly unnerved—we screamed a bit—and didn't look at the body much beyond a passing glance before I dialed 911. Once he arrived, Sprayne had seen the look on my face and after one or two questions at the scene of the crime, had asked if I wanted some air, which I unequivocally did. Now he was going to do his follow-up where the air was.

"I saw a man running out, and the door flew open and

stayed open," I said. I figured it was best not to admit too much up front. Some cops are hostile to PIs (even if I knew I wasn't a *real* PI), and I didn't know yet if this guy was one of those.

Sprayne let a little air out through his nose and shook his head slightly. "I'm going to give you another chance, and keep in mind that I've run your name through the system."

"This one's not bad," Maxie said. I thought Sprayne looked a little shopworn, but everyone's entitled to an opinion. Maxie hovered over his head and stared at the iPad on which he was taking notes. "He knows you have a PI license," she added.

Aha. So he'd wanted to give me a chance to come clean before I crossed a line into illegality. I appreciated that. Perhaps he fell into the okay-with-PIs category. I nodded at Sprayne to acknowledge his courtesy. "I'm a private investigator, and I was following a man who came to this address. He was inside for less than five minutes before he came running out looking terrified and drove away."

"That's better," the detective said. "Let's try and keep the answers on this level of honesty from here on out. What's the guy's name?"

"The guy's name?" I asked. Suddenly I was back at the restaurant the night before, stalling by asking questions instead of answering them.

"The guy you were following," Sprayne said tolerantly. "The one who went into and out of Joyce Kinsler's house so fast. What's his name?"

"He's not *that* great," Maxie said. That was little help.

He was a cop, and I had no reason not to tell him, but I hesitated. "Do I have to answer that one?" I asked.

"You answer questions with questions, have you noticed that?"

"Do I?"

Sprayne did not smile, but he didn't appear to be angry

either. "Yes, you have to answer. This is the investigation of a death, possibly by suicide, but you never know. If someone was here besides you, I need to question him. So I'll ask you again, and I'd like the answer in a declarative sentence, please. What was the man's name?"

"David Boffice," I reported dutifully.

"You were tailing him?" Sprayne asked.

Tailing. That was so Sam Spade. "Yeah, I was tailing him, Copper. Wanted to put a shadow on him so I could see if he was up to some hanky-panky, see?" I'd gone for Sam Spade, but it came out more Edward G. Robinson. Was that progress?

"Who are you, Elliot Ness?" Maxie asked. She floated over and looked at Sprayne's iPad again. "He's looking up the questionnaire you filled out when you got the innkeeper's license. He knows about the house, and he knows you have a daughter. He probably knows how much you weigh." *That* was distressing, but I fought off the frown I wanted to send her way.

"Are you nervous?" Sprayne said. My suppressed frown must have come across as an expression of anxiety.

"I just saw a woman hanged from her kitchen ceiling with an extension cord," I told him. "I might be a tad on edge, yes."

Again, a small nod from Sprayne. "Who is your client?" he asked. "And please don't answer by saying, 'My client?' because that would just be rude."

Confidentiality is important to a PI because clients don't like their names being bandied about. Divulging a client's name can result in your losing any potential cases you might otherwise have been given. Luckily, I could care less about that. "Helen Boffice," I said immediately.

"David's wife?"

I nodded. "She thought he might be cheating on her and wanted me to follow him and catch him in the act, so to speak."

"And Joyce Kinsler?" Sprayne tilted his head in the direction of indoors.

"She was the woman Helen suspected was stealin' her man," I told him.

"And what did you find out?" Sprayne prompted.

"That Dave Boffice likes Nathan's hot dogs and sometimes visits his mother-in-law at lunchtime," I told him truthfully.

It took him a moment, but he seemed to get what I was saying. "But today he came here." Sprayne wasn't stupid, and he wasn't a stiff. "You didn't have a personal stake, did you? Maybe a thing with Dave Boffice?"

My face probably flushed with anger. "No, as a matter of fact I'm dating the owner of a paint store," I said. "Where do you come off with a crack like that?"

"Wanted to see your reaction," Sprayne answered. "Don't take it personally."

"It was personal. How can I not take it personally?"

"I sincerely apologize, okay?" Maybe he even meant it. I didn't answer.

"You should dump Josh and go out with this guy," Maxie suggested, probably just to annoy me. I gave her an irritated look and then pointedly looked at the wedding ring on Sprayne's left hand, for her benefit. If Sprayne caught that look, he didn't say anything. No doubt so he could better embellish it later when he told his wife about the crazy lady he'd interviewed at the scene of the suicide.

"Dave Boffice," Sprayne said again. "This was his first time here that you saw?"

"Yes," I told him. "This was the first time I'd seen Dave come here, and the first time I've ever been here." No need letting him think *I* was a suspect. In a suicide.

"So this Helen Boffice was pretty mad?" Sprayne asked me. "Wanted to get pictures of her hubby in the act so she could divorce him and take all his money?" It's hard to be subtle about asking if you think someone is capable of violence. Especially when using the word *hubby*.

"No, actually she wanted to get the pictures so she could blackmail him into being an obedient husband for the rest of his life," I said honestly. "Weird but true. They seem to have a somewhat competitive marriage."

"And I thought mine was tough," he muttered.

"Ooh," Maxie said. "*Unhappily* married." I refrained from giving her a look that would kill because what would be the point?

"Based on what Helen told me, they're both very career-driven," I said. "I've never spoken to Dave."

"You get a license plate on the car he was driving?"

There are times I'm actually embarrassed by being a lousy investigator. "I really should have, shouldn't I?" I said.

"Forget it. We can run the records. What kind of car was it?"

"Nissan Altima. Metallic Slate. 2010 or '11, definitely since the redesign. Charcoal cloth interior. No detailing, just plain vanilla." I got that from Maxie, who was reading off Sprayne's iPad. He was checking to see if I knew my business.

Sprayne stared at me a moment, then wrote all that down. "Clearly you weren't paying very close attention," he said.

"You always this hilarious?" I asked.

"My wife thinks so."

Maxie looked disappointed. I wasn't.

There was no point in asking Sprayne for any information on Joyce Kinsler's death because I was his key source on the incident, and I hadn't been especially helpful.

To be honest, the whole thing had shaken me pretty badly. I'd put on my best sassy demeanor with Sprayne to hide my near total anxiety. In the car on the way home, I ignored Maxie, and the instant I got into the house and satisfied myself that the guests were either out or in the backyard (Cybill was performing something that resembled yoga or sumo; I couldn't tell which, but it required a mat), I sought out Paul, who wasn't hard to seek out.

He was already in the kitchen, hiding from the guests, waiting for me to arrive, and pacing in the air. I wouldn't have been surprised to see him wearing a trench coat and smoking a cigarette, but Paul hadn't even smoked when he was alive. Now he probably figured he should have tried it; what would have been the harm?

Maxie had gotten inside before me and apparently explained the situation, because Paul's first words were, "Are you all right?" Paul, bless him, never holds a grudge.

I took a beer out of the fridge and opened it, then sat down on one of the barstools by the center island I had installed when we moved in. "I'm okay," I said. "You'd think I'd be a wreck."

"It'll hit you later," he told me. Always helpful.

Maxie came down from the ceiling. "Melissa's not in her room," she said anxiously.

I blinked. "I know," I told her. "She's still at school."

Maxie stopped, head down and feet still on another floor. "Really? It's not three o'clock yet?"

Paul and I stared at her. "No."

She seemed frazzled. Maybe something could actually get to her, and she was just covering. She shook her head as if to clear it, then grinned an evil grin. "Another guy was hitting on her," she told Paul. "A cop."

Paul's face got even more serious, if such a thing was possible. "The detective on the case was flirting with you?" he asked. He was probably trying to calculate how that might affect the investigation. Or he was jealous.

"He was not hitting on me," I said. "He was interrogating me. And anyway, I'm not interested."

"No? How come you haven't called Josh and told him you found a dead body yet?"

Okay, so that was a good question. I had thought of calling him right after I'd gotten off the phone with 911 to report Joyce's death, but the memory of his chilliness last night—probably with good reason—had left me unsure of how reassuring he would be.

"It's not that," I told Maxie.

"Uh-huh."

"Alison's romantic life is irrelevant," Paul reminded us. I felt there was no need to rub it in but stayed silent. "What's important is the way Joyce Kinsler died. Do you think she committed suicide?"

"The woman was strung up with an extension cord like a noose," I said. "I seriously doubt she died of natural causes."

Paul shook his head. "Of course not. The question is whether she did it to herself."

I can't say it hadn't occurred to me, but hearing Paul express the thought aloud gave me a little jolt. "You think someone killed Joyce?" I breathed.

Paul regarded me. "What have I always told you?"

I recited like Melissa did when she was in second grade, in a singsong voice that indicated rote memorization without any shred of comprehension. " 'An investigator never makes an assumption without facts but always keeps all possibilities open.' "

Paul nodded. "So is it possible, based on what you saw, that someone killed Joyce Kinsler?" he asked.

I didn't want to conjure up that mental image again, but I wasn't being given a choice. I tried, against the emotional tide, to recall exactly what the crime scene had looked like, but it was hard. I'm not used to seeing dead bodies. I'm just used to seeing dead spirits. There's a huge difference.

"It was a fairly normal-sized kitchen," I said, closing my eyes to visualize the scene more precisely. "Entrance from the living room and double glass doors leading out to a back deck. There were exposed beams running across the ceiling that were supposed to look like oak but were probably stained pine. Joyce was almost exactly in the center of the room, hanging from the main support beam, maybe a foot, foot and a half off the floor." I opened my eyes and looked at Paul.

"Was there any blood on the floor or anywhere else?" he asked. "Any signs of a struggle?"

I considered carefully. "No. Nothing I saw. Everything looked exactly right, except Joyce without her feet on the ground."

"Interesting," Paul said.

"What's interesting?"

"Nothing was out of place." Paul paced some more. "She was hanging in the middle of the room."

"I'm pretty sure I said that."

"What did she jump off of?" Paul stopped and looked at me. "If she set up the hanging to commit suicide, she'd stand on something, fix the cord around her neck after throwing it over the beam, and then jump off whatever she stood on. If there was nothing out of place, I assume that means there was no overturned chair, no platform that would have been under her feet."

I thought back to the image in my brain again. "No. Nothing. The table and the countertops were too far away."

"Did you see a note anywhere?" he asked.

"No."

"Interesting," Paul repeated.

"Do you think you can find her on the Ghosternet?" I asked.

Paul looked dubious. "It's probably too soon; she probably hasn't gone through whatever Maxie and I did when we found ourselves still here." He pointed a finger at me. "Don't forget; she might not show up as a ghost at all." People don't, not always.

There was a knock at the kitchen door, and I heard Beth Rosen's voice peep through. Sometimes, because I inform the guests that the kitchen isn't open for meals, they think they can't come in at all, and I don't really discourage that impression because it gives me a safe haven to talk to the non-living members of the household. "Alison?" she asked quietly. "Are you in there?"

I walked to the door and opened it toward me. "Hi, Beth," I told her. As far as she could tell, there was no one in the kitchen but me. "Come on in."

She walked in and looked around. I worried for a moment that she'd heard me talking to Paul, but she was a Senior Plus guest so was at least aware that there were supposed to be ghosts in the house. "How can I help you?" I asked. You talk like that in the hospitality business.

"I don't want to bother you if you're . . . busy," she said.

I spread my hands. "Not at all. Please, tell me what you need."

"It's . . . well, it's the spirits you have in the house," Beth said. I wasn't crazy about the way she said it; there was far too much concern, even fear, in her voice.

I successfully fought the impulse to look at Maxie; I couldn't imagine any of the guests being this worried about something Paul would do. "What about them?" I asked, possibly allowing too much of an edge to creep into my voice.

From behind me, I heard Maxie saying, "Whatever it is, it wasn't me."

Whatever it was, it was definitely her.

"Well," Beth continued, "I don't want to complain. I mean, we certainly knew there would be, you know, ghosts in the house when we booked the tour. And watching them interact with us every day has been really exciting." There was definitely a *but* coming in this sentence.

I decided to accelerate its arrival. "Has there been a problem, Beth?" I asked.

"Yes, I'm afraid so." She bit her lip and looked worried. "But I don't want to get anyone in trouble or anything."

I stole a quick glance at Maxie, who shrugged, which

could either mean, "I don't know what she's talking about" or "Whatever."

"There's no need to worry," I told Beth. "Just, please, sit down and tell me what's wrong." I gestured toward the barstools at the center island.

Beth nodded and sat down on one of them. I took a position next to her and saw Paul hover into view at my side, seemingly interested in watching Beth's face as she spoke.

"I don't worry about the presence of the spirits in the house," Beth began. "Like I said, it's one of the reasons we wanted to come here. But," and there it was, "I was led to believe—that is, *we* were led to believe—that there was no danger involved in the tour."

"There isn't," I said. "The spirits in this house are absolutely not dangerous, I promise you." Paul nodded, perhaps involuntarily.

I couldn't see Maxie behind me, but I'd have bet she was not nodding in agreement.

"Perhaps that's true," Beth went on. "But I've seen something I consider to be considerably more disturbing, and I have to say, it probably goes beyond the parameters of what I—*we*—can be comfortable with."

Beth's circling around whatever was bothering her threatened to take up the next two years of my life, and that would be inconvenient because I had to pick up my daughter from school in ninety minutes. "What have you seen, Beth?" I asked.

"Well, why don't you come with me and I'll show you," she suggested.

That seemed like the quickest solution to this problem, so I nodded and followed Beth out of the kitchen and to the hallway. We walked down to the game room entrance in silence. Paul followed behind, but Maxie zoomed ahead, stopping just in front of me as we were reaching the archway that leads to the game room.

There, on the paneling I'd labored so long (okay, I

labored for an afternoon) to paint white, was a haphazardly scrawled message that appeared to be painted in blood. It read:

"Humans must not breech these walls
Daemons' souls are fed
Any humans entering
Will surely become dead."

"Okay," I said. "I can see the problem."

Fifteen

It took a while to reassure Beth that the ghosts (I didn't mention Maxie, over her protest, by name, but it was implied) had just been acting playfully and intended no one any harm. But from the way Beth was talking, I got the impression that Harry was the more frightened of the two. He had not even been brave enough to come ask me about it and was now hiding in their bedroom on the second floor. Beth went upstairs to reassure him.

Once she was out of the room, Paul examined the message and determined that it was in fact written in red marker and not blood. That was both good news and bad news because it meant that the writer wasn't quite as gruesome and sadistic as we might have thought, but marker would in fact be harder to wash off the wall than blood. There's a reason they call it permanent marker.

So I found myself going into the basement to find a

roller, roller tray and the white paint I'd used on the paneling. This was a message that had to be extremely gone before any of the other guests stumbled across it.

Paul followed me into the basement. "It wasn't Maxie," he said.

"I know it wasn't Maxie. Maxie would never use the word 'daemons.' Who says that?"

From upstairs, in the direction of the game room (where Maxie had been asked to try to clean up the message with a scrub brush and Mr. Clean), came, "I heard that."

"I'm saying, I really don't think Maxie wrote that on the wall," Paul reiterated.

I got the roller tray out of my tool chest (bottom shelf, with the larger items) and looked at him. "I know," I said. "It wasn't Maxie. I'm inclined to believe it was Cybill trying to stir up support for her house exorcism."

"We have no evidence," Paul said.

I gathered up all my supplies, including a drop cloth to cover any spills while I repainted the wall, and headed for the stairs. "I'm not going to prosecute," I said. "I don't need evidence."

"If you're going to accuse one of your paying guests of doing material damage to your house," Paul reminded me as I climbed and he floated up the stairs, "you really don't want to be wrong. You're a businesswoman."

I stopped at the door to the upstairs. "I really hate it when you're right," I told Paul.

He smiled. "I'm not always crazy about it myself," he said.

"So what do I do?"

"Stay quiet and observe," he said.

"You know that's not my strong suit."

"Nonetheless."

I went through the door and walked to the game room, paint in hand.

* * *

I did eventually call Josh later in the day but got his voice mail. I couldn't help wondering if he was truly busy or if he just ignored my call out of testiness over last night. Driving Melissa home from school, I considered getting her to call him just to check but decided that was a hysterical, manipulative response. Besides, I'd have to tell Liss why she was doing that, which was enough for me to decide against it.

As Paul had advised, I didn't confront Cybill in the house but kept careful scrutiny on her movements, which were minimal. Mostly she stayed in her room (chanting was not infrequently heard through the door) or spent her time out in the backyard watching the waves from the dune overlooking the beach. That's a nice peaceful way to spend a spring afternoon, and I've done it myself, but with Cybill it seemed somehow a little creepy, like someone waiting for a sign.

I decided to wait until the next day to report back to Helen Boffice. Just because I'd seen her husband at the scene of Joyce Kinsler's death (which was probably a suicide) didn't mean I had to call Helen immediately.

Neither did the three voice mails Helen had left me already. The police had probably already talked to Helen and Dave, for that matter. I had nothing to tell her that they couldn't.

I spent the evening putting a second coat on the defaced wall in the game room, with my father supervising. Melissa was upstairs doing homework, which probably meant watching television, since her homework rarely took more than half an hour because she's a genius (A bragging mother? Moi?). Hey, even eleven-year-olds need to decompress after a day at the salt mines.

"So you've got a dead homeless guy in a gas station bathroom and a dead adulteress hanging from her kitchen ceiling," Dad was saying. "You lead an interesting life, baby girl."

To be honest, I figured talking to one's deceased parent while painting over an anonymous threat that likely came from someone pretending to be a ghost was somewhat more unusual, but Dad had a point. "And yet, what I'm worried about is a guy," I told him. I could always talk to Dad about anything. Mom, you had to avoid certain areas. Like real life.

"Josh from Madison Paint?" Dad considered, then pointed at my work. "Watch the drip."

I corrected my brush technique and told him, "The drip is the one I married."

"Don't get me started. Look, as I understand it, your problem with Josh is that you like him, but you don't trust him."

I stopped painting and looked at Dad. "What do you mean, I don't trust him? I trust him fine."

My father folded his arms. "Then why don't you tell him about us? Me and Maxie and Paul?"

"Mom never told *me* she could see ghosts," I said.

"She didn't want you to know . . ."

". . . because she thought I'd feel bad that I couldn't do it. She didn't give me the opportunity to be okay with it. Now who are we talking about not trusting?" I asked.

"This isn't about your mother," Dad said. "Why aren't you telling Josh?"

"Seriously?" I blinked a couple of times and went back to my second coat. "This is not your normal off-the-rack situation. He'll think I'm nuts. And to tell you the truth, I'm not sure he'll be wrong." Maybe everything since that bucket of wallboard compound hit me in the head had been a hallucination. I'd just been dreaming all this time.

"If you don't trust him to believe you about seeing ghosts, you don't trust him, baby girl," my father said.

"How do you trust somebody with a story like that?" I asked. "No sane person would believe it."

My father considered me for a moment. "Let me ask you

this," he said. "If you were still married, would you tell your husband what was going on?"

"Did Mom tell you she could see ghosts before you died?" If you don't have an answer, turn the tables on your questioner.

Dad's eyes got a bit sad. "As a matter of fact, she did," he said.

That put a damper on the conversation, so I painted silently for a minute or two.

Dad changed the subject. "Now, what are you thinking about this room?" He could always make me feel better by talking about the nuts and bolts of old buildings like the one I own.

I finished covering over the disturbing message on my wall, which would now be slightly whiter than the others in the room. Dad said he'd think about uses for the room but would head for Mom's house now. He seemed concerned about me, in a loving way. It made me feel bad that I was making him worry, so now my day was complete. I went back to thinking about the two cases I had agreed to investigate (I know I said I was off the job, but you didn't think I meant it, did you?). Paul and Maxie were not anywhere in the immediate vicinity, so I could ruminate. And not call Josh. Or I could go upstairs and watch TV with my daughter . . . nah. Had to have a plan for tomorrow.

The Boffice matter seemed to be completely out of my hands now, I decided as I straightened up the library. The police were handling Joyce's death, something I had not been asked to do.

So the focus should now be on Everett's murder, I decided. The pictures Paul had examined hadn't given us much to go with, so tomorrow would be a day of getting in touch with the homeless veteran's ex-wife and family members as best I could, especially trying to find the son Maxie couldn't yet locate. There had to be a reason someone cared enough to want Everett dead, but at the moment, there wasn't one suggesting itself too plainly. Or at all.

But Josh was nagging at my mind. Was Dad right about my not trusting him? Could I trust that *anyone* would believe the truth about my life these days? Why wasn't Josh calling me back (and why did I sound like I was back in junior high school)?

My phone rang in my pocket, and I pulled it out, hoping Josh had gotten my psychic signals. Nope. Another call from Helen Boffice. I couldn't duck her forever. Besides, she was undoubtedly calling to fire me from her case, which was fine with me. I picked up.

"Helen, I'm so glad you called. I don't know if you've heard what happened." I was in fact sure she had, but I was covering.

Her voice cut me off before I could say any more, and it sounded . . . what was that tone? Irritated? Impatient? Angry? "I heard, all right," she hissed. Her voice was low, making me think Dave might be nearby and Helen was concealing the conversation. "The police just left. I'm just hoping you got some pictures in the past couple of days that will accomplish the goal we set forth." The goal we set forth? Who talks like that?

"I couldn't get photos," I said slowly. "Mostly because Dave went to the mall for lunch one day and to visit your mother the next. When he drove to Joyce Kinsler's house today, she was already dead."

"My mother?" Helen asked. Could she have chosen a smaller point to pick up on from what I'd told her? Next she'd be asking me what he'd had for lunch at the mall.

"Yes. He visited her yesterday. They seem to get along well." I was speculating, but there hadn't been loud shouting, and Margaret O'Toole had given Dave a peck on the cheek when he left.

Helen didn't say anything for a long moment. "Listen,"

she finally said, her voice now hard as marble, "I want you to find out who killed Joyce Kinsler. The police seem to think *I* might have done it, and that's impossible. I need to know if it was Dave. Find out everything you can that might point to him."

"Helen," I said, "I'm not sure I can—"

"I'll double your fee."

She hung up and did not pick up when I called her back.

Sixteen

"I haven't heard from Everett for five years," said Brenda Leskanik late the next morning. We were sitting on a deck overlooking Route 18 North in Old Bridge. Brenda, when I called, had said there wasn't much to tell but agreed to talk to me if I came to her, which I was happy to do. But she didn't want to meet in her home. "A public place," she'd said. "Everett is a touchy subject."

The restaurant where we'd met, Bernardo's Slice of Heaven, was normally a pizza place with a little twist of new cuisine. But in the late mornings and afternoons, Bernardo's was essentially a coffee shop, and the patio (really a rooftop) was the outdoor seating area, where she and I were sipping coffees. I was avoiding the thought of a chocolate chip muffin that had been calling to me at the counter when we ordered. The urge to go back downstairs and rescue it from its captivity was strong.

I had decided, after not mentioning the call from Helen to anyone in the house and sleeping on it for a night, that I was under no obligation to follow up on her demand that I investigate Joyce Kinsler's death. Helen hadn't hired me for that, and I hadn't accepted the case. I didn't have to do it. It felt great.

"Did you know what had happened to him?" I asked. "About his homelessness?"

"I knew," she said flatly. Brenda was a woman in her forties who had never been beautiful but had a look that elicited respect first. She wasn't severe, didn't intimidate, but her military training certainly came through in her every word and gesture. "At first I tried to help out, you know, find out where he was and offer to give him some money, but he wouldn't take it. Said it was bad enough he couldn't give me child support."

"I heard you left the Army because you were pregnant," I said. "They don't require that, do they?"

Brenda shook her head, but she clearly wasn't happy about the question. "No, they can't do that," she said. "They just make it clear that it'll be so much more difficult to raise a baby if you're in the service, and then they let you make the choice. I made the choice to leave. Frankly, I was ready to get out anyway."

"Why?"

She shrugged. "Not everyone is a career soldier. I got into it to pay for college, and when I got out, I had enough money for that. I also had a husband and a son. I ended up working a job and studying at night, but I never got to see my son. Left school without the BA, but I had an associate's degree and that was enough to get me onto a management track at one of the chain stores at the mall. Got me and Randy health benefits, things the Army didn't offer after I got out."

"Randy is your son?" I asked.

Brenda closed her eyes for a moment. "Randy *was* my son. He passed away seven years ago."

Why hadn't Maxie found that? She'd said something

was odd about Randy's records, but she couldn't figure out what. "I'm so sorry," I said.

Brenda shook her head. "There's no way you could have known. Randy developed a drug problem in high school, left home, didn't want to have anything to do with us."

"What happened?"

"Drugs," she said, "then a motorcycle accident. He ended up at the bottom of a ravine near an offshoot of the Passaic River. The bike was so smashed, they could've fit it into the trunk of a car. A small car."

Brenda looked so shaken, I didn't have the heart to ask more. "It must be incredibly hard for you."

She sniffed a little but looked at me with clear eyes. "The fact is, it's not that much different than when he left. Sometimes I have to remind myself of what happened."

"What happened to split you and Everett up?" I asked, changing the subject. "You and he met in the Army. He must have been impressive enough for you to marry him. How did he end up homeless?"

"Everett was *very* impressive when I met him," Brenda told me. "He wasn't like the other guys in our outfit. Didn't come across as all kinds of macho frat boy when everybody knew we were all scared to death every single day. He was a real human being, you know? Just happened to be carrying a rifle and dressed in uniform. That made an impression on me over there."

"It wasn't the same when you got back?" The wind was picking up, but it didn't look like it would rain anytime soon. The breeze on the rooftop actually felt good, and the smell from the kitchen, where no doubt more chocolate chip muffins were being baked, was quite wonderful.

"No," Brenda said. "It wasn't the same. Well, that's not true. It was the same—or he was the same—for a while. He was still Everett. He still treated me like a person and not a different species. That happens in the service, you know, women are sized up on the first pass, and they're either the ones guys want or, you know, not. Everett wasn't ever like that. He always related to me as Brenda."

"So what changed?" I was hoping Paul would make sense of all this from the recording I'd informed Brenda I was making. It was just as well she'd agreed to it—the wind up here would have made a secret recording from inside my tote bag pretty much unintelligible.

"I'm not sure. Everett started telling me about people talking to him. People I couldn't see. People who weren't there. I figure he'd had a schizophrenic break somewhere along the line, but he was never diagnosed because he refused to go see a doctor." Brenda was dry-eyed and absolutely steady relating this; she wasn't happy about what had happened to Everett, but it was so far back in the past that she was no longer shaken by it. He wasn't her husband any longer, and now he was dead. It was sad, but it wasn't going to touch her. Not anymore.

"He heard voices?" Suddenly this story was hitting a little too close to home.

Brenda nodded slowly. "He came home one day from work and said he'd heard someone talking to him when no one was there. Said he didn't understand it, but he figured he'd better listen to the voice, like in that movie where the baseball gods talk to Kevin Costner."

"Field of Dreams," I said. Like that was the important part.

"Yeah. And the voice was telling him to quit his job and go follow his dream in life."

I waited, but that was all Brenda said. "What was his dream in life?" I asked.

"That was just the thing. He didn't have one." She shrugged.

"How old was your son then?" I asked. It was a painful subject I was sure, but I knew Paul would ask me later, so I pushed on through.

"Maybe eleven or twelve. It was the last year Everett

was living with us, so I guess that's about right." Brenda looked off into the distance as if there was something there other than a highway with cars going by. Maybe there was.

"Do you think . . . I'm sorry, but I have no other way to put this . . . do you think that maybe that was when things with Randy started to go in the wrong direction?" I hated myself for asking, but it might lead to something. Okay, so I was grasping at straws, but I really didn't see Brenda as the killer and I needed a theory.

"Yes," she answered in choked tones. "It certainly didn't help. That's such a pivotal age anyway."

"Did Everett say whether he ever saw anyone, or was it just a voice? Voices?"

"There was more than one voice, for sure, at least two and maybe more," Brenda said, still staring into the past and not focusing on me at all.

"Besides telling him to quit his job, what did they say?" I asked.

Brenda blinked, finally seeming to remember I was there, and looked into my eyes. "I guess they told him to leave Randy and me," she said.

"I bet that made you mad," I said.

Brenda didn't acknowledge the implication. "It sure did," she said.

"You froze me out," Paul said.

"I took a little time to gather my thoughts, that's all," I told him. "Look, I realize the investigations are very important to you, but the fact is, they can be dangerous to me and there are still things that people can do to hurt me. I try to avoid those whenever possible."

"And the Dave Boffice case?" he asked. "That's dangerous?"

"Ask Joyce Kinsler."

"I've tried," Paul answered. "I haven't had any luck yet."

We were in the den, with no guests around at the moment, although at least Cybill would be back after lunch. The two couples were both going on car trips; Tom and Libby Hill to the Seaside boardwalk—what was left of it—and Harry and Beth Rosen to see Lucy the Margate Elephant, one of the few attractions in the area undamaged by the storm: a six-story wooden elephant you have to see to believe. Harry and Beth, in an attempt to believe it, were going to see it.

"I understand it's scary to see a woman dead like that," Paul said, doing his best to be reasonable. "But that doesn't mean you should quit the case."

"I'm not *quitting* the case," I said, doing absolutely nothing to appear reasonable. "I'm done with the case because there is no case. Dave Boffice is not cheating on his wife with Joyce Kinsler. I was hired to find out, and I found out. Where do I send the bill?"

"Helen called and said she wanted you to find out what happened to Joyce, and find out quickly," Paul countered. "If you're not going to do that, as a *professional,* you should at least call and let her hire someone else."

"Consider it done," I said. I even intended to do so.

"All right," Paul answered, but he didn't appear to think it was even a little right. "What about Everett Sandheim?"

I probably scowled. I felt like I scowled. "That one's proving tricky," I told him honestly. "There are a lot of directions to go in, and I don't know which one's best."

"What about the window?" Paul asked.

"The window?" The answering-with-questions had become a reflex.

"The men's washroom window at the gas station," Paul answered. "You were supposed to find out whether it was large enough . . ."

"Why can't I just measure the window?" I said.

Paul stopped floating, was completely still, and looked at me. "What?"

"Why can't I just measure the window? Why do I have to go through it?"

Before he could answer, my cell phone vibrated in my pocket, and I pulled it out. The number wasn't one I recognized, but it was local, so I answered it.

"Ms. Kerby?" the caller said. I knew that voice. From where did I know that voice?

"Who's calling?" I asked. I'm not admitting to anything until I know whether the person on the other end of the conversation is a raving maniac. It's a rule I have.

"Detective Sprayne of the Eatontown Police Department." Oh, yeah. *That* was where I knew that voice.

"What can I do for you, Detective?" I asked.

"I have some more questions about Joyce Kinsler," he said. "Can we meet for coffee?"

More coffee. So I'd sleep less tonight; what the heck.

He gave me the name of a diner near the Eatontown police station, and I agreed to meet him there in twenty minutes.

"I have to make this quick," I told Sprayne when I arrived. "I have to pick my daughter up from school in an hour."

"You have a daughter?"

I was aware he knew that already; he was making small talk. "Quick," I reminded him.

"Okay," Sprayne said. "Here's the thing. We don't think Kinsler hanged herself."

I took a breath. "Because there was nothing under her feet. Nothing for her to jump off of."

Sprayne's eyes widened, and he tilted his head in respect. "Very good. The only person we're sure was at the scene anytime around when Kinsler died was your pal Dave Boffice," Sprayne said. "And you, of course. But I've done some checking, and you don't have a motive for killing Joyce Kinsler."

"That's sweet, Detective," I said. "I feel so much better."

Then it hit me—had he researched me beyond what his iPad had told him at the scene? "What do you mean, you've done some checking? On me?"

He pulled a reporter's notebook from his inside pocket and opened it to a page. "You are the owner of a bed-and-breakfast in Harbor Haven," he began.

"It's a guesthouse. I don't serve breakfast." It's become a knee-jerk response at this point.

"Fine. A guesthouse, at 123 Seafront Avenue. There are rumors your guesthouse is haunted. You have an eleven-year-old daughter named Melissa who is in the fifth grade at John F. Kennedy elementary school in Harbor Haven."

"You were just pretending to be surprised I had a daughter," I said.

"People like it when you ask about their kids," he said. "You are . . . let's say in your late thirties, were once married to a Steven Randell, ended in divorce. You got your private investigator's license about two and a half years ago but don't use it much. You're currently dating a guy who works in a paint store."

"He owns the paint store, and where did you get *that* from?"

Sprayne smiled. It wasn't exactly kind, but it had that bad-boy quality that some women (like Maxie, for example) find appealing. "You told me," he said.

Oh, yeah.

"Great. So you've researched me. I appreciate your leaving out my weight and how many times per week I change my sheets." The irritation in my voice sounded real, but it felt fake. I can't explain it.

"I can look those up if you want me to," he said playfully.

Was the married guy *flirting* with me? That was something I certainly didn't need. "What did you want to know from me, Detective?" I was pushing this back toward the case if it killed me.

"We've talked to Dave Boffice," he said, his voice once again a model of professionalism. "We told him about Kinsler, and he had the good taste not to act surprised. Said he'd gone there and was so spooked by finding her that he went straight home. Says he didn't call 911, because he was in shock. He claims he was at the Monmouth Mall getting a Nathan's hot dog when Joyce died."

"Do we know exactly how long she'd been dead when I got there?" I asked.

"Not yet, just an estimate. More than an hour, less than twelve."

"I would have seen if he went to the mall, and he didn't. Either way, he was there right before me and ran out with a look on his face that would indicate he'd seen what I saw a couple of minutes later." I avoided saying "seen a ghost" since, well, I guess that seemed less shocking to me these days. For instance, there was a transparent woman, I'd say in her early fifties, dressed for 1966, hovering over the booth next to ours, but we hadn't spoken.

"Do you think he had time to do anything?" Sprayne asked. "Contaminate the crime scene? Maybe straighten up what Kinsler would have been standing on before she died?"

"It's possible. It would have only taken a few seconds to stand a kitchen chair back up or something, but why would he bother? What difference would it make to him if everything in Joyce's kitchen was neat and tidy except for the dead woman hanging from the rafters?"

Sprayne shrugged. "You can't answer the question until you have facts," he said. "We don't have facts yet." Something Paul would have said.

"Anyway, it was well after Joyce had died," I pointed out. "Dave definitely didn't kill her while I was outside watching; he wasn't in there long enough, and your report shows that she was dead awhile before we got there."

"Let's say he did kill her earlier in the day," Sprayne

suggested. "Is it possible he knew you were follow-ing him?"

So this was going to be about what a lousy detective I am? Only *I* get to say stuff like that! "I really don't think he did," I told Sprayne, making sure my jaw muscles didn't clench. "There was no sign he knew anyone was on his trail. Why?"

Sprayne cocked an eyebrow; he had noticed my tone. "Don't get excited," he said. "Nobody's casting aspersions. If Boffice knew he was being followed during his lunch breaks, he might have killed Joyce sometime earlier, and then put on a show about how shocked he was because he knew he was being watched. Deflect suspicion."

Dammit. That made sense.

"It's just a scenario. I don't have anything to go on yet," Sprayne said with a shrug. "Have you spoken to Boffice yourself?"

My lips curled. "What kind of detective do you think I am?" I asked.

Another shrug. "I don't have any facts about that, either."

"No. I've never spoken to Dave Boffice," I admitted. "What's he like?"

Sprayne smiled, but only with one side of his mouth. "The blandest, most average guy you ever met in your life," he said. "Off the record."

"But you still suspect him?"

"That's one of the reasons *why* I suspect him." Sprayne waved to the waitress and made that writing gesture that people think means "bring me the check, please," and peo-ple who have waited tables believe signals that you're an imperious jerk. It's all a question of perspective.

"Are we done?" I asked. I didn't actually want any more coffee anyway, not that he'd bothered to ask first.

"Unless you have something else to add," Sprayne said as the waitress brought our check. and he made a show of picking it up, which, let's face it, he should. "I didn't expect to have an amazing lead come out of this meeting."

"Then why did you call me?" I asked, leaving out the part about how it had wasted both our time.

"Your scintillating conversation," he deadpanned.

Seventeen

I called Josh when I got home—to be fair, he'd actually returned my call—and I told him about finding Joyce's body. He asked if I wanted him to come over, and I said yes, after thinking about it, but that he should wait until after the store's usual closing hour.

Paul wanted the rundown on my meeting with Detective Sprayne, so I gave it to him sans hilarious banter. Maxie was doing some research into Dave's business, which was keeping her busy for the moment. "So Detective Sprayne agrees with us, that Joyce Kinsler was murdered," Paul said, stroking his goatee. "David Boffice certainly has to be a suspect, but I imagine Helen would be as well, wouldn't you say? The wife angered by the affair, deciding to eliminate the competition? If there was an affair."

"What do you mean, 'if there was an affair'?" I asked.

"We don't have proof. We only have Helen's word for it. Don't assume, Alison." Paul loves nothing better than to school me on his personal theory of investigation. I don't mind it, but I'm not sure it helps. Me.

"If there was no affair, why did Dave go to Joyce's house?" I asked.

"A good question. We're dealing in speculation, and I don't like that." Paul rubbed his eyes. "If there was an affair, or even if she just *believed* there was, Helen would be a natural suspect."

I was repairing a small leak in the sink in the downstairs powder room: not a big deal, but annoying enough to warrant attention. I do minor plumbing, but nothing big. Dad wasn't around—he must have been at Madison Paint with Sy and Josh—or he probably would have insisted on doing the repair himself. "But the thing is, Helen didn't seem to want to eliminate the competition," I told Paul. "She wanted to intimidate her husband."

"Killing Joyce would certainly accomplish that goal, don't you think?" Paul countered.

"I think she just wanted Dave to know she knew about the affair," I said, climbing out from under the sink. "Killing Joyce would be too final, too oversized a response to what she was trying to accomplish. It was about getting the upper hand, not about something as final as death." I tried the faucet, and it no longer leaked. Am I good, or what? "Besides, it's not our case anymore. The Eatontown police will handle it." That was my story, and I was sticking to it.

Paul sputtered but didn't respond. Melissa, who had been in the kitchen with Mom learning how to make macaroni and cheese, appeared in the doorway. "Mrs. Murphy is on the phone," she said. "She wants another progress report."

Groaning is not attractive, but I've found it's sort of involuntary.

I keep the landline in the house for a few reasons, although I use my cell phone mostly for personal and business calls. Having the phone in the house covers me if the

cell phone needs recharging, if cell service is interrupted
for some reason (it had been out for almost a week after the
storm, along with electrical power), and if guests who don't
have cells might need to use a phone while staying here.
Also, I've never gotten around to canceling the service, and
some visitors actually do look me up in the Yellow Pages
and call to make reservations. But if Kerin Murphy was
going to start calling me at home, that might be enough to
reconsider canceling.

"Can you tell her I left the country?" I asked. "Nowhere
far, maybe just Venezuela." But Melissa gave me one of her
looks—the one that indicates she's more mature than I
am—and I trudged out to the den, where the landline sat
on a side table, to take Kerin Murphy's call.

"Why are you calling me at the house?" I asked Kerin
as soon as I picked up the receiver.

"Because you never gave me your cell-phone number,"
she answered. That was true, and I had been hoping she'd
take the hint, but life just doesn't work like that sometimes.
"Luckily, your home number was in the book. What do you
have to tell me about your investigation?"

"You can't expect progress reports every day, Kerin,"
I said.

"I certainly can, and I do," Kerin answered in her best
businesswoman tone. "I hired you to perform a professional
function, and as your employer, I am entitled to regular reports
on your progress toward the achievement of that goal."

"Did you read that in a self-help book on being a successful businesswoman?" I asked. Maybe I could get
myself fired for insubordination. It wouldn't be the first
time. "Look. I met with Everett's ex-wife. She hadn't seen
him in years. His son is dead. I called his father and got the
woman who's overseeing his care at an assisted living
facility in South Carolina. I haven't gotten to his sister yet,
but I have calls in. What is it you're expecting?"

"Results. We hired you because you claim to have certain . . . abilities. We want you to exercise them."

Tom and Libby Hill walked in through the front door as I tried to talk sense into a woman who had once baked individual chocolate soufflés for a second-grade bake sale. I lowered my voice. "I do not believe a ghost killed Everett Sandheim," I told Kerin. "I've seen no evidence of that." Not much, anyway.

"You're being evasive," Kerin shot back. "Was it one of your ghost friends and you're afraid to say so because it will ruin your reputation?"

This conversation was passing the edges of ridiculous and heading for . . . something beyond ridiculous. But Tom and Libby, standing discreetly by and trying to look like they weren't listening, were listening. I had to be careful with my response.

"Why, that's just silly," I attempted, trying to sound like Kerin had suggested that I might be working too hard or should plant palm trees in the front yard. "That's just not what is happening here."

"Then what *is* happening?" Kerin demanded. "You're the one who sees ghosts. You base your whole business on it. Do you deny their existence?" I couldn't do so in good conscience, because Maxie was floating down from the ceiling and Paul had wandered in from the bathroom.

I kept the light tone in my voice, which might have been my biggest triumph of the day. "I'm just saying that I haven't got anything to report yet, and that you should expect an operation like this to take a little time. It's not the kind of thing that can be completed quickly."

Tom Hill made a show of examining an "antique" I had on a shelf over the fireplace. It was a small figurine of a sea captain holding a fish, and I'd picked it up at a flea market in Englishtown for seventy-five cents because I felt the guesthouse should have something ocean-ish. Maxie hates that thing, and as with most such issues involving interior design, I am loath to admit she is right.

"We're not paying you all that money to stand still," Kerin said.

If she thought that was a threat I'd take to heart, it was necessary for me to disabuse her of that assumption. "If you're not happy with my service, I can recommend some alternatives in the area," I said. "Feel free to call them."

Kerin's voice took on a growl. "Oh no," she said. "You're not getting out of it that easily. I'm going to call for a status report *every day* until this case is solved. You can count on it." That was it; I was definitely having the landline disconnected.

"And I can assure you that you'll hear about every bit of progress that is made," I said. My tone wasn't fooling anybody. "Nice to hear from you, Kerin." I hung up before she could make some other threat. I just wasn't in the mood.

"Man," Maxie drawled. "Some customers are so demanding."

I turned directly toward Tom and Libby. "Sorry to keep you waiting," I told them. "What can I do for you?"

Libby walked over and Maxie assessed her but said nothing. That's not unusual for Maxie; I think most of the time she'd like to pretend there are no guests in the house, though she does love to amuse herself by interacting with them at the spook shows.

"Alison," Libby began, "Tom and I were wondering if you might be able to move us to another bedroom in the house."

Paul's eyes narrowed. He has a sense about when things aren't quite right, and it appeared to be surfacing with Libby's not terribly unusual request.

Mentally, I went through my room inventory. There were three guest bedrooms being used at the moment, the Hills and the Rosens in two of them, and . . .

Of course. "Your room is right next to Cybill's, isn't it?" I asked.

Libby tried to avoid my eyes by looking at the picture frame on the table next to her, but she nodded. "Yes," she said. "The chanting goes on well into the night, and it's something of a . . . problem for us, you understand. We don't want to be a bother."

"It's not at all a problem," I assured her. "I have another room you can move into right away, right here on the first floor, where you won't be disturbed at all. Is that all right?"

Tom broke in before Libby could answer. "That would be great," he said. "You have no idea how that woman has been keeping us awake. I mean, I don't want to run down anybody's religion, but I need to sleep, you know?"

"Tom," Libby admonished.

"Don't worry about it," I told them. "I'll get you a key to the downstairs bedroom right now." They both seemed quite relieved and went upstairs to pack their belongings for the long journey down one flight of stairs.

"There's more to Cybill than you'd expect," Paul suggested as I walked toward the kitchen to open the locked cabinet where I keep the room keys. "She believes she has a mission here, and I don't think it's one that's especially helpful."

"She's a pain, he's saying," Maxie chimed in. "And I agree. Let's boot her out."

"You two seem to forget that I need this guesthouse to succeed so I can keep my daughter in shelter and food," I growled. "You guys do what you do, and let me do what I do. I'll go deal with Cybill." And it was at that moment that I realized I didn't know exactly where Cybill was. So much for trying to keep close tabs on her. "Uh, you two don't happen to know where she is right now, do you?"

They looked at each other. "Oh, we wouldn't want to step over the line," Maxie said. "You do what you do. We'll do what *we* do." In an instant, they were both gone.

I sighed. I probably should have been a little more diplomatic in dealing with the ghosts, but there are days when they're like close friends and days when they're like annoying insects. Today was a day to hide the can of Raid.

I pushed the kitchen door open and found Mom and Melissa putting the final touches on a macaroni-and-cheese casserole I happily would have eaten now, even though it hadn't officially been cooked yet. "The bread crumbs create a crunchy crust on top," Mom was saying. "You put it in the oven, and we'll clean up while it bakes." Okay, so it wasn't *baked* yet. These technical terms were overwhelming.

"Hi, guys," I said with a veneer of cheerfulness that couldn't hide my fatigue. It had been a long day, and it wasn't close to over yet. "How's dinner going?"

"We're baking it now," Melissa answered.

"Melissa did it almost all by herself," Mom told me, as Liss slid the baking dish—did I own a baking dish, or had Mom brought that with her?—into the oven.

Liss tried to hide her beaming pride but failed pretty seriously. "Grandma told me what to do every step," she said.

"Don't be modest," Mom told her. "It was you all the way." It was such a nice gesture, and Melissa was so happy, that some of the weight on my neck seemed to ease.

"Is Dad coming over later?" I asked Mom. "I wanted to ask him about something."

"I don't know," Mom answered. "Is it important?"

"Not really." I wanted to talk to my father about the white paint I'd used, which wasn't exactly covering the red marker on the walls. The weird message underneath was still showing through. It occurred to me that I could also ask Josh when he arrived. If we were speaking to each other. I walked to the locked cabinet where I keep room keys while Mom and Melissa set about cleaning up the countertops, which didn't need that much cleaning. Mom has always made it a policy to wash and put away as she cooks, so by the time she's finished there isn't a huge cleanup job left to do. I looked over at Melissa. "Thanks for making dinner, baby," I said.

"Dinner?" Melissa asked, a sly smile on her face. "Macaroni and cheese isn't dinner. It's a . . . side dish, right Grandma?"

I got the key out and locked the cabinet again as Mom answered her, "You've got it, honey. We'll get to the rest in a minute."

I walked out of the kitchen and found Tom and Libby ready and waiting at the hallway entrance with their two suitcases on the floor next to them. "This is so good of you," Libby told me. "I hope we're not being unreasonable."

"Not at all," I assured her as I led them to the downstairs suite, which has its own bath. I usually charge more for it, but under the circumstances I thought it was the perfect solution. "You're entitled to a relaxing vacation, and I'm happy to do anything I can to help."

Before we got to the bedroom door, Paul appeared at the other end of the corridor, and his face told me what he had to say was important. That's never good.

"Here we go," I said, my voice rising about half an octave. I unlocked the door and opened it, and handed Tom the key. "Enjoy the new room," I said. Normally with the suite, I give a little tour, showing the guests the bathroom attached and reveling in the extra space, but that's really just to show off why it costs more than a regular room, and it appeared that I should be in a hurry.

"Oh, I'm sure we will," Libby told me. "It's beautiful." Since I had worked fairly hard on that room when we moved in, I was proud to hear her say so. But Paul had business, so I wished Tom and Libby well and hightailed it for the game room, the closest private space for me to talk to invisible people.

"Okay, what's up?" I get abrupt in such situations, particularly when I was less than thrilled with the day to begin with.

"There's someone here I think you need to meet," Paul told me.

Josh would be here in forty-five minutes. Mom and Melissa were putting some elaborate dinner surprise together in the kitchen, perhaps because of that. I had guests in the house, and a crazed local posse was displeased with me because it was taking me more than two days to find out who repeatedly stabbed the local homeless guy in a gas station bathroom. Another client would undoubtedly be upset that I wasn't looking into who had hanged her husband's mistress with an extension cord. And a loopy self-described exorcist wanted to rid my house of, among other people, my father.

"I'm not sure I need to meet more people right now," I told Paul. "Where is this person, and how do I get out of the meeting? I'm guessing this is someone who's . . ." I try not to use the word *dead* to describe people when Paul is around. He's sensitive about no longer breathing.

"Yes, it's someone like me," he answered. "And he's waiting in the basement. I think it's important you meet with him."

But before I could answer, I saw a transparent man, in his sixties if I were any judge, rise up through the floor into the game room. He was wearing a heavy wool peacoat and a knitted wool hat. Maxie changes her clothes about once a minute, and Paul will occasionally appear in something other than his traditional jeans and flannel shirt, but this guy had clearly died in winter and hadn't given any thought to his attire since.

"Alison," Paul said, "this is Matthew Kinsler."

Uh-oh. "Mr. Kinsler?" I said.

"Yes," the man said. "Joyce Kinsler was my daughter."

Eighteen

"This just isn't fair," I said.

Matthew Kinsler looked at Paul for some sort of explanation. Paul didn't answer him but turned his attention to me. "Mr. Kinsler wants to engage our services," he said.

There weren't many ways a dead man could have discovered a private investigator specializing in such cases. "You put out an ad on the Ghosternet again, didn't you?" I accused Paul.

He held up his hands in front of him. "Nope," he answered.

"I heard about you from someone I know," Matthew explained. "There aren't a lot of detectives who can see us."

I felt my eyes narrow. "Who?" I asked.

"Who, what?"

"Who? What person, or spirit, that you know recommended me?" I crossed my arms. "How do I even know you *are* Joyce Kinsler's father?"

Matthew cocked an eyebrow. "Her kitchen had exposed beams and no center island, and still had unpacked boxes from when she moved in two months ago. She drove a 2005 Toyota RAV4, until last Thursday, when she'd just bought a new Acura. And when she was eight years old, she got her finger stuck in a car window and we had to take her to the emergency room. She had a permanent crook in her left index finger. And she cried most of that night. Is there anything else you want to know?"

I leaned on one of the windowsills. "I'm sorry," I said. "I didn't mean to hurt you any more than you've already been hurt."

He shook his head. "I can understand your uncertainty. But I can tell you that Arlice Crosby recommended you. She speaks very highly of you."

I wouldn't have thought the service Arlice had received was much worth recommending. But she was a dear, generous woman. Paul smiled behind his hand; he'd told me word of mouth would build our business. His hand was transparent, so hiding the smile was less effective than he might have hoped. The fact that almost all our clients were dead and couldn't pay was irrelevant. To him.

"How do you know Arlice?" I asked Matthew.

"I hang around a bit at Hanrahan's, the tavern over on Ocean Avenue—spent a bit of time there when I was alive," Matthew answered. "Arlice drops by now and again, and we have struck up the occasional conversation. When this happened to Joyce . . ." He trailed off.

"How did you find out where I live?" I asked. "How did you get here?" Maybe I could prove to him that he'd come to the wrong place, and he would go away and not ask me to look into Joyce's death. That would be good.

"Arlice told me where you live. And you're in the phone book," Matthew answered, with a slight tone of *duh*.

That was it. I had to get unlisted from the phone book as soon as I had a spare moment to find out how you did that. Which would probably be sometime when I reached my mid-seventies. All I managed was, "Oh, yeah."

"I wasn't there when my daughter passed," Matthew said without prompting. "I was just roaming around on the beach, watching the tide come in. And by the time I got back to her house, just to look in on her, she was already . . . in the body bag." He bit his lip and then took on a determined look to keep from doing whatever ghosts do in place of tearing up.

The afterlife, I have discovered through trial and (mostly) error, is not an orderly place. Paul couldn't contact Joyce and ask her how she died because people seem to take at least a few days to "reawaken" as ghosts, and some apparently skip this level of existence entirely and are never visible spirits; the rules are fluid at best. The afterlife seems to be run by the same people who brought you the Internal Revenue Service.

"I'm sorry," I repeated. "I wish there were something I could do." And halfway through the word *something*, I knew I'd made a monumental tactical error.

"There is," Matthew said. "You can find out who killed my daughter. I can't pay you, but I can figure out a way to get my ex-wife to write you a check, maybe do it myself. I'm very good at forging her signature. How much do you need?"

"Mr. Kinsler . . ."

"Matthew."

I really didn't want to get to know him, because that would make me feel even worse. But I said, "Matthew. I don't need you writing checks on your ex-wife's account for me. I'd end up in jail for forgery."

"But I'd be the one doing the forging," he protested.

"I doubt they'd try to lock you up."

Matthew nodded. That was true.

I wanted to be careful and not point the finger at the Boffices. I'd never met Matthew before, and an angry ghost has a lot of resources at his disposal. "It's not the point, anyway," I continued. "I'm concerned that you think I can do something the police can't do. I know the detective on the case in Eatontown, and he's doing everything he can to find out what happened to your daughter. You don't need me, Matthew, honestly. Let the police do their job."

"I never trusted a cop in my life," Matthew Kinsler said. "I'm not going to start now."

"Detective Sprayne is very good," I said, despite not knowing whether he was even competent at his job. "He'll find out what you need to know, and if you follow him around, you'll find out just as soon as he does."

Matthew shook his head. "You'll care. You'll get some justice for my daughter," he said. "You have a little girl. You know how it feels. Please, Ms. Kerby, don't say you won't help me. You may be the only detective in the world who can look me in the eye and tell me what I need to know. I have no place else to turn. You have to help me."

I hate it when they're persuasive. Especially the dead ones. Paul looked at me with puppy dog eyes, begging for the challenge. I felt like throwing him a liver treat.

"Okay," I grumbled. "Tell me what you know."

It turned out that Matthew didn't know much about his daughter's death, but he knew plenty about her life. "I didn't stick around when that Boffice guy showed up. He's been visiting Joyce since around the beginning of the year, first in her old place in Avon and now the new one in Eatontown," he said. "I left whenever I saw him. There are things a father never wants to see, no matter what."

He'd seen his daughter receive Dave at her home a number of times, he said, and didn't like the look of the guy from the beginning. "He even wore his wedding ring," he said. "Didn't even try to pretend."

Matthew also noted that Joyce was out of the house more often after Dave left. She had taken drives with Matthew in the car (of course, Joyce had no knowledge of her

father's presence), and he thought she'd actually driven to a
house he came to believe was Dave and Helen Boffice's
home. She'd just sit there and watch the place, he said,
much as I had watched Dave drive to his various lunchtime
rendezvous. She'd never gotten out of the car to so much as
ring the doorbell.

But as for the day Joyce died, Matthew had no knowledge of her comings and goings. His sojourn to the beach—
something he did infrequently, he said—had kept him
from his daughter's last moments, and he actually choked
up when he spoke of it.

"Maybe I could have done something," he said. "Cut the
cord down or something. If I'd been there . . ."

"There was no way you could have known," I told him.
"Just let me know if you hear from your daughter at all. If
she becomes, you know . . . like you, she'll have very good
information to share."

Paul nodded in approval and Matthew, looking determined,
went on his way, although I had no idea as to where he'd go.
Ghosts have a lot of time on their hands, and while some
(like Paul) are tied to specific locations, many (like Maxie)
have very little limitation in terms of territory. Matthew
could literally be anywhere.

There wasn't time for Paul and me to strategize further,
because Josh arrived, on time as always, for the dinner
Mom and Melissa were busily preparing in my kitchen
(which would no doubt be cleaner after they cooked than it
had been after I'd cleaned it). He'd said hello to them on the
way, as he entered through the kitchen door after parking
his car behind the house.

I told him all I knew about Joyce Kinsler's death and the
little that had happened regarding my investigation into
Everett's. We talked about our respective days, and while
the mood wasn't chilly, it had the air more of two friendly
acquaintances catching up than people who'd been dating
for months. Josh seemed to be studying me, watching for a

sign of something I couldn't identify, and I wanted to tell him about the ghosts in the house and couldn't find the words. This wasn't good.

Melissa came in to tell us that dinner was ready, and the four of us—with occasional intrusions by Paul and Maxie, who wanted to discuss investigations and make comments about Josh, respectively—had dinner quietly and without serious incident. Which I guess was a plus.

It was all so civil and unexceptional that by the time we'd gotten through clearing the table, I was convinced that Josh would never come back, and that was making me sadder than I would probably have anticipated.

That was it, I decided—tonight I'd tell him about the ghosts. If he was going to run off screaming into the night, at least it would be because he knew the truth.

Of course, the first thing I had to do was get rid of all the other people, living and dead, in the house. Which could prove tricky, especially since guests were starting to return from their dinner excursions.

"Maybe Josh and I will go out and get some ice cream for dessert," I suggested as I started the dishwasher. Mom and Liss, who had been accepting accolades and discussing how to cook beef short ribs (that had been the surprise entrée, and it was excellent) and macaroni and cheese, stopped for a second to consider what I was saying.

Josh must have sensed that I wanted to talk to him in private. He is a very intuitive man. "Sounds like a good idea," he said. "Let me get my jacket, and we can get going."

"Ice cream?" Mom said. "Isn't that a little heavy after that whole dinner?"

In my family, turning down a dessert is a sign that someone has been diagnosed with a terminal disease. I stared at her. "Really?" I asked. "Are you okay?"

"Yeah," Melissa chimed in. "I'm thinking of skipping dessert tonight. Why don't we get out the karaoke machine?"

I looked over at Josh, who didn't seem nearly as

confused as I was but who certainly was not pleased by this turn of events. "Is something wrong, Liss?" I said.

"No. Why do you ask?"

"Because the last time you turned down dessert you had to have your appendix out." Out of deference to my daughter's level of embarrassment, I chose not to mention her recent ice-cream-related stomach problems.

"No," my daughter lied, "I'm just in the mood for some singing. Let's get the machine out; what do you say?"

Paul looked at me and shrugged. Whatever this gambit was about, nobody had brought him into the loop. Maxie looked bored, which meant it wasn't about her.

I pursed my lips. It was involuntary, I swear. "I say something's up, and you're not telling me about it."

I noticed an interesting look on Josh's face after I said that.

Melissa nodded. "I didn't want to say anything, because I thought you'd get upset."

"I'm already upset. What?"

Mom pointed to the front door. "Out there," she said. "Don't get upset."

Clearly, they believed whatever was out there would upset me. Subtle, no? "What, out there?" I asked.

"Let's take a look," Josh said and headed for the door before anyone could argue with him. I was right on his heels.

We walked out onto the porch and looked out into the street. A car went by, which wasn't unusual. The lawn had been mown fairly recently. This, too, was hardly cause to keep me inside the house. But Mom and Melissa, presumably because they didn't want to upset me, stayed inside and did not attempt to explain themselves.

Maxie showed up and looked out into the street. "I don't see anything," she said.

Paul, still observing Mom and Melissa, had not yet started toward the door. He probably was looking for telltale signs of conspiracy. He always said it was best to watch the subject when they were focused elsewhere; it was the time they were least conscious of their reactions. But he didn't seem to be getting anything useful.

I looked at Josh and shrugged. "They're my family," I said. "I suppose I should be concerned."

"Every family has some quirks," he said. "Mine has a guy who got his MBA and then decided to buy into a paint store." It was the first glint of humor from him since before our "celebratory" dinner, and I was glad to see it.

Harry and Beth Rosen started up the walk and saw at least two of us on the porch. We greeted them, and Harry shook his head. "You hate to see this in such a nice neighborhood," he said.

That was an interesting opening line, so I suppose there was a moment when Josh and I looked blankly at them. "Something wrong?" I asked.

Behind me I heard Maxie gasp, then growl a little. I turned.

Painted on the wall next to my front door, in the same red marker that had proved so difficult to get off my paneling in the game room, had been scrawled, "FLEE, MORTALS! THERE BE GHOSTS HERE!"

Mom appeared at my left shoulder. "We just didn't want you to be upset," she repeated. I ignored her.

Josh and I took in the sight. I didn't look at his face. I was too busy trying to get my jaw to unclench.

"That's it," I said. "Now they've pissed me off."

Nineteen

"It wasn't me," Cybill Hobsen said. "I have no idea why you would think it was me."

Despite Paul's pleas for restraint, Mom's reminder to act professional and Josh's clear desire to get away somewhere and talk, I had given in to my impulse to confront Cybill in her room.

"You have been disappointed with me for not asking you to 'cleanse' my house of ghosts," I reminded her through the tiny opening I could manage between my lips. "I insisted the spirits here were not dangerous, but you disagreed. This was your way of trying to prove me wrong."

"It most certainly was not," Cybill responded. "But if you wish, I will pack my things and find my way back home. I will, however, feel it necessary to report your conduct to Mr. Rance at Senior Plus Tours. I don't appreciate being accused of vandalism."

"You didn't find a red marker in her belongings," said Paul, floating just behind me and being an irritating purveyor of conscience. "It's entirely possible she *didn't* write either message."

I forced myself to exhale and softened my voice. "I really hope you won't do that, Cybill," I said. "Please don't leave."

"I don't know." Now she was playing coy. "I don't want to stay if I'm not welcome here."

"Of course you're welcome," I said, wondering if I meant that even a little. "I was upset at finding graffiti on my house, and I overreacted. Can we try to go on as if this unfortunate scene hadn't happened, please?" There are times even I am appalled at how quick I am to pander to a paying customer.

"That depends," Cybill said.

Depends? "On what?" I asked before I could think it all the way through.

My phone vibrated in my pocket. I resisted the urge to pull it out. Whoever was calling would have to wait until I'd defused this situation, the one that I had fused in the first place.

"Are you *sure* you don't want me to cleanse the house?" she asked.

"I'm quite sure. It wasn't any spirit that lives in this house who wrote those words, I assure you." Even Maxie wouldn't have done that; she had too healthy a respect for the integrity of the house. She never would have defaced it.

Cybill, predictably, looked disappointed. "I still think a quick ritual would heal the house," she said. I didn't know the house was sick, but I did not comment on that.

"Tell you what," I countered. "Suppose we schedule a ceremony for Sunday night, before everyone goes home. Not one that would banish the ghosts from the house, but one that would protect it from outside entities. Can you do something like that?"

Her face brightened visibly. "I can!" she said. "I would

be delighted to seal this house from outside spirits." I made a mental note to be sure that Dad was here before the ceremony began, on the one-in-a-million chance that Cybill could actually do what she said she could.

"That would be wonderful," I told her. "I'm so grateful."

"I'll begin preparing immediately," Cybill said and went into her closet. "I might need a different robe."

I walked out of her room and started down the stairs. I heard Paul behind me say, "You might just be successful at the hospitality business yet."

"But not the investigation business," I said quietly.

"You're getting better all the time."

"We're nowhere on anything," I reminded him.

"That's usually when we do our best work." Paul has a somewhat rosier picture of our attempts at detection than I do.

I walked downstairs, where Melissa was bringing Harry and Beth some coffee, and went back out onto the porch. Josh was still out there, closely examining the red words on the clapboard next to my front door.

"What do you think, Doctor?" I asked him. "Will the patient survive?"

"I wish it were paint," he said. "That would be easier to remove. This might actually require something on the order of sandblasting to get down to a surface that will be free of the marker, and that would mean you'd have to repaint the whole exterior of the house."

That sounded tedious and fairly expensive. I was not pleased, and I must have looked it. "Luckily, you have a friend in the paint business," Josh said.

I wasn't sure what that meant. "A friend?" I asked.

And my cell phone rang again. I pulled it out just to check and saw that the caller was Phyllis Coates at the *Harbor Haven Chronicle*. I made a low sound in my throat. "I'm sorry," I told Josh. "I have to take this." He nodded, his face impassive. "Just hang on."

Phyllis sounded rushed, which isn't the least bit unusual. "I'm just getting this, but it might help you," she said. "There's been no arrest yet, but I know the cops have interest in someone for Everett Sandheim's murder."

I immediately thought of Brenda Leskanik, Everett's ex-wife, but I realized that was because she had the only reason I knew of to be mad at him. And she hadn't really seemed all that mad. "Who are they looking at?" I asked Phyllis.

"Marv Winderbrook," she said. "The owner of the Fuel Pit."

What possible motivation could Marv have to kill a homeless man in his gas station's men's room? "Why?"

"Mostly because they don't seem to have any other suspects," Phyllis answered. "But also because Marv had applied for a restraining order to keep Everett from using the restroom at his station."

"I think I need to talk to Marv," I said wearily. It had been the one thing too many while I juggled two cases and a complement of guests.

"You'd better hurry," Phyllis said. "He could be in jail by morning."

"You think I need to go tonight?" I looked at Josh, who managed with Herculean effort not to roll his eyes at all.

"Hey, you're the private eye," she answered. "I just write for the local rag." That's Phyllis for *yes*.

In my mind's ear, I groaned. Outwardly, I said, "You don't happen to know where he lives, do you?"

"Right behind the station," Phyllis said. I could hear the smile in her voice, and one day I would have to get her for that.

I disconnected the call and looked at Josh. "I really want to stay here and talk to you. You need to understand that."

"I could come with you," he said.

I wished he could. But if I was going back to the Fuel Pit, and I really needed to do the measurements on the bathroom window, then I needed to take another passenger with me. That could be Josh, certainly. But if there was ghostly activity in the restroom, he wouldn't see it, and I'd be inside talking to Marv.

I needed to go with Maxie.

So reluctantly—make that *very* reluctantly—I shook my head. "This one I really need to do by myself," I told Josh. "It's business."

His face closed off like it had at the restaurant. "Fine," he said.

"Believe me, it's not—"

"I know. It's not that you don't want to stay, but you can't. And you can't really explain why that's the way it is, right?" He sounded sad, rather than angry.

"I don't have time. You have to take me on faith this one last time. I want to be here. I want to talk to you. I *will* talk to you, hopefully as soon as I get back. And I'll tell you whatever you want to know. But right now I have a narrow window of opportunity, and I just don't have the time for anything else. I don't think you're the kind of guy who wouldn't be able to understand that. Are you?"

"I'm not sure," Josh said.

That was a body blow. "You're not?"

"No. That last sentence was so twisted I'm not sure what you're asking me. Am I not the kind of guy who wouldn't understand? What does that mean?" He allowed the hint of a smile to peek out from under his frown.

A small amount of hope perked me up. "Stay here," I urged him. "Hang out with Mom and Liss if you want. As soon as I come back, we'll talk."

The smile faded. "I don't think so," Josh said. "I have to get up early. We can talk tomorrow. Right?"

I nodded. But I couldn't say anything.

* * *

"I'm not going back in that bathroom," Maxie insisted.

She hovered lightly over the passenger seat of the Volvo and stared at me, but I was driving and watching the road. "Nobody's asking you to," I told her. "I just want you to take this tape measure and get the dimensions of the window. You can do that from the outside." I had taken a tape measure from my toolbox, and now I extended it to her. She hid it in the pocket of the trench coat she liked to wear when we were out on what she had taken to calling a "mission."

"If there's somebody inside, I'm not looking," Maxie said.

"Please don't. I don't want somebody inside to see a flying tape measure. That's all I need." I turned right. The Fuel Pit was at the end of the street on my left. At this time of the evening, there was no problem finding a space to park directly across the street. "I don't see you rushing in to check it out," Maxie told me.

"I'm going to be in the back talking to Marv," I reminded her. "Try not to be too loud."

I'd actually called Marv and asked if I could come over to talk, and since he knew me from being around town (I often point guests to his station, and Marv knows that), he agreed but sounded puzzled about the reason for my visit. I'd told him I was coming as a private investigator but not that I'd heard he was the prime suspect in Everett's murder. There are things one simply doesn't mention, darling.

"Just get the dimensions," I reminded Maxie. "You don't need to do any more than that."

"Don't worry, I won't," she assured me. And then she was gone.

I met Marv in what he called his sitting room, which was a studio apartment of sorts in what had obviously once been a garage behind the Fuel Pit. He had closed the Fuel

Pit for the night. Many of the area's gas stations are open 24/7, but Marv runs the place almost entirely by himself and isn't on a major highway, so with the gas rationing after the storm he started closing at nine every evening and never stopped. He is a tall, thin, scrawny-looking man with an Adam's apple that could be seen from space, but he had combed his hair and was wearing jeans and a polo shirt instead of his usual oily overalls. He was trying, and I appreciated it.

"I told the police everything I saw, and I gave them the security tapes," he told me once I mentioned Everett's name. "I don't know what else I can tell you, Alison."

"Tell me why you were requesting a restraining order against Everett," I said. No sense in beating around the bush.

Marv waved a hand; the whole thing was irrelevant. "I wasn't *really* going to go to court," he said. "I just wanted a piece of paper to show Everett so he wouldn't spend his days in my men's room, keeping actual customers away, you know? Some days he'd just set up shop in there like it was the Waldorf. I started to feel like I should bring him room service."

"When did that start?" I asked. "I never saw him anywhere except outside the Stud Muffin."

"Two, maybe three months ago," Marv estimated, his eyes rolling up as he grasped for the figure. "I'd let him go in and, you know, clean up every once in a while, but all of a sudden it was a regular thing with him, and he'd stay in there a really long time. I don't like to think about what he might have been doing."

Now that he brought it up, I didn't want to think about it, either. "Still, going to the police department and filing a petition, even if you didn't intend to go through with it, was pretty serious," I suggested.

Marv thought about that and nodded, conceding the point. "The fact is, the last few months Everett started creeping me out," he said.

I heard a scraping noise outside the window and looked, but there was no sign of Maxie. I wondered if she was doing something to the window that would draw attention to herself, but Marv didn't seem to notice, so I just plowed on. "Creeping you out?" I asked.

"He started telling me he was hearing ghosts," he said. "I mean, no offense, Alison, but that's fairly creepy." It was lovely how the locals respected my position in town.

I know you can't hear my tone of voice, but that was meant sarcastically.

And to be fair, the idea of Everett hearing ghosts was doing a decent job of disturbing me, as well. Did my future include sitting outside the Stud Muffin in a series of winter coats, telling people about Paul and Maxie and asking for spare change? Best not to think about that.

"No offense taken, Marv," I said, although I wasn't entirely sure that was true. "Did Everett say specifically what he was hearing?"

Marv must have figured I was asking out of professional curiosity—that I wanted to compare Everett's spectral experience with my own. That wasn't far off the mark, but I really wanted to know if there was any indication whether Everett had been hearing *real* ghosts or if they were voices in his head that would be explained by a possible mental illness. In any event, Marv flattened out his mouth in an expression that was supposed to indicate thought and said, "He told me he was hearing ghosts. Someone he knew, he said."

Whoa. "I guess it's possible," I heard myself say. It was really just a thought that came out because I hadn't thought to guard it. "He didn't say who?"

"Nope," Marv answered. "You couldn't get much from Everett, but the ghost thing makes sense, sort of. Because that door was locked from the inside, and there wasn't no way somebody could have snuck in, stabbed Everett all those times, and then snuck out." He considered for a moment and then looked at me. "Why don't you just find Everett's ghost and ask him what happened?" he asked.

"It doesn't work like that," I told him. Still, I'd asked Paul, who can contact other ghosts, to put out the occasional bulletin for Everett and Joyce Kinsler. And of course, so far there had been no responses he could report.

"Too bad," Marv said.

I think he would have elaborated on his sentiment, but there was a very definite sound from outside. And it was a sound I really didn't want to hear. The sound of breaking glass. From the direction of the gas station.

Specifically, the men's restroom.

Maxie.

"What was that?" Marv said, I think rhetorically, and stood up to head for the door.

"I didn't hear anything," I tried, but it was far too late. Marv had already pulled a jacket off a hook near his entrance, and all I could do was follow him out the door.

We—that is, Marv with me holding up a decidedly lagging rear (no comments!)—were downstairs and at the gas station in less than a minute. For the first half minute or so, even with the lights on, neither of us saw anything.

The difference was that I knew where to look but didn't want to give the information away.

"Psssssst!" Seriously? Maxie was floating around in a tree limb about fifteen feet up over the garage structure that housed the restrooms, saying, *"Psssssst!"* as if Marv could have heard her and she had to be discreet. I closed my eyes in exasperation for a moment, collected myself and looked up.

Of course, I didn't say anything, but she knew she had my attention. "It wasn't my fault." I considered telling her she should have that imprinted on one of her signature black T-shirts, but the whole "not speaking to the ghost in public" thing made the situation a little trickier. So I simply made a face that indicated I thought her statement was, let's say, suspect. "Really!" Maxie insisted.

I looked at Marv, who was still scouting around the grounds of his station, saying, "I was sure I heard glass breaking" and scratching his head. I'd never seen anybody actually scratch his head when he was thinking before; it was sort of quaint. He hadn't looked in the key area just yet. He would soon enough, so I had to think of something to say.

But Maxie wasn't making my thought process any easier. "I'm telling you, I just dropped the tape measure and it broke the window," she said. "So it's really sort of *your* fault."

I couldn't help it; that made me look directly at her, no doubt with my eyes bulging. "Well, you gave it to me . . ." she attempted.

"Oh, my," Marv said, and I turned to look, all the while knowing exactly what he had found.

Sure enough, the window to the men's room was smashed. And it was clearly smashed from the outside, because shards of glass had fallen inside the bathroom. What *was* lying outside on the grass, shining brightly under Marv's key-chain flashlight, was my tape measure. He walked over and picked it up, examined it.

"That's weird," he said.

"It sure is," I decided to agree. "Why'd somebody go out of their way to break your window with a tape measure? Why not use a rock? Why do it at all?" I wanted to add, "Am I babbling?" but decided against it.

But Marv was examining the tape measure and not the damage to his window. "It's got initials on it," he said.

Oh, yeah. I do that sometimes, so my tools won't get mixed up with someone else's, or in case I leave them somewhere . . . I'm a little OCD, okay?

"A.K.," Marv went on, and it actually took him a second. He turned to me. "You last name is like Kerber, or something like that, isn't it, Alison?"

"Kerby," I said. He had me dead to rights. I almost stuck out my hand to introduce myself.

"Is this yours?" Marv asked. He was truly confused, and given that we'd been sitting a few feet away from each other when the glass had broken, he had every right to be.

I considered telling Marv the tape measure didn't belong to me, but that would require so many verbal hoops to jump through that I honestly didn't think I could pull it off. Mom had always told me that the person who tells the truth doesn't have to remember the lie. "Yes, it's mine," I told Marv, and held out my hand. He actually handed me the tape measure. "I'll pay to have the window fixed."

"I don't understand," he said, which indicated that he was an intelligent man. He looked around to see where my accomplice might have gone. She was up in the tree, for once not finding the situation hilarious, which was almost a refreshing change of pace for her. "Why would you want to break my bathroom window?"

"I don't. Didn't," I told him. "I didn't want to break your window, and I didn't break your window. But someone did, and they used my tape measure to do it." That was all true. Mom didn't say you had to tell them everything and make an idiot of yourself.

"That's good," Maxie said from the tree, where she was pretending to sit on a limb. "It's all true, and you're covering your tracks." My eyes narrowed, because I was covering *her* tracks, but I couldn't honestly claim to have had no hand in the night's activities.

"How'd they get your tape measure?" Marv asked. I'm not sure if he was being suspicious or simply thinking aloud, but I felt an obligation to answer him.

"They must have gotten it out of my car," I said. Okay, now I was skating on very thin truth—but technically the tape measure *had* made the trip here in my car. Feel free to look at it any way you like; that's the point of view I was taking.

"You leave your car unlocked?" he said, incredulous that any self-respecting Jerseyan would allow such a careless breach of security.

"The backdoor of the wagon doesn't lock," I said, which, unfortunately, was true. "They could have gotten in that way." They *hadn't*, but they could have. If there had been a they.

"Better get that fixed," he said. "Bring the wagon in this week, I'll take a look."

Wow.

Marv and I agreed that I'd pay for a new pane of glass and install it myself. But for the time being, he fit the open space with a piece of plywood and said he'd clean the glass out of the restroom himself, "because it's the men's room, and you oughtn't be there, Alison." He believed in his heart that I had made it to my late thirties, married and had a child, and I had never realized that men's and women's restrooms have different equipment. You had to like Marv.

Except now the police seemed to like him for Everett's murder, although I had no clue—literally—why they would.

Maxie floated down to the car quickly, probably aware that I was annoyed with her and might drive away and leave her to find her own way back to the guesthouse. She stayed silent for a while as I drove, but her head kept turning to me and then toward the window. She sat (or simulated sitting) in the passenger seat, not getting in my line of sight, but not climbing into the backseat where she could be, quite literally, invisible.

Finally, she could no longer contain herself. "It wasn't my fault," she said again.

"I don't want to talk."

"But it *wasn't*. I didn't *mean* to drop the tape measure—I got startled. A little." She looked away again, and now it was my turn to wait until the urge got too strong to avoid speaking.

"Startled by what?" I managed to say.

Maxie turned her head slowly toward me to heighten the

drama of what she wanted to say. "There was someone in there," she said.

I blew out some carbon dioxide. "Impossible," I told her. "Marv locks the door to the bathrooms when he closes the station, and he checks to make sure they're empty before he does."

"That's just it," Maxie said. "It wasn't somebody who would get stopped by a locked door."

I really didn't want to ask the next question, but what choice did I have? "You mean whoever was in the men's room was a ghost?"

"Probably," she said. "There was a guy in there, and I'm pretty sure he was like me. You know, not exactly alive."

"Yeah. I know." I thought for a moment. "Was it Everett?" If so, we could turn the car around, park somewhere unobtrusive, and just *ask* him who had stabbed him. Case closed. I looked for a place to make a *K* turn.

"I don't think so. He was too clean," Maxie answered. So much for the *K* turn. "It was a guy, though. I mean, thank goodness."

"Why is it better that the ghost was a man?"

"Well," she said, "it *is* a men's room."

Twenty

Josh had painted over the latest vandalism on my house as well as could be expected, which was ridiculously nice of him considering what a lousy girlfriend I'd been since pretty much ever. It was a temporary fix; the words were still visible, but not *as* visible. Then, Mom reported, he'd made his farewells and gone home.

I, on the other hand, had spent the evening discussing a murder in a public restroom with a gas station owner and a dead interior designer. Such was the state of my social life these days.

Paul, of course, had wanted—and gotten—a full report from me on the exciting incidents at the Fuel Pit. And the goatee stroking he'd done indicated this was either very thrilling or extremely perplexing, or both.

"We have two very puzzling cases," he said after I'd retreated to the kitchen for a bowl of Edy's slow-churned chocolate. I wasn't sure from his tone whether that was a good or a bad thing. I knew which way I'd have voted, but no ballots had been handed out.

Apparently, my house was not a democracy, and worse, I wasn't the dictator.

"You could say that," I told him. "I'm feeling just a little in over my head." Like, two stories over my head.

"Don't worry," Paul assured me. "It's all under control."

"Sure, from where you're floating."

Mom, who also reported that Melissa had gone to bed reluctantly a half hour before, looked at me with sympathy, understanding what kind of day I'd had. "What should we do, Paul?" she asked, getting the conversation back on track.

Paul was clearly relishing his role as head of operations for our detective agency. "First, don't panic. It's a good sign that things are starting to happen. In Everett Sandheim's murder, we're seeing evidence that there was indeed another spirit involved, or at least that there's one at the scene of the crime now. You're going to have to go back and talk to that spirit, Maxie."

Maxie, who had been cruising around the room horizontally like Cleopatra on a barge, stopped dead in what would have been her tracks and stared at him. "Me?" she wailed. "Why me?"

"For one thing, because you can get in and out of there without anyone knowing. And because we don't know this ghost. It's possible he is dangerous and violent," Paul explained, his voice never betraying anything resembling emotion. This was strictly procedure. "There's nothing he can do to you, so you are the logical choice to interview him as a witness."

"I'm not going back in there," Maxie protested.

"There's no reason for you to be afraid," Mom told her.

"I'm not afraid. I'm grossed out."

"You'll be keeping Alison out of danger, Maxine," Mom

went on. "That's very important to me and to her father, and especially to Melissa."

Maxie pouted, but didn't shake her head. "You're not playing fair," she said, and rose up very close to the ceiling, in order to make a hasty escape if any more responsibilities were flung in her direction.

Paul shrugged that off and looked down at me (he had risen a bit when Maxie did, probably without thinking). "And you should see if Lieutenant McElone has the final medical examiner's report yet," Paul continued. I didn't want to talk to McElone again if I didn't have to, and I realized that I probably didn't, because Phyllis would get it from her special "friend" at the ME's office before McElone got it. I'd call Phyllis in the morning. "Then you should check to see if any of the other homeless people in town might have known Everett or had reason to wish him gone."

"Other homeless people?" I said. "In Harbor Haven? I don't think we *have* any other homeless people. I figured Everett was the franchise."

"I'm sure there are at least a few," Paul said. "The lieutenant will know who they are and where they can be found, as well."

"Man," Maxie marveled, "you are so insensitive." She started whirling in slightly tighter circles but not any faster.

"Maxine," Mom scolded.

"Sorry, Mrs. Kerby." A familiar refrain. She vanished into the ceiling.

"Now," Paul said as if nothing had interrupted him (it's a coping mechanism for him), "about the Joyce Kinsler case."

Ugh. I really didn't want to think about that one. "I think it's too much for me," I said to Paul. "You brought in her father and guilted me out, and that wasn't fair. I don't know what to do for him."

"I'll tell you exactly what you should do." My father's voice came from behind me; naturally, I hadn't heard him come in. "You go help that man find out what happened to his daughter."

I turned to face him. "Oh, Dad," I whined. "You, too?"

"Me especially," he said. "Who would know better what it means to want to protect your daughter?"

"You've managed, a couple of times," Mom reminded him. She likes to build him up. It's rough on Dad, being dead and everything.

"It's not the same thing," he said. "Alison" (he only calls me "baby girl" when we're alone with family; the man is sensitive), "Paul is going to tell you what you should do, and you're going to do it, okay?"

I couldn't argue with my father even when he was alive. Now the level of guilt was exponentially higher, and he was playing it. "Okay," I managed.

"Good. Paul, I'll leave it to you." And Dad vanished up into the ceiling, probably to go watch Melissa sleep. He says he finds it comforting; I think he's standing guard. My father was a successful handyman in his life, and in order to be successful, he had to deal quite a bit with clients. The ones he worked for loved him, and the ones he didn't work for respected him. He had a good touch with people.

That made it all the more incongruous that Dad really doesn't like crowds. Even now, he comes around to my house after the guests are in their rooms and the daily group meetings in the kitchen around dinner are over. He sees Mom when she's alone, goes to Josh's paint store to sit in with a few of the old painters, living and dead, and the rest of the time, he has a few places he likes to spend time thinking and looking at the ocean.

The five of us in the kitchen was probably a little more than he was up for this time of night.

I turned toward Paul. "Fine," I said. "You've got the whole world conspiring against me. What is it I'm supposed to do about Joyce Kinsler?"

"You need to talk to Helen Boffice," Paul said. "Outline

for her exactly what you intend to do, of course, leaving out the fact that we have a second client." Paul likes to think of the ghosts we help out as clients, and on my polite days, I refrain from pointing out how they don't ever pay me.

"My client is Helen," I told him now. "She's the one who signs the checks." This wasn't one of my polite days. I'm pretty sure the last one was in late 2006. "What am I asking her?"

"Exactly where she was when Joyce died would be a nice piece of information, but wait until late in the interview for that one." Paul sometimes gets a little tilt-y when he's thinking hard about a case, and now he was listing to his right, at an angle to the floor. It was just a little distracting, and with the second bowl of Edy's (What? I was upset) going down a little rockier than the first, a little nauseating.

"You want me to ask a potential murder suspect for her alibi at the time of the killing?" I asked. Mom looked concerned and took a spoonful of Edy's for herself. Like daughter, like mother.

He stopped, straightened himself (thankfully) and focused his attention on me. "Yes. Why?"

"Nothing. Forget I brought it up. So if that's what I'm saving for late in the interview, what do I ask to break the ice?"

"Ah!" Paul said, pointing his finger in the air. "That's the interesting part."

But he was interrupted by Maxie, who descended from the ceiling in her "I'm carrying something" trench coat. "You've *got* to see this!" she said, pulling my Stone-Age laptop from the coat. She drifted over to Paul and showed him the screen.

It took a few moments. "Wow," Paul said.

"Wow?" I figured I'd ask.

Paul seemed to remember there were other people in the room. "Maxie has found something about our client."

I felt a rush of excitement. "Kerin Murphy?"

"Helen Boffice," Paul answered. Damn. "It seems David is not her first husband."

That was interesting, given that she had not listed a first husband on her intake form. But it was hardly amazing. "So she was married before," I said. The obvious question *So what* went unspoken.

Until Mom said, "So what?"

"It's more than that," Maxie said. "Helen's first husband died."

Hmmm . . . "A questionable death?" I asked.

Paul shook his head. "Cancer. But there's something Helen didn't tell us. Apparently, her first husband was a very successful man in the food-service business. He ran concessions in many of the area's arenas and stadiums."

It was starting to sink in for me, but Mom got it sooner. "He left her money?" she asked.

"Four million dollars," Maxie said.

"I think I have a new first question to ask her," I said.

Twenty-one

Helen Boffice suggested we meet at the Stud Muffin the next morning, which actually was somewhat convenient for me. After I saw her, I was going to see Phyllis, then McElone, and if I had time after that, I'd meet Jeannie for lunch before going back to the Fuel Pit to install the new window before heading back to the guesthouse for the afternoon spook show. I got to the Stud Muffin a few minutes early and almost overlooked Helen when she came in punching something or another up on her iPad—I'd forgotten how small she was; at first glance, she looked like a very businesslike teenager. Paul, Maxie, Mom and I had spent some hours trying to digest the idea that Helen Boffice was a widow with four million dollars in her bank account. Helen and Dave didn't live extravagantly; my house was probably worth more than theirs. Neither of them had a luxury car. But the records on file indicated she had plenty of money. It was decided (by Paul, pretty much all by himself) that I shouldn't ask her about the money, since it didn't seem to have an immediate connection to the case and needed "further research." "Wait until we know what we want to ask," he said.

"Sorry," Helen apologized when she finally looked up from her iPad. "I'm backed up on a week's worth of orders, and now there's this thing with Joyce Kinsler." Honestly, that's what she said: "This *thing* with Joyce Kinsler."

"Yeah, about that," I replied. "I need to know whether you think Joyce was seeing anyone other than your husband." Paul had suggested more delicate wording, but Helen's lack of regard for a dead woman, whether she'd been cheating with Dave or not, rubbed me the wrong way. I'm not sure there was a right way to rub me in regard to that particular subject.

Helen looked momentarily surprised. "Other men?" she said, I think rhetorically. "I guess it's possible. I hadn't really thought about it before. Why do you ask?"

Now I was the surprised one. "Because if Dave didn't kill Joyce Kinsler, I have to wonder if there was someone else who might have been involved with her and have something of a beef." I was talking fast; normally I would have come up with something better than "a beef."

"Oh, you're wrong. Dave killed Joyce, all right." Helen took a dainty sip of her latte.

I sat there and stared. Suddenly, the pumpkin muffin in front of me didn't seem quite as appetizing. After word-shaped thoughts started back in my brain, I said, "You're certain?"

"Oh, completely. He was just putting on a show for your benefit. He probably strung her up hours before he led you there." She might as well have been explaining how Dave had used Drano to unclog the upstairs bathroom sink.

"Did he tell you he'd done that?" I asked, moving the tote bag to my lap so Paul would be able to hear this conversation better when I got home. "He said that he'd killed Joyce Kinsler?" I could let Detective Sprayne know, too, but maybe I'd let McElone call him.

"No, of course not," Helen said, still as proper as a schoolmarm. One who was drinking a latte and explaining how her husband had murdered his mistress. One who could have quit her job and moved to Aruba if she'd wanted to. You have to watch those schoolmarms. "He would never admit that to me. It would give me the upper hand. Dave couldn't possibly allow that."

My eyes started to hurt. That was the explanation for why I had to squint so hard. "If he didn't tell you, how can you be so sure he killed her?" I asked.

"Oh, he had to," Helen said, waving her hand in a "don't be so naïve" gesture. "See, I got an e-mail from old Joycie early that morning, confessing about their affair. Once Dave knew the cat was out of the bag, he couldn't possibly let her live. That would give me—"

"The upper hand."

"Precisely. He knew I'd be able to hold that over him for the rest of our lives. With Joyce gone, he could deny everything, say she'd committed suicide because she was crazy, that the e-mail was a sign of her craziness, and then I couldn't possibly get an advantage." She dusted a crumb from my muffin, which I hadn't touched recently, off the table. No doubt it was trying to get the upper hand on her.

"Do you have a marriage or a poker game?" I'm fairly sure I hadn't expected that to actually come out of my mouth.

Helen raised her eyebrows and shrugged. "Our marriage is a competition," she said. "I'm not ashamed of that. When two successful people come home from work, they can't simply turn off their personalities at night. We remain who we are, and we are very competitive people. This is how we live."

If you call that living, I thought. "So you're just guessing that Dave murdered Joyce Kinsler to . . . get some leverage on you?"

Helen shook her head just a tiny bit. "I can prove it. His

right hand has a mark on it, right across the palm, the kind of mark you'd get if you had to pull really hard on an extension cord for more than a couple of seconds. Looks painful." She seemed pleased about that. She kept her own left hand covering her right, just to drive home the idea of control.

"Did you tell the police about it?" I asked.

"I told them. They didn't seem to care about the mark on his hand."

"Where does Dave say he got that?" I asked.

She snorted, daintily. "He says it's a burn mark. That he had to open the hood of his car and check the radiator, and he leaned on the edge of the hood too hard, says he burned it."

"You don't think that's true?"

"I don't think Dave knows how to open the hood of his car," Helen sneered. "I practically have to show him how to open the gas cap every time we pull into the station. And he thinks he can convince me he was making a repair on the engine? Please."

Mentally I cut out the call to McElone, as this evidence was so circumstantial Judge Reinhold would throw it out of court. But if there was a visible mark on Dave's palm . . . "Did the police detective notice the mark on Dave's hand when he was questioned?" I asked Helen.

"Oh, Dave hasn't been questioned in Joyce's death," Helen said, as if explaining that the Earth is indeed round. "They think it was a suicide, or that the wife might be involved. They always look for the easiest answers."

I knew that neither of those things was true but couldn't imagine why Helen thought it necessary to lie to me about it. "Really," I said. "I'm surprised. That's lucky for Dave, I guess."

"Not so lucky. I'm going to make sure he knows I'm on to him." Helen looked like a chess master who had just figured out how to end the game sixteen moves from now.

"Threaten to call the cops. Teach him to underestimate me. I'll show him who has—"

"Don't say it," I said.

"Well, you're having a week, aren't you?" Phyllis Coates said.

We were standing in Phyllis's "office," a cluttered room filled with paper, about four percent of which Phyllis actually needed or, if she were being honest, could identify even after reading it. There was a hot plate with a pot of horrendous coffee sitting next to a pile of old bills, notes, outgoing invoices and for all I know, laundry lists, just waiting to start a fire that would take down three city blocks. This, to Phyllis, was the way you ran a newspaper.

"A week," I echoed.

"You've got two dead bodies and a whole truckload of questions." Phyllis made that sound like the best time a girl could wish for. Clearly, we were of different sensibilities. But I loved her like a crazy old aunt, and she saw something in me that probably wasn't there. "So this Boffice woman says her husband killed his girlfriend because he wouldn't let her have the satisfaction of catching him playing around?" She reached into a drawer in her "desk," which was a large cabinet that had a chair next to it, and pulled out a pair of half-glasses on a chain, which she put around her neck.

"Since when do you need those?" I asked. Phyllis's eyesight had always been sharp as a razor.

"I only need them when I wear contact lenses for distance," she answered, with some shortness in her voice.

"Contact lenses?"

"Do you want to talk about the story, or what?" Phyllis doesn't care much for getting older. She says the only thing that's worse is *not* getting older.

"The story, of course. So Helen Boffice has millions of

dollars that she doesn't seem to be spending. Is it possible she paid somebody to kill Joyce?"

Phyllis, perhaps still smarting from my talk of her eyewear, had a sour expression and waved a hand. "Possible. Anything's possible. The question is what can we prove." Phyllis seems to believe I'm a member of her staff, which is doubly astounding because she doesn't have a staff. "I'm going to find out what I can about her finances, but a lot of that stuff isn't public. Still, if she made a million-dollar withdrawal from her bank account, it should send ripples out somewhere." I didn't tell her Maxie was running an online search in the same area.

"That's the only reason I can think of that she wouldn't tell me about the money," I said.

"Why? Does everyone who sees you on the street give you a full financial disclosure?"

I decided to change the subject. "Sorry. So did Marv get arrested today?" I asked.

I'm not sure if it was the contact lenses, but there was a twinkle in Phyllis's eye. She waved a hand. "Marv's not getting arrested," she said.

Huh? "Then what was that frantic phone call about last night?"

She chuckled. "I thought you needed a kick in the pants on this one, so I made sure you got out there to do the interview." She looked at me. "It worked, didn't it?"

I thought of the conversation I could have had with Josh, the one that was currently causing me digestive distress because I still had to have it, and moaned. "You have no idea what you did to me," I told Phyllis. But there was no changing her; to be Phyllis's friend, you signed up for Phyllis. It was usually worth it.

She seemed to find that amusing. "Helen Boffice," she insisted. "She says her husband Dave strung up this Kinsler woman?"

"That's about the size of it," I said. I start talking like

I'm in the middle of the newsroom at the *Daily Planet* and it's 1952 when I go to see Phyllis at the *Chronicle* office. I sort of love it.

I was thinking of eras past because the ghost hovering over Phyllis's head, visible only from the chest up through the ceiling, bore a very striking resemblance to Cary Grant. I was wondering where Cary Grant died, although I was sure it was not in Harbor Haven. Of course, he would have had plenty of time to get here. I started to wonder if Cary Grant was a fan of the Jersey Shore. I wondered if the current rebuilding efforts would satisfy him.

"Do you buy it?" Phyllis asked, snapping me out of my Cary Grant reverie.

I considered pouring myself a cup of coffee, then looked at the decades-old coffee pot and the washed-once-this-month mug sitting next to it, and decided to give up coffee for the rest of my life. Eating, too. "I don't know," I told her. "She seems positively sure about it, but she has absolutely no actual evidence. Their marriage might be bizarre enough that she'd set him up as a suspect just so she could claim some kind of advantage over him. I wonder if they have a scoreboard in their bedroom, to keep track of who's in the lead."

"Do you think it's possible Helen killed Joyce Kinsler?" Phyllis asked me.

Unlike Helen, I don't like accusing people of things until I have clear, tangible evidence that I can say absolutely proves that person did whatever is being discussed. It's an ironclad rule with me. "I'd be surprised if she didn't do it," I said. Perhaps *ironclad* was overstating it.

"And on what are you basing *that*?" Phyllis wanted to know. As a reporter, she really does have to wait until there's proof before saying something.

"I get a vibe," I said.

"A vibe," Phyllis repeated, bringing me back on topic. If the ghost said anything, I'd know for sure if he was Cary

Grant. Have you ever noticed how you can't say *Cary* or *Grant* separately? It has to be *Cary Grant*.

"I think Helen is scary." Cary Grant, because I decided I would tell Mom and Melissa that's who it was, looked a little stunned. I shook my head just a tiny bit, which Phyllis must have thought was a comment on Helen Boffice, and Cary Grant clearly saw as something of a disappointment. He rose up into the ceiling, silently. My loss.

"I don't think that's a lot to go on," Phyllis lamented. "Luckily, I have a little bit more." Reporters get into the business not for the wealth and glory (I'll insert a space for guffaws) but because they are, to a person, the biggest gossips on the planet. There's nothing a reporter likes better than knowing something before everyone else.

I could play along. "Like what, Mata Hari?" I said. "Spill."

"The cops talked to Dave Boffice, but they're not looking too hard at him."

"You have sources with the Eatontown police?" I asked.

She fixed me with a look. "You think there are places I *don't* have sources?" Touché.

"What about Everett? Did the ME issue a report yet?" I asked.

Phyllis grabbed a reporter's notebook off the tumult going on atop her desk. She flipped to a page. "Not formally. They're not exactly authorizing overtime for the death of a homeless guy in a gas station men's room."

"A homeless veteran," I reminded her. "You'd think they'd have a little more respect."

"Wouldn't you." Phyllis consulted her notes again. "Unofficially, Everett died of blood loss brought on by forty-seven small stab wounds to his chest, arms and neck."

"Forty-seven?" I gasped.

Phyllis took off her reading glasses and nodded. "Apparently someone had a very small knife and a lot of time on their hands."

"What about the knife?" I asked.

"What about it?"

"They didn't find it, but the door to the men's room was locked from the inside. What do they think happened to the knife?"

Phyllis regarded me for a moment. "The medical examiner doesn't really deal with questions like that, but if you ask Lieutenant McElone . . ."

"My very next stop," I assured her.

"Excellent." Phyllis snapped her notebook closed. "Then you don't need me to duplicate the information."

I waited, but she seemed determined not to tell me anything else about Everett's death. I waited some more. That didn't work any better. "This is about the glasses thing, isn't it?" I asked.

"Only partially," Phyllis said. "Go talk to McElone."

It suddenly occurred to me that lately I had been treating the people close to me pretty badly. I didn't know why that was the case, but I had a feeling it had something to do with the tension between my idea of my relationship with Josh and the fact that I live with two dead people. Ghosts, more than anything else, are inconvenient when one is trying to find romance.

I went and talked to McElone.

"Why am I talking to you?" Now, that was more like it. I could always count on Lieutenant Anita McElone to be consistent. No matter what the situation, I would be an annoyance to her. There's something comforting in that kind of reliability.

"How many times are we going to do this dance?" I answered back. "You're going to complain about me gumming up the works for the police, I'm going to tell you that I have a client and besides, I'm only trying to help, and eventually, you're going to be grumpy but admit that I'm not a total screwup and tell me what I need to know. So can we jump to that part now?"

McElone never—*ever*—cracks a smile in my presence, and she wasn't disappointing now, either. "You had me up to the point where you weren't a total screwup," she said.

"Everett Sandheim," I reminded her.

McElone made a low noise in her throat and punched her computer keyboard for a moment. She looked at the screen, which she insisted on keeping turned away from me. The fact that I was in the chair in front of her desk, and she would have only been able to show me the screen by turning it completely around and away from her view, was a likely excuse.

"The ME report hasn't come back yet," she said. I waited, but that was it.

"I know," I told her. "I'm going to go with loss of blood from forty-seven stab wounds made with a small knife."

The lieutenant didn't even have the decency to look surprised. "You talking to Phyllis Coates again?" she asked.

"I'm not at liberty to reveal my sources," I answered. Then I realized that was something I'd overheard only Phyllis say, so McElone had gotten her answer. Time to shift the focus away from how smart she was and back to how smart I was. "What happened to the knife?" I asked.

"I'm thinking it entered Everett's body forty-seven times," she said. "What else do you want to happen to it?"

She was being intentionally obtuse. "Nice try," I said. "What you're telling me is that the Harbor Haven Police Department has no idea how someone stabbed a man forty-seven times in a gas station restroom and then got out with the door locked from the inside?"

"Maybe it was a very drawn-out suicide," McElone said, but she couldn't even make it sound like she believed what she was saying.

"Then I'll ask again: What happened to the knife? If he killed himself, where did the knife go? You didn't find it in the room. If he *didn't* kill himself, how did the killer get out while leaving the door locked?"

"We're looking into the possibility Houdini did it," McElone said.

I wasn't having a great detecting day, and besides, I was frustrated on about eighteen different levels. "Come on, Lieutenant," I said. "How about we both stop wasting our time and try to cooperate with each other? Is there something I can do that could help you?" I caught myself quickly enough to add, "Besides leave?"

"That was going to be my first choice," she admitted.

"What do you say? Can I do something for you? Something related to the investigation?" A thought struck me. "Helen Boffice has four million dollars from her first husband," I offered.

"We know."

Damn. "Okay, what *else* can I do?"

McElone's office is really a cubicle; there are no permanent walls, no door and no privacy. So it shook me a little when she stood up to look over the partitions and make sure no one was listening, then sat down and leaned over her desk, gesturing for me to do the same.

Her voice dropped to a barely audible whisper. "Are you still in on the whole ghosty thing?" she asked. "Can you really talk to dead people?"

There was something completely *wrong* about those words coming from McElone's mouth. The idea that the person who most disdained the idea of ghosts, who was creeped out by my house, who rolled her eyes whenever I showed up, would be asking me about being the ghost lady, was disturbing on more levels than I could identify in the moment. "It's possible," I managed. "What do you need?"

"Can you get in touch with Everett and ask who killed him?" she rasped. Then she put her head back and laughed, unable to hold in her merriment any longer.

Truly, the woman had a future in stand-up comedy. At

least, in her own estimation. "When I see him," I mumbled. Okay, so it didn't make me feel *that* much better, but it was something.

It took McElone quite some time to get herself back under control, and even after the hilarity had subsided, she still bubbled over with a few more "What you can do to help" and one "Ask Everett who killed him," which set her into another brief giggle fit. It was like the Bizarro World McElone had taken over, and I had to wait until the sober real one could get back across the border into reality.

"You're a serious wit," I told her. "I'm just barely hiding my hysterics."

"I am damn funny," she agreed. "No, you can't help me. But I'll tell you what. Just for giving me such a good laugh, I'll give you something for free." The fact that she'd never given me anything for money came to mind, but if she was feeling generous, this was not the time to be snarky.

"What's that?" I said, trying to sound neutral.

"You know Everett used to spend most of his time outside the Stud Muffin," McElone said. That wasn't exactly heart-stopping news, so I nodded and waited for more. "But lately, he'd been spending more time at the Fuel Pit."

"I know; Marv told me. So what?" I asked.

"There's a little colony of homeless that camp not far from there, so I went down to talk to a few of them after Everett died. Most of them scatter when they see a uniform, but I went in civilian clothes and brought sandwiches, so a couple were willing to talk to me."

Touching story though this was, I was finding my patience wearing thin. Forget that I'd had no idea there even were more homeless people than Everett in Harbor Haven; she wasn't getting the satisfaction of a reaction out of me. "You're a wonderful Samaritan, Lieutenant. If you'd like me to contribute to the homeless sandwich fund, I'll be happy to make a donation. But what has this got to do with anything?"

"If you're going to be that way . . ." She started straightening the absolutely nothing out of place on her desk. (It was like McElone's cubicle had seen Phyllis's office and used it as a negative role model.) I think she might have rearranged a paper clip by one millimeter. It was excruciating.

"I'm sorry, Lieutenant. I'm having a really bad week."

"Good thing it's Friday," she said.

"Thank goodness," I agreed. "So please, can you tell me what you found out when you fed the people at the Fuel Pit?"

"No, but maybe you'd like to go down yourself and talk to a woman named Cathy. She knew Everett pretty well, and she has a theory about what happened to him."

"What's Cathy's theory?" I asked.

"She wouldn't tell me." McElone regarded me, daring me to respond. I didn't. "She wouldn't even talk to me—a couple of the others told me she was Everett's pal, and others said there was no such person as Cathy. So you're going to go over there and charm your way into her heart," she added.

"You want me to go talk to a woman named Cathy who's homeless, who might not exist, but if she does, she could be either mentally ill or addicted to something . . ."

"Don't stereotype," McElone warned.

"My apologies. So you want me to go and ask this woman, who wouldn't tell *you* something about what happened to Everett, what happened to Everett? And you think she's going to tell *me*?" I had, in my life, had better ideas.

"You said you wanted to help," McElone reminded me.

Twenty-two

"I'll give you this," Mom said. "You don't go to the same old place for lunch every time. Which is just as well, since there's no food here."

"Take it easy," I told her. "Once I do this, we'll find lunch, okay?"

"I wasn't complaining."

I had called Marv, who informed me he'd gone ahead and replaced the windowpane himself ("it was no biggie"), so now Mom and I were standing at the edge of a parking lot, about a half block behind the Fuel Pit. The lot backed onto a crusty, uncared-for dune that, if you walked for ten minutes, would eventually lead to the beach. There was a partial shelter built, maybe by FEMA after the storm, that could comfortably contain maybe seven people.

And gathered around it were perhaps twenty homeless people of both sexes and various ages, the youngest around thirty and the elder statesman, a rather redolent fellow named Irv, claiming to be in his late seventies. He looked more like he'd been one of the first passengers off Noah's ark.

"I don't know no Cathy, but there's someone in the ladies," he said, pointing in the general direction of some brush at the top of the dune. "What do you want with this Cathy?"

I had to choose my words carefully; they'd already been visited once by the police about Everett, and they hadn't told Detective McElone anything. "We're not a tourist attraction," a man named Will had said to us when we'd first arrived. "Go to the beach, if you can find it. Look past the knocked-down houses."

"I hear that Cathy knew a man named Everett Sandheim," I said. Irv started to look annoyed, but I didn't give him time to voice his irritation. "I knew Everett, and I'd like to talk to her about him just a little. I don't know if you heard, but Everett's gone now."

"Everybody knows that," Irv sputtered. But he was distracted. He pointed. "Maybe that's Cathy," he said. He pointed at a tree and walked away.

After a moment, a woman emerged from the trees. The first time I saw Cathy Genna, I thought she might be a ghost. She was so pale and thin that she might have looked transparent in the right light, and the way the sun hit her at midday, there wasn't a great deal of difference visually between Cathy and the woman floating next to her. Except that that woman was dressed for a day out in 1898, and Cathy's feet were on the sand.

"Wow," Mom said.

That was unquestionably the right word; it was clear that Cathy had once been very beautiful indeed. Back when she still had a full head of hair and a full set of teeth. And when the clothes she was wearing were something other than what had obviously come out of a Dumpster, or several Dumpsters. Cathy was in her mid-to-late forties and had a glazed look in her eyes, as if she were looking at something that wasn't there, or wasn't visible to the rest of us.

I knew the feeling.

I approached her cautiously, but smiling (which felt phony). Mom hung back, not because she was afraid but because she doesn't like to invade people's personal space. She's too polite. I don't have that problem.

"Everett?" Cathy asked.

"Everett Sandheim," I said. "I'm Alison Kerby, and this is my . . . friend Loretta."

Mom chuckled. "Friend," she said. "I'm her mother." She held out a hand, but Cathy didn't take it.

"Yes," Cathy answered, as if that meant anything.

I had to stumble on. "Um, I sort of knew Everett, that is, we both sort of knew Everett, and now that he's gone, well . . ." My voice just trailed off. I think my mouth might have kept moving out of sheer momentum. I had nothing left that could be reasonably thought of as conversation.

Fortunately, that is not a condition that has ever afflicted Mom. "We're trying to figure out what happened to Everett," she said. "The police say you knew him. Did you?"

Cathy looked at Mom, then at me, through slits for eyes. "You're not cops?" she challenged.

Mom laughed and shook her head. "Do I look like a cop?" she asked.

Mom is in her sixties and does not look like a cop, so Cathy laughed, too. "No," she admitted. "So who are you?"

I was now just a spectator and Mom was the star, so I let her run with it. "We're just people from town. We saw Everett around; we tried to help him out when we could. But when we heard what happened to him, we thought it wasn't right that nobody was trying to find out who killed him. So we figured we'd try."

"Everett was your homeless guy," Cathy said. "There's all of us here, but Everett was the only one everybody saw."

"Until the cops told us about this place, we never knew

you were here," I admitted, just to remind everyone that I was there. "I'm sorry about that."

Cathy waved a hand in indifference. "That's the way we want it," she said. "I don't need people coming and bringing me soup. I just want them to leave me alone."

"What about Everett?" Mom said.

"I knew Everett," Cathy said, looking away. "I knew him better than anybody else around here. He liked me, so he told me stuff."

"Stuff?" I had found my voice. Cathy appraised me, but I couldn't tell what she was thinking. "What kind of stuff?"

Cathy recovered from her moment of unease and looked me right in the eye. "He said he saw ghosts," she said. "Ha! Ghosts."

I nodded. "What did he say he saw?" I asked Cathy.

"Okay, I was wrong," she answered, scratching at her neck with chipped fingernails. "He didn't say he saw ghosts."

That didn't help. "He didn't?"

"No. He said he *heard* ghosts. That's different, right?" Cathy nodded once to emphasize her point.

"Yes," I agreed. "That's different. But it was ghosts? More than one?"

"Oh, yeah. Everett said there were two ghosts, a guy and a girl. I'm hoping they were married or something; that'd be good." Cathy looked around, keeping an eye on the area, always vigilant. That was the impression I got, anyway.

"What did the ghosts say to Everett?" I asked.

"What?" Cathy seemed easily distracted, as if her attention span didn't necessarily reach to the end of a sentence.

"The ghosts," I reminded her. "What did they say to Everett?"

"You believe in ghosts?" Cathy asked.

I didn't know which way to play it with Cathy, but I figured it was best to play along with her to get better information. And anyway, there was what Mom always said about telling the truth. "Yes, I believe in ghosts," I told her. Mom nodded once, to indicate that she also knew about ghosts and also that I was brilliant for saying so. She can do that with one nod.

Cathy searched my eyes, which I took as a good sign; she didn't seem to like eye contact. "Yes. You do, don't you?" She busied herself for a minute by kicking something in the sand that turned out to be an empty plastic water bottle. She pulled it up and put it in a worn canvas supermarket bag she had strung around her shoulder like a purse. "Ghosts. Funny things. Tell you the damnedest stuff."

"What did they tell Everett?" I reiterated.

"Told him someone was gonna die," Cathy said. "They didn't mention it was gonna be him. Damn unfair of those ghosts, if you ask me."

I absorbed what she'd said for a moment. "The ghosts told Everett someone was going to die?"

Cathy thought for a long moment. "It was maybe two weeks ago. Told me he'd been hearing ghosts talking. I said I had lots of friends who hear voices, and he said no, this wasn't voices, this was ghosts, and he knew because he recognized one of the voices, and it was somebody who was dead."

"He knew one of the ghosts he was hearing?" I asked, once again confirming a point she'd made. "Did he say who it was?"

"Oh, yeah," Cathy said. But she didn't say anything else, choosing instead to sit down heavily on the sand and start searching through the grocery bag.

"Who was it?" I asked.

"His son," Cathy said, her head almost inside the canvas bag. "He said he was hearing the voice of his dead son. Now imagine that." She pulled a feathered hat from the bag and admired it. "I thought I'd lost this; what do you know?"

* * *

"His son!" Paul was on the verge of giddiness with the latest information. "What can that mean?"

"I don't know," I told him, "but if you can raise Randy Sandheim on the Ghosternet, it might really speed up this investigation."

Paul nodded briskly; that had been his thought as well. "I'll do that in a minute. It's fascinating, though. But this Cathy said he heard two ghosts?"

"Yes, but she didn't say if he knew the other one, a woman."

We were meeting in Melissa's room, which I don't like to do when she's not there, but now that Tom and Libby were downstairs, they were likely to hear echoes of me talking to "myself" in the kitchen or the game room with no one else present in the house and no competing noise to cover us. Paul had been anxious to hear the news, and Maxie had been working on digging up more about Helen Boffice's millions.

Maxie was trying very hard to look, as Paul would say, like a helpful operative. Dressed conservatively (for her) in a pair of skintight jeans and a black T-shirt bearing the words "Available for Weddings and Bar Mitzvahs," she hovered near the ceiling, holding the notebook computer on her lap, legs straight out in front of her as if she were sitting up in bed.

"Helen's money is interesting," she reported.

"Interesting?" I asked. "How is money interesting?"

"Because she's had it for eight years, since her husband died, and she's been married to Dave for six. There's no indication she ever spent any of her inheritance at all. Until four months ago." Maxie suddenly "grew" a green visor on her forehead and a pair of glasses that I guarantee did nothing to improve her vision.

I tried to move around behind her to see what was on

her screen, but Maxie was too high up. I like to think she wasn't intentionally keeping me away, but she does love the spotlight and adores being told she's done good work.

Paul rose up to look, though. "Really!" he said, exactly the reaction Maxie would want. "What happened four months ago?"

"That's what's *interesting*," she told him. "She's been deleting—"

"Withdrawing," Paul corrected.

"Fine, *withdrawing* big chunks of money, almost once a week, but in cash, so there's no way to know where it's going." Maxie looked at me. "So that's interesting, right?"

"Yeah," I said. "That's really good work, Maxie." Give her what she needs, you'll get more back. "So how do we trace the money?"

Maxie stared at me blankly. "Huh?"

"How do we trace it? How do we find out what she's been using it for?"

Her expression indicated I needed some remedial education. "We don't," she said. "I just told you that."

I looked to Paul for help. "So how does this help us?"

"Any and all information helps," he said. "We'll have to determine how, though, when we get more."

That wasn't a huge help itself.

"So what's my next assignment, boss?" Maxie asked Paul.

"Since when are you Samantha Spade?" I said.

They ignored me. Which was probably wise. My mind was still asking when could we talk to Josh, and my stomach was telling me it was best if we didn't.

"Try to find out if there were any increases in Dave's bank accounts, if maybe she was giving him the money," Paul told Maxie. "I can't imagine why she would, but until we know for sure, we can't eliminate any possibility."

Maxie saluted him like a soldier. "Gotcha, chief." She was putting on a show, though I couldn't figure out who the audience might be.

"But while you're at it," Paul continued, "see what you can find out about Joyce Kinsler herself. The more information I have, the better the chances I can contact her directly once she moves to this level of existence, assuming she does."

"I'm on it," Maxie said. I think she pretended to crack a piece of gum in her mouth, too. She suddenly changed back into a trench coat, put the laptop inside and vanished. Probably up onto the roof. She says she does that because the WiFi access is better up there, but the fact is, Maxie does her best work alone.

"She's up to something," I said.

I hadn't even realized Paul was listening. "Don't make assumptions, Alison. It inhibits your development as an investigator."

"I'm not that concerned with my investigative development right now, Paul. I'm concerned about Everett Sandheim and the dead son he thought was talking to him, about a weird ghost in the men's room at the Fuel Pit, about having to deal with Kerin Murphy, about Helen and Dave Boffice and who killed Joyce Kinsler, about someone writing beware messages on my house for no particular reason, and about the fact that Josh is coming over after dinner and I have to tell him something I'd rather not tell him." That last part sort of slipped out before I could think about it, and I had no choice but to complete the sentence.

Paul cocked an eyebrow. His eyebrows were getting a real workout today. "Really! What is it you don't want to tell him?" Usually, Paul has issues with guys I date, but up to this point he'd been remarkably un-judgmental about Josh. If this was an opening salvo in some effort he was dreaming up to discredit Josh, he'd picked the wrong moment.

I fixed my gaze on him the best I could; Paul is not exactly what you'd call completely there at any given moment. "I have to tell him about you and Maxie," I said. "Because I want to prove to him that I trust him."

Paul's face showed no reaction. "I think that would be an error," he said. "The rumors about this house are best left just rumors. Even Senior Plus Tours doesn't have any proof of us. Bringing in another person who would know that there really are people like Maxie and me here would be extraordinarily dangerous. And it would be an invasion of my privacy."

"Your privacy!?" I couldn't believe what I was hearing. Even the part I was saying. "You think me telling my boyfriend about you would make this house a tourist attraction? Newsflash, pal: This *is* a tourist attraction, because I need it to be! That's incredibly selfish of you, Paul."

"After all we've built over the past year and a half, you want to risk our operation by telling a man you've known only a short time about us?" he shot back. "Do you realize that your emotions might be getting the best of you?"

"Do you realize that you're jealous of every guy I look at twice?" I countered. "That you don't think any one of them is interested in me for myself? You think every man I meet has an ulterior motive."

He gave me a look.

"Okay, so sometimes they did. That's not the point. What I'm saying is, this is not about *you*." Except that it was, at least partially, about him and Maxie.

It's not easy to turn on your heel and leave a ghost in your wake. For one thing, they can move through walls, so closing a door behind you doesn't really have the same resonance as it would with someone more corporeal. For another, ghosts don't have the disadvantage of having to travel on legs; their speed is modulated, up to a point— they can't fly at seventy miles an hour—but they can move quicker than the living can.

None of that mattered because of the glimpse I caught of Paul's stunned face, and he did not follow me when I left the room.

Twenty-three

It was a little humiliating four seconds later when I then had to go back up the stairs, look Paul straight in the eye, and say, "Okay. Now, what was I supposed to be doing on the Joyce Kinsler case?"

Paul being Paul, he didn't make me suffer for my outburst. Very patiently, he answered, "You need to explore the possibility that someone other than Helen or Dave might have wanted Joyce dead. We know she didn't kill herself, but we don't know the motive, and we don't know if there was an aspect of her life that might have made a difference. I've spoken at length to her father while you were away. There are some possibilities."

Which was how I ended up in Katrina Holm's house in Spring Lake the next morning.

Katrina was a very nice, very attractive lady in her early forties. But when I'd asked her on the phone if I could come up to talk about Joyce Kinsler, she had sounded almost offended.

"I'm not sure why you'd ask," she'd said. "Joyce was my friend, almost my sister. She's dead now. I'm mourning. Can't you get whatever information you need from someone else?"

"I completely understand and hate to impose," I'd answered. "But it's entirely because you were her closest friend that you can provide the kind of insight no one else can offer." A little flattery never hurt. "I promise it won't take long."

Her voice softened a little. "Can't we do this on the phone?"

Paul, who could hear both sides of the conversation, shook his head. I knew he always wanted me to see the expression on the subject's face and get a sense of the feeling in the room.

"It would be much better if we could talk in person," I said. "I'll make it as convenient for you as I can. I have to be in the area anyway." Sometimes it's best to make the person you're asking think they're helping you out. I don't know why it works, but it does.

And so I was now sitting in Katrina's living room, a pitcher of lemonade on the coffee table and Katrina herself on the sofa opposite me. I sat in an upholstered chair. Katrina hadn't offered anything more than the lemonade yet, and so far I'd only asked the softest of questions. The voice recorder next to me was probably bored.

"When you said that Joyce was like a sister to you," I began, "well, do you have a sister?" That seemed pretty innocuous, and Paul always said to start with something easy to get the subject comfortable. In this case, I wasn't diving right in and trying to prove anything about Katrina. I had no reason to think she'd murdered Joyce Kinsler. I had no reason to think she didn't, either. This was a fact-finding mission.

"No, and maybe that's one reason Joyce and I were so close." Katrina was already biting her lip a little; the more sensitive questions were going to be tough to ask. "Because we both needed somebody to talk to like that. I'm just now starting to realize how much I'll be missing her for the rest of my life."

I avoided biting my own lip and went on. "When is the last time you heard from Joyce?" I asked Katrina.

"Just the day before . . . it happened," she answered after a moment. "And the thing is, she didn't sound the least bit unusual. Just the same Joyce. We talked about *American Idol*, can you believe it? And then we hung up, and the next thing I knew . . ." Her voice trailed off.

"Did she mention Dave Boffice that day?" I asked Katrina.

Katrina looked puzzled. "Why would she?" she asked.

I didn't know how to answer that, so I dodged. "I have to follow up on everything."

Katrina shook her head with an incredulous look. "No, she didn't mention that guy. Why does it matter? They barely knew each other."

Well, that made perfect . . . *huh*? "They weren't having a torrid affair?" I was so thrown, I was using words like *torrid*.

Katrina gave me a stare best reserved for someone who tells you the world is hexagon-shaped. "No!" she said. "Joyce said he was some guy she worked with."

"So why mention him at all?" I asked, congratulating myself for not saying *torrid* again.

"She said he used to come over once in a while and complain about his wife," Katrina answered. "I thought that sounded weird, but Joyce told me he needed an ear, and she provided it."

That didn't smell right. "Did she mention anything about his wife's money?" I asked.

"No. Why? Did she have some?"

I sat in my car and wondered about my life. But mostly, I watched the door of the office building and waited for Dave Boffice to walk out.

I hadn't told Paul I was going to see Dave, but it was inevitable, and here I was. I did keep the voice recorder in my tote bag, so I'd tell Paul about it later. I hadn't called Josh. I hadn't called Phyllis. I hadn't even called my mother. Maxie had been absent when I'd left, which really hadn't bothered me, but suddenly I felt very alone.

The police had questioned Dave (despite what his wife had told me—a call to Sprayne confirmed it) and probably gotten more out of him than I would have. But if I was going to investigate Joyce Kinsler's death—and after her father had visited, it was a given that I would—I needed my own information. It didn't make sense that Joyce hadn't told her best friend, Katrina, about her relationship with Dave. Was Joyce lying to her best friend? Or had Helen truly been mistaken about Dave and Joyce's "affair"?

It was Saturday, but I suspected that Dave would be in his office. From Helen's description and everything I'd witnessed, he didn't seem to have much of a life outside of his work. Sure enough, his car was parked in his customary space, despite there being many fewer cars in the lot than usual. Dave was a serious creature of habit.

I was right, and before too long, he appeared at the glass doors. I marveled at the idea that he would put on a suit to go to work on a Saturday. The butterflies in my stomach became hummingbirds and started flying around, which was odd. I wasn't afraid of Dave—he was so bland he didn't inspire fear—and had interviewed people about crimes before. I attributed the nerves to everything else that was going on in my life and got out of the Volvo to approach Dave before he could reach his car and drive away.

He didn't seem to notice me until I was only a few feet from him; he was reaching for the keys in his jacket pocket. "Mr. Boffice?" I began, and he turned his head to face me.

"Yes?" he asked. Then he looked at me more closely. "You," he said. "You've been following me around."

So much for my stealth skills.

"Yes," I admitted. "I want to ask you about Joyce Kinsler."

His expression didn't so much react as freeze. He did not move one facial muscle, and that gave the impression of great tension. It was a little scary.

"This is not the place," Dave said through clenched teeth.

"Where is the place?"

"Follow me," he said, opening his car door. "That should come naturally to you."

I had to run to my car to keep up.

We drove to a Dunkin' Donuts about two miles from Dave's office. Once inside, I ordered an iced decaf (I had enough stimulation on my own right now) and eschewed the baked goods to show Dave how professional I was. It's hard to be taken seriously when you're eating a muffin. Dave one-upped me by not ordering anything.

"Is that why you were following me?" he asked in a hushed voice once we had sat down at a table far from the counter. "To find out about Joyce?"

I saw no reason to be evasive. "Yes. Your wife hired me to find out if you were having an affair."

Dave's bland face showed something that incongruously looked like relief. "My wife," he said. "You mean she hired you to confirm that I was having a relationship with another woman so that she could use it to blackmail me. Isn't that a little closer to the truth?"

I didn't answer.

"Helen is the most competitive person I've ever met," Dave said. I wasn't sure if he was talking to me or himself. "But this is beyond the pale."

"You think your wife killed Joyce Kinsler so she could win?" I'd been thinking it, but I tend to discount anything I think as unhelpful to the investigation. Paul does the thinking; I do the . . . whatever this was.

Dave looked stunned. "Helen? Kill Joyce?" He seemed

to mull it over for a moment. "I wouldn't put it past her, but I don't think she did. I'm not sure she could handle it, physically." It was true that Helen was a small woman, and hanging someone took considerably more upper-body strength than, for instance, shooting them.

"Do the police think you did it?" I said. I couldn't be sure, and I didn't want to ask Sprayne any more questions if I didn't have to.

Dave's mouth flat-lined. "Probably. They think I was sleeping with Joyce, after all. They questioned me for two hours."

"You *weren't* having an affair with Joyce Kinsler?" So what Katrina told me had been true?

"Of course not. I take my marriage vows seriously. Helen thought what she thought, but Joyce and I were just friends."

"Just friends," I repeated. It's the declarative-sentence version of answering a question with a question. I like to mix it up.

"Well, you were following me. Did you ever see me in a compromising position?"

He had a point. Sort of. "I only followed you for a few lunch hours," I said. "It's possible I just caught the wrong days."

Dave's eyes lost focus; he stopped looking at me. "A few lunch hours," he said. Now *he* was doing it.

I decided to plow on. "I agree that Helen might not have been strong enough to kill Joyce, but she has a lot of money," I said, deciding on the spot to play that card. "Could she have paid someone to do it?"

Dave stood abruptly and put five dollars on the table despite not having ordered anything. "I have to leave," he said and was out the door before I could react.

I could have followed him, I suppose, but his quick exit stunned me, and I sat there for a full minute.

Then I picked up the five bucks and left.

* * *

"He ran?" Paul texted when I was back, sitting in my car—ghosts can't be heard over the phone, but he can use a cheap phone I'd bought to text me when I was out. I'd given the *Reader's Digest* version of my day, and when I said Dave Boffice had let slip that he thought his wife was morally, if not physically, capable of killing, and then fled, Paul had shown quick interest.

"Yup," I texted. "I feel like I'm the child of a sticky divorce. Mommy and Daddy are fighting because they each think the other one killed somebody."

A text came from Paul. "Talk to Sprayne."

As it happened, Detective Michael Sprayne had recently called me with an enticing promise of "new info" to share on the Kinsler case. I hadn't wanted to talk to him, strictly because I'd have to hear about it from Maxie, but I realized now I had no choice.

I put the phone back into my tote bag and walked from my car to a park bench where I'd agreed to meet him.

I stopped to turn on the voice recorder as I entered the park. Detective Sprayne, in a T-shirt and jeans on a Saturday morning, was already on the bench in question and gestured toward me. He looked less rumpled than either time I'd seen him before. Which was weird, since the last time he was in a suit.

"I don't get it," I told him, all business. "Out of the blue you call me with new information on Joyce Kinsler. Is there something you think I can tell you to help your investigation?"

Sprayne, who was making a show of being relaxed by stretching his legs, shook his head. "I just wanted to share," he said.

That made no sense. A police detective sharing information with a private investigator with no obvious advantage?

"You are really a cop, right?" I said. "You don't act like other cops."

He grinned and sort of chuckled, more a snort. "I've found some stuff, and I can't figure out what it means," he said. "I thought if we talked about it, we might be able to make sense of it. Is that so impossible?"

I'd never met a cop who would feel that way, and there was something about the way he was grinning that made me think he was at the very least exaggerating. But if I could find out something that might help Paul, I was game. "Okay, shoot," I said, and immediately regretted saying that to a cop who carried an actual gun.

"I talked to your pal Dave Boffice yesterday," Sprayne said when I was finished. "He said everything you want a witness to say, almost had me convinced he had nothing to do with Joyce Kinsler, was just a friend of hers, went over to her house to complain about his wife."

Exactly what Dave had told me. "*Almost* had you convinced," I echoed back, and told him what Dave had said to me. "What changed your mind?"

I saw a ghost watching the kids at a nearby playground, like a caring grandparent seeing to their safety. Sprayne took a moment and answered me. "Did a few routine checks on Boffice," he said. "Just the usual stuff, tax records, recent cell phone, employment history, that sort of thing." I made a mental note not to get in trouble with the authorities.

"You found something unusual?" I asked. Dave seemed such an average guy, anything out of the ordinary would be a surprise.

"Yeah, we found something. Up to about seven years ago, there was no such person as David Boffice." He let that sink in for a moment.

I stopped watching the ghost and stared at Sprayne. "What does that mean?"

"Exactly why I'm here conferring with you."

"No, I mean what do you mean, there was no such person as Dave Boffice seven years ago?"

"I'm saying that he had no birth certificate, no record of attending any school, no employment history, no tax records, no phone records, no credit cards. Then all of a sudden he starts to appear on official records just a hair under seven years ago. Now, what does that mean?" Sprayne took a sip of his coffee and blinked, the first time he'd done so in a while.

"It beats the living heck out of me," I said. "Are you certain?"

"The fact is, the only David Boffice I could find died seventeen years ago at the age of eight."

David Boffice was dead? I wondered if Paul could find him.

Twenty-four

"How do you track a person who didn't exist until seven years ago?" I asked.

Paul didn't have time to answer, because my phone rang. I had foolishly forwarded the calls on my landline to my cell phone when I left the house that morning, and now the cell was ringing with Kerin Murphy on the other end. I considered not answering, but then Kerin would just come to the house, and that would be more than I could handle at the moment.

"Hi, Kerin. I've been working the case and should have something for you soon. Nice talking to you."

But she saw my ploy and raised me an indignant, "Not so fast, Alison! I'm concerned about your investigation, and I want satisfaction!"

Satisfaction? "Are you challenging me to a duel, Kerin?" I asked.

"Don't be cute. You've been ignoring me and treating me like an annoyance since this began." I opened the phone to speaker mode so Paul could hear the other end of the conversation. I could see Maxie's feet and calves hanging through the ceiling, but most of her was upstairs with Melissa, who was ostensibly doing homework. As for Maxie . . . it's hard to know what Maxie is doing at any given moment, even when you can see her doing it.

"I don't think I've been doing that," I countered, mainly because it seemed like the kind of thing I would say if I meant it.

"Well, you have. I've been monitoring your progress, and you have been spending more time on some other investigation while I'm paying you good money to solve Everett's murder." Paul shrugged. Since he can't be heard over the phone, and not by Kerin under any circumstances, he could speak freely. "It's been difficult to juggle both cases," he admitted. "But we haven't been ignoring Everett Sandheim. You still need to get the dimensions on that window, though."

I gave him an exasperated look. "I'm working both cases," I said to Kerin. "Everett's murder is just as high a priority, but if you feel you haven't been getting the service you deserve . . ."

Kerin cut me off. "Don't tell me to take my business elsewhere again, Alison. I intend to make sure you see this through, and I want something done quickly."

"What is it you want done quickly?" I asked pointedly.

"Something!" Well, that was clear. "And now that the people you've been following around are moving out, you should have more time to concentrate on Everett. Honestly, I don't see how—"

I'd been just sort of half-listening, but Paul's eyes widened to the size of hubcaps and he pointed at the phone. "What did she just say?" he shouted.

Maxie dropped down through the ceiling. "What's the racket?" she demanded. "We're trying to concentrate on Apples to Apples up here."

Playing a board game with a ghost when she was supposed to be doing math? My daughter had a lot to answer for. Not to mention, Maxie should have been tracking down Dave Boffice's existence prior to seven years earlier.

"What did you just say?" I echoed back to Kerin. "Who's moving out?"

"You know, the milquetoast-looking guy," Kerin said, her tone adding an intimation that I was even a bigger idiot than she'd imagined. Paul gasped.

"Wait a minute—how do you know what I've been doing?" I said.

Kerin was very matter-of-fact. "You've been following that man all week!" she said. That wasn't an answer to my question, but what she hadn't said answered it well enough.

"I've only driven past his house once. How do you know where it is?" Then it hit me. "Wait a minute—you've been following me?"

"Well, *someone* had to make sure you were doing the work you were contracted to do," Kerin answered. "And now you can get to it because those two won't be in town anymore. I drove by their house to see if you were there, and I saw a big van in front of their house, loading cartons out of the garage."

"Call Sprayne," Paul said quickly. "Get there now."

I hung up on Kerin, which was the highlight of my day.

Maxie insisted on coming along, and I didn't argue. There was no point to it, and there was no time. I even had her find the directions to the Surf Drive home of the Boffices from the first time I'd used my portable GPS to get there. Maxie's manipulation of the device must have been a treat for anyone pulling up next to my car. The idea of a GPS unit floating in space was the last thing on my mind at the moment.

I'd left a message for Sprayne. Kerin, by the way, had called me four more times, but I had ignored the calls.

"What does it mean if they're moving?" Melissa asked. Yes, I took my daughter with me when confronting some potentially violent suspects. Even though Paul could certainly have kept an eye on her, and she really needed very few eyes kept on her anyway, I was more concerned that it would have appeared odd to the guests for me to leave my eleven-year-old daughter alone in the house while I stormed out on some unspecified mission. Besides, Melissa is really good at spotting the things I miss. Maxie, after programming the GPS, read a magazine in the backseat.

"It can mean a lot of things," I answered. "And we don't know that they're moving. We only know that Kerin Murphy says she saw a van loading cartons in front of their house."

"Right. So that means they've decided to keep all their stuff in boxes now?" Maxie said with an edge to her voice.

"We're making no assumptions until we have facts." I could recite the Gospel of Paul with the best of them. Maxie snorted.

"How long before we get there?" I asked Melissa, who was in charge of the GPS. A lot of people mount those things on the dashboard, but I keep mine in the cup holder in the console. It had nothing to do with the fact that the first time I'd used the dashboard thing, I'd turned the unit the wrong way and it had broken off.

"Two more minutes," Liss reported.

"I hope they're not already gone," I said to no one in particular.

"Too bad for you," Maxie said as we pulled onto the Boffices' street. If there had been a moving van in front of the house, a relatively modest McMansion type in the center of the block, it was no longer there. No movers were loading boxes. The garage door was not open and the front window had no curtains or drapes.

It sure did look like Helen and Dave had moved out.

There was a car in the driveway, but when I pulled up in front of the house, I deduced—trained detective that I am—that it belonged to Detective Michael Sprayne, who was already standing at the front door, scowling. His demeanor did not become the least bit brighter when, after insisting above protests that Melissa stay in the car, I got out and joined him there.

"Your pals are minimalist decorators," he said without looking at me.

"You're welcome for the tip," I countered. "What makes them my pals, anyway? You didn't have a unit keeping an eye on them, and now it's my fault?"

"Believe it or not, we don't have a cruiser available to watch every house that has a crime suspect with no indication of flight risk living in it." Sprayne looked through the side window next to the door. "There's nothing inside."

"Newsflash," I said.

"I don't have a warrant," he mused. "I suppose I could get one."

"You new to this?" I saw Melissa looking at Sprayne through the car window. She did not seem impressed. Melissa is an excellent judge of character.

Sprayne turned, finally, to scowl at me. "You know how many murders we get in Eatontown a year?" he asked.

"None?"

"None."

"So the crime rate has gone up. Anyway, you want to get into this house, right?"

He nodded. "But I don't have a warrant."

I reached over toward the door. "I don't suppose you've tried the knob." Sure enough, it turned and the door swung open.

"Still don't have a warrant," Sprayne said.

"The door was wide open. Besides, you didn't open it; I did. You can arrest me for breaking and entering into an empty house if you feel like it."

"I don't feel like it." He walked inside, but I noticed he felt for the gun under his left arm first.

I held up my hands, palms out, toward Melissa, telling her to stay in the car. She pouted but knew better than to disobey me on this one. Maxie wouldn't have let her out anyway.

Sprayne was already in the living room, gun still holstered, when I walked in. The place was, as advertised, completely empty. There were some indentations on the carpet where the furniture had stood, one or two—no more, certainly—scuffs on the walls (which were all painted white) and one of the many ceiling fans in the living room, kitchen, dining room and family room, which were all visible from where I stood, had some dust on its blades. That was it.

"Welcome to generic house," I said.

"Does look like everything is gone," Sprayne answered.

"Doesn't look like there was much here to begin with," I noted.

"No, you're right. The walls are too clean, the ceiling is perfect, there's no smell of lingering cooking. You have to wonder if anyone ever lived here at all." He dropped his right hand to his side, no longer reaching for his weapon, and walked into the kitchen. "Look here." He pointed to a mark on the carpet. "I've seen this shape before." It was rectangular and deep, meaning a solid piece of furniture had sat there. "Grandfather clock."

"Fascinating. Let's search the house."

I opted to take the staircase to the second level. I looked into the upstairs bath, which was exactly like one in a model home, and then walked into the master bedroom suite.

Matthew Kinsler was floating there, looking less distraught than disappointed. "I missed them," he said. "If I'd known, I would have gotten word to you. That gumshoe in your house would have heard me if I'd sent a message."

"What are you doing here?" I asked.

He snarled. "I came by to check on that Boffice guy. Figured I'd come here to see if the bastard would say anything about her. But he was gone by the time I got here."

"You think he had something to do with what happened?" I asked.

From downstairs, I heard Sprayne call up. "Clear down here. You okay?"

"I'm fine," I yelled back, then turned and stage whispered to Matthew. "I don't have much time. What do you know?"

"Nothing more than the last time I saw you," he answered in his normal voice, which made sense. "One thing that's weird, though. Did you notice anything about Joyce's house?"

I must have looked puzzled because he went on without waiting for an answer. "Every picture, every photograph in that house, is gone. Used to be everywhere," he said. "What would someone want with her pictures?"

"Kerby!" Sprayne insisted from the staircase.

"Coming," I answered him. I looked at Matthew and shrugged. I couldn't risk talking again, so I waved at him and turned back to the stairway.

Sprayne was standing there, weapon drawn, then saw me walking toward him and holstered his gun. "I figured someone had you at gunpoint," he said. "What took you so long?"

"It's lovely you're so concerned about my well-being," I said. Better to change the subject. "Let me ask you something," I said. "Did you notice anything strange about Joyce Kinsler's house?"

Twenty-five

"No photographs," Paul said. If his goatee had been real, he surely would have rubbed it off by now. His furious stroking of his own facial hair was making *my* chin chafe. "No photographs in the house." It was becoming his mantra.

"Maybe there was a treasure in one of the pictures and the person who killed her wanted to get it," Maxie suggested. We were having our current conference in the kitchen, where my mother was expected any minute. She was going to teach Melissa how to cook lentils. I had quit cooking class, my dismal failure to be expected given that I hadn't paid the slightest bit of attention, so I was just cleaning up the kitchen.

"I really don't think it's treasure they were after, Maxie." Melissa, who is always patient with everyone (having learned that from being patient with me), had no trace of irony in her voice. "Besides, why would they take *all* the pictures?"

"Exactly," Paul agreed before I could be sarcastic. "And Matthew said there used to be a lot of them, right, Alison?"

"That's what he told me. He said there were family photos and pictures of Joyce with friends everywhere. She never married, so maybe she liked to have pictures around to feel like other people were there."

Paul stroked even harder, if such a thing were possible. "The Boffices moved out of their house, and Joyce's photographs are missing," he said. He was clearly thinking out loud because he didn't look directly at any of us. "There has to be a connection."

"If we knew the name of the moving van company, maybe Sprayne could find out where the Boffices' stuff was going," I suggested. "Should I go back and check with some of the neighbors?"

Paul looked at me with the pride of a teacher whose student just mastered a basic algebra equation. "That's very good!" he said. "But you could ask the one person we know who saw the moving van . . ."

Oh no. "Kerin Murphy?" I said. "Do I really have to go and ask her for help?" The thought made my stomach quiver. If you've never had a stomach quiver, trust me, it's not something you'd want to experience.

Melissa looked out the back window. "I don't think you'll have to go and ask," she said ominously.

Sure enough, Kerin was at the back door, and she'd already seen me through the window in the kitchen door, so I couldn't pretend I wasn't there. I would have to pretend Paul and Maxie weren't, but that was little solace. "Let her in," I said to Liss.

Melissa unlocked the door, and Kerin, her face taut (no doubt with some surgical help) and severe (all on its own) strode in at ramming speed. "How *dare* you hang up on me!" she demanded. "I've called you four times since then and you've ignored my calls! You—"

"Hello, Mrs. Murphy," Melissa said. "How's Marlee?" Kerin's daughter and Melissa were no longer in the same class. There had been some scandal when Marlee was held back for a year after fourth grade.

Kerin semi-froze, realizing Melissa was there, and she had to put on her Perfect Mom persona. She pivoted in a blink and gave Liss a ghastly warm smile. "She's just fine, sweetie," she cooed. "She misses being in class with you." Melissa, who had never gotten along with Marlee, masked the fact that she knew Kerin was lying.

"That's nice," Liss said.

Kerin nodded, acknowledging that she was, indeed, nice, and patted Melissa on the head, which was about as condescending a move as she could improvise at the moment. "Now I have some business to discuss with your mommy, dear." And she walked past Liss like she was a mannequin in the juniors' department.

"Somebody needs to take this witch down a notch," Maxie suggested. Except she didn't say *witch*. I don't often agree with Maxie, but you can count that as one of those rarities.

"You haven't been taking this investigation seriously," Kerin hissed at me when she came closer. "You haven't been taking *me* seriously. That's going to stop."

"Did you notice a name on the moving van in front of Dave Boffice's house?" I asked her.

She stopped advancing, stunned. "What?"

"The moving van. You said you saw the moving van being loaded at Dave and Helen Boffice's house. Did you notice the name of the van line?" I had decided to play offense, right around the time Kerin dismissed my daughter as a silly little girl. There are some lines you don't cross. (It wasn't much, really, but it was enough under the circumstances.)

"I . . . the van . . . I don't know," Kerin said.

"Think. You said you saw a van. What color was it?"

Paul nodded in approval. "People remember more than they realize," he said. "Walk her through the steps."

"Yellow," Kerin answered. "Now. You've been—"

"Okay, yellow," I cut her off. "What color was the lettering?"

"Black, of course," she said, as if I should have known that.

"Was there a picture on the side of the van?" I looked at Maxie, then at the ceiling. She nodded, understanding my signal to her to use Kerin's clues to look up moving companies online, and went upstairs to retrieve the prehistoric laptop.

"Yes," Kerin told me. "There was a picture of a truck on the truck. I mean, how stupid is that?"

"Praise her for her help so far," Paul advised. I gave him an annoyed look, which Kerin seemed to find puzzling. "Go ahead," Paul continued.

"That's great," I said through clenched teeth. Melissa nodded encouragement. "You're doing really well. Now. Do you remember anything else about the van? Like what the name on the side might have been?"

Maxie appeared in her trench coat, which allowed her to conceal the laptop as she traveled through walls. She took up a position behind Kerin so that anything she did would be out of Kerin's field of vision.

"It started with a *K*, I remember," she said slowly. "I always notice *K*s because it's the same as my name." Luckily, the ceiling fan was masking the quiet click of the computer keys, because Kerin didn't seem to hear them.

In the interest of the investigation I refrained from hitting her over the head with a frying pan. "That's good. Anything else?" I asked.

"Koban's!" she said triumphantly. "It was Koban's Van Lines. I remember because—"

I didn't care why she remembered. "That's great! Thank you, Kerin! You were fantastic!"

"Really?" Kerin asked. "I didn't think I'd remember, but I did."

"Yes, you did," I said, ushering her toward the back door. "You were a huge asset. Thank you for coming by."

"Oh, it was nothing!" Kerin gushed. "I'm always happy to be of help."

"Great," I told her. "We'll see you soon. Thanks so much for pitching in."

"Not at all. Call me anytime." She would probably be halfway home before she realized she hadn't gotten to yell at me the way she wanted to.

That bought us the time we needed. "Maxie?" I said as soon as the back door was closed (and the shade over its window drawn).

"Yep, I've got the phone number for Koban's," she said and read me the number.

I punched the mover's number into my cell phone, but from the den I heard Cybill calling for me. I started to disconnect the phone, but just at that moment, there was a click on my phone. "Koban's. How can I help you?" The voice was male, middle-aged, and completely disinterested. Melissa waved a hand at me and walked to the kitchen door, indicating she'd handle the guest for now.

"Hi. I'm a private investigator working on a case, and I need to know where one of your vans took some things today," I said. There was no point making up a cover story, I figured. He'd either tell me or he wouldn't.

"What?" the guy asked. I reiterated my mission. "You're not the cops?" he said.

"No, I'm a private investigator," I told him. I noticed Paul's hand covering his eyes (sort of—both are transparent—did that mean he could see through his eyelids? I probably didn't want to know); clearly I'd done something stupid.

The guy hung up. .

I stared at the phone like it had done that on its own. Paul looked down at me with something approaching pity in his eyes. "You never tell them you're a PI," he said. "They don't have to talk to you." He might have mentioned that earlier.

"Well, I'm not the cops. I can't tell him I am. I'm pretty sure that's against the law."

"There are ways to imply it without saying it," he reminded me. "But it's too late now."

Melissa walked back in. "Cybill wanted your opinion on what gown to wear for tomorrow night's performance or whatever," she said. "I told her blue."

"Nice choice," Maxie chipped in.

"Liss," I said, suddenly inspired, "can you do your grown-up-lady voice? The one I always tell you to use when someone calls and I'm in the shower?"

Melissa dropped her voice half an octave and said, "Sure. Why?"

I looked up at Paul, who gave me a "why not?" expression. "It's pretty convincing," he said.

I told Melissa what I wanted her to do, and she really seemed to enjoy the idea. She used the prepaid cell phone I had bought for Paul (I wasn't going to let the moving guy see Melissa's phone number) so that the Koban's guy wouldn't recognize the number I'd just called from.

"Koban's," I could hear him say through her phone. "How can I help you?"

"Hello," Melissa said. If I'd closed my eyes, I would have thought . . . it was my daughter doing an adult voice. I know her pretty well. "This is Helen Boffice. Your company moved me from my home today."

She held the phone a little from her ear so we could hear the man say, "Ms. Boffice? Right. The emergency job. What can I do for you?"

"There's a vase missing," Melissa answered. She even pronounced it "vahse," an ad lib on her part. "I'm wondering if you'd found anything in the van."

"We didn't take your vase," the guy said defensively

(and using the traditional New Jersey pronunciation with the long *A*). "Our guys are honest, lady."

"Oh, I'm sure they are," Liss assured him. "I thought perhaps it had been left on the truck by accident. Do you have my new address?"

There was an ominous pause on the other end of the line. "Okay, who is this?"

I don't know what a jig is, but if we had one in the house, it was definitely up.

Melissa, however, is cooler under pressure than Dairy Queen soft-serve. "I told you, this is Helen Boffice," she said, adding a hint of irritation to her voice. "Do I need to speak to your supervisor? I'm asking you to confirm the address so you can deliver the *vahse* if you find it."

When he spoke again, the suspicion in the man's voice had been replaced by concern that he had insulted a paying customer, a feeling I know fairly well. "I'm sorry, Ms. Boffice, but you know from both your moves that we have a very strict policy of not giving out that information on the phone. I can't break it, even for you, honest." The poor guy was actually worried that my eleven-year-old was going to have his employment revoked.

"Sir, I have no desire to cause trouble at your place of work," my daughter told him. "But that is a valuable family heirloom (I didn't even know she knew the word *heirloom*), and I want to ensure that you have the correct address so that it can be returned." Sometimes that child scares me more than living with two ghosts.

"Well, why don't you give me the address, and I'll just write it down here?" the man offered.

Melissa didn't miss a beat. "I want to make sure that you had the right address before, so there was no chance of a mistake."

The suspicion came back into the van man's voice. "Didn't the moving men show up at your house with everything else you own?" he asked.

That got Melissa, finally. She gasped a little and stammered, "Uh . . . uh . . . uh . . ."

Paul slashed his finger across his throat and Liss hit the End button on the phone. "I'm sorry," she said to me as soon as the call was disconnected.

I gave her a hug. "Oh, baby, don't be," I said. "You were terrific." Liss broke into a wide smile; she loves to get praise and likes to hear it from adults the best. She is an adult waiting to happen, when she's not a little tiny girl. I so love that kid.

"Didn't either of you hear that?" Paul asked. "The man said she should know about their efficiency from *both* her moves. Helen moved twice, probably recently, or he wouldn't have had it on the screen in front of him."

"What does that mean?" Melissa asked.

Maxie intently clacked some keys. "You're right," she told Paul. "Helen contracted the movers two weeks ago, and they moved some stuff of hers."

"To where?" I asked.

"I don't have that, or I could tell you where they moved this time," Maxie said.

"So we still don't know where the van went," Liss pointed out.

"Let me work on that," Maxie said. "I might be able to trace it if I can find the license number of the van on a video camera from the security system at the Boffices' old house."

"Good," Paul said. Then he turned to me. "In the meantime, you have an old piece of business to settle."

I felt my brow wrinkle up, faster than usual. "I do?"

"Yes. We still need the dimensions from that men's room window."

"Will you get off that?" I asked. "It's small, okay? I wouldn't be able to fit through it. I eyeballed it."

He just gave me his patented Paul admonition face.

"Okay, I'll get my tape measure. But I'm not going there

alone." I turned to Liss. "And no, you're not going. There's a ghost we don't know in that bathroom."

She thought about arguing but saw my expression and realized she didn't have a chance. "Who's going to pretend to babysit me?" she asked.

"I'll call your grandmother."

"So who will go with you to the Fuel Pit?" Melissa asked.

"The one person I would actually like to take with me to a men's room at a gas station," I said confidently.

Twenty-six

"I don't understand why I'm here," Kerin Murphy said.

I didn't admit it, but I could understand her confusion. Kerin had probably just made it back to her house when I called and said I wanted her to come with me on an "errand" related to Everett's murder. I hadn't mentioned that it involved a visit to the bathroom where he died, and I hadn't said anything about our standing in the mud looking through a window that Marv had repaired. (This time I'd informed Marv I'd be out there doing some snooping so he wouldn't be upset to find the two of us behind his restroom structure, and in return he'd assured me that no one was inside, which would have been a deal breaker.)

"You wanted to see action in the investigation of Everett's death," I reminded her. "This is action. You're here so you can see it."

"You could just report back to me on your progress," Kerin suggested, her nose wrinkling despite no discernible hint of an unusually unpleasant odor. This was the kind of place that you felt *should* smell bad, even if it really didn't.

"Since you've been so *concerned*," I explained, "this way you know I'm not slacking off on the case." And maybe I could figure out why Kerin was pretending to be so concerned about Everett and his murder.

Kerin kept quiet, mostly because the obvious thing to say would've been that she knew I wasn't slacking off, but she wouldn't give me that modicum of respect. We had an interesting relationship.

I approached the window with my tape measure. I measured horizontally, vertically and diagonally and wrote the dimensions on my arm in ink. Kerin looked disgusted, so maybe this wasn't a pointless exercise after all.

Then I took a deep breath and looked through the window.

The brand-new window was pretty clean, so there was no difficulty seeing in. More accurately, there wouldn't have been any difficulty, if there hadn't been a cheap slat blind hanging in front of the windowpane.

"What are you doing?" Kerin asked. "You got the measurements. Let's go."

"Just a second. There might be a ghost in there. After all, you're the one who wanted to see me catch a ghost for killing Everett." She asked for the ghost lady; she was getting the ghost lady.

"Oh, seriously," Kerin said. There wasn't anyone around for her to show off to, so she was revealing her true colors. "There isn't any ghost. Must we play that game now?"

"It's all part of the service," I answered cheerfully. "I'm going inside."

Her tone was flat. "What?"

"You heard me. Marv said there's nobody inside. I'm going to look."

"It's the *men's* room," Kerin pointed out unnecessarily. Her reluctance to enter overcame my general unease at the prospect. If Kerin didn't want to do it, it must be worth doing, right?

"You can report me to the restroom-etiquette police whenever you like," I told her, walking around the side of the structure to get to the front door.

Of course, I did stop at the door to compose myself. If there was someone not-so-alive inside, it might not be someone very friendly. We were working with the potential of a killer ghost, after all. I didn't relish the prospect.

Kerin came up a pace or two behind me, as if to allay any thoughts I might have that she'd possibly have my back if there was trouble. "Well?" she asked.

"Keep your earrings on," I said, given she was wearing some dangling models that were actually quite nice. "I'm getting prepared."

Her eyes narrowed. "You don't need to put on a show for me," she groused.

"It's all I can do." I didn't turn around to see her face; I'm sure the picture I had of it in my mind was fairly accurate. Just before I reached for the doorknob, which Marv had told me would be unlocked, I added, "By the way, there's a ghost of a man in a tuxedo right behind you." Which was true. (Who dies wearing a tuxedo in a gas station? He must have traveled from elsewhere.) "He has a kitchen knife sticking out of his chest." Which wasn't.

Kerin turned to look, gasping, and I turned the door handle. Before she could react any further, I had the door open and was taking a tentative step inside the restroom.

It was, as one might expect, small, with all the requisite equipment, including a stall with a metal door that showed remarkably little sign of rust. Marv didn't run the most luxurious ocean liner, but it was a tight ship, and it was clean enough, contrary to Maxie's horrified descriptions. The mirror was free of graffiti and cracks, and the floor had been mopped in recent memory.

There was no one visible in the room.

I turned to look in every direction, performing almost a complete 360-degree spin, and had satisfied myself to the point that I was about to exhale and head for the door again. Mission accomplished, nothing to report.

Except then there was a sound from inside the stall. Not my worst nightmare, but definitely in the top twenty.

It was a low sound, one that at first I thought was mechanical. But it was not; it was the sound of a person . . . or an animal. Something with deep tones, for sure, and not necessarily happy ones. I reached into my tote bag for something to defend myself with, but a pack of spearmint gum (sugar-free) and a small change purse didn't really seem very threatening at the moment. Neither did the map of Ocean County, the tape measure, the lipstick case, the small bottle of Snapple I hadn't even opened two days ago—should have put that in the fridge—or the voice recorder. I made a mental note to get a roll of nickels the next time I was at the bank. You can wrap your hand around it and hit someone, and it hurts more, or something.

Besides, how often do you need a nickel these days?

I called myself a few choice names mentally and moved carefully toward the stall door, doing my best to make as little noise as possible in case this really was a hostile spirit; no sense making it mad. Every step sounded like the rap of a snare drum to me, but the person—living or dead—inside the stall didn't seem to hear me. The rumbling sound continued. And just as I got to the door and slowly reached out my arm, I recognized it from my married nights with The Swine.

No, not that. Someone was snoring in there.

Ghosts don't really sleep, but they do become sort of incapacitated sometimes. I know Paul has to recharge his batteries and usually does so at night when it's quiet; Maxie seems to be on a permanent charge, but she's always grumpy in the morning. So it could still be a ghost inside.

I moved my hand slowly to the door and was just about in contact with it . . .

"Alison!" Kerin yelled from outside the men's room door. "Come on! Is there someone in there, or not?"

The snoring stopped. I made a mental note not to take Kerin on any more stakeouts and pushed the stall door open.

There was indeed a ghost inside, floating in a sitting position, legs straight out as if he were stretching them. He wore a crisp Army uniform, and a cap with the number and name of his outfit on it, though the light was bad and I couldn't read it. His hair was short and neat, his skin clear, his face shaved. It took me a long moment to recognize him.

"Everett?" I attempted.

"Ghost Lady," he answered. His voice was clear and steady, free of the rasp I remembered. His eyes had lost the film I knew.

"You look . . . really good," I said.

Everett hovered out from the stall, presumably to give us more room and provide some sense of decorum in a decorum-free zone. "I know," he said. "I appear to have cleaned up a little."

"A little?"

He laughed. "Okay, more than a little. But I remember you. You always treated me well, and I never really got to say I appreciate that."

"Nothing special," I said.

Everett regarded me with a look that said otherwise. "You'd be surprised."

I had so many questions. I'd spoken to murder victims before, but the ghosts had never been so conscious so soon after their deaths, and none of the others I'd spoken to had known who killed them. This was great! There would be no detective work necessary on this one—Everett could just tell me what happened, and I'd find a way to prove it. Simple.

But first I had to figure him generally. "Why do you look so different?" I asked. Usually when I saw ghosts, they appeared pretty much the way they looked at the moment they'd died. Dad was a little less wan and thin than during those awful last days, but he still didn't appear to be decades younger. Everett was clearly in a pre-homeless state.

He looked at me funny and asked, "What do you mean?"

"I mean, you're all neat, your hair is cut, your beard is shaved. How come you don't look the way I remember you?"

"I've cleaned up," he said, his tone indicating that should have been obvious. "I did not present the way a member of the United States military should. It was unfortunate."

Uh-oh. Maybe this wasn't going to be so simple. I was starting to get a sinking feeling in the pit of my stomach.

Then it got worse. Everett went on, "The only thing I can't understand is why I'm not able to leave this restroom. There's nothing stopping me from walking out the door, and yet I can't seem to make it outside." He stopped and looked at me. "Believe me, this isn't the kind of place you want to spend a lot of time."

Oh, boy. Everett didn't know.

Then it got even worse than that. Kerin opened the restroom door a crack and shouted in. "Alison! Are you coming out? Did you find a ghost, or not?"

You can always count on Kerin Murphy to make things more uncomfortable.

Everett didn't react immediately. He looked away, silent, clearly digesting the question Kerin had asked. After a moment, his voice sounded a little more brittle, even after he cleared his throat. "Were you expecting to find a ghost in here, Ghost Lady?" he asked.

"My name's Alison," I said, which managed both to make our conversation more normal and also allowed me to sidestep his question.

Everett nodded, brows down and serious. "Alison," he said. "Am I . . . did you think . . . why are you here, Alison?"

Kerin opened the door a bit wider. "Alison?" she said.

"Come on in," I told her. Why shoulder this one by myself when I could make Kerin feel bad, too?

Kerin inched her way into the room. "Um . . . is there someone in here?" She looked, as most people who don't deal with ghosts regularly do, at the ceiling. She could see the ceiling perfectly well, so I didn't see the point, but that's what they do.

"I'm in here," I pointed out.

"Not *you*." Kerin might be a little freaked out, but she was still Kerin.

"What do you think?" I asked.

"She can't see me?" Everett asked. That really seemed to hit him hard. I'd been right. He didn't know he was dead, and now the knowledge was coming down on his head like a ton of Bruce Willis.

"No, she can't, Everett," I told him. "I'm sorry."

"Everett?" Kerin asked. "Everett is in here?" She was staring almost directly at him, and started swinging her arms, as if trying to hit the being she couldn't see to prove there was someone there.

Everett started to rise, something I've seen happen to Paul and Maxie when they're really taken aback by something. "Then I'm . . . Ghost Lady. I'm dead, aren't I?"

"I'm really sorry," I repeated.

"Do you think you're convincing me?" Kerin asked. "You think I believe you found the ghost of a dead homeless man in the men's room?"

Everett backed up in midair and put his hand to his mouth. It was sinking in, and it was a terrible reality, as bad as a man can get. His eyes were staring straight ahead, but I got the impression he couldn't see anything. Ghosts don't breathe, of course, but there was a rumbling coming from his chest that seemed to simulate hyperventilating.

"It's okay, Everett," I told him. "It's going to be okay."

"Oh, really," Kerin said. "You're not impressing me, you know."

I focused on the ghost and refrained from telling Kerin that impressing her was currently four-thousandth on my priority list, just beneath "look into laundry detergent alternatives." Everett blinked, trying to absorb his new existence in a moment. But it was, I knew, going to take a long time for him to adjust.

Unfortunately, I didn't have that kind of time. "Listen to me," I said to him. "I understand you're really freaking out right now, and I don't blame you. But I need you to focus. I need you to tell me what happened, and how you got here. Can you do that?"

Everett shook his head. I'm not sure whether he was telling me he couldn't help or simply rejecting what had happened to him.

"You can talk to the air all day," Kerin said. "I'm going back outside." She turned and left. Can't say I was all that upset. In retrospect, it would have been better if she hadn't shown up at all. My bad.

There wasn't much time; the one thing Kerin was right about was that I couldn't stay in here forever. I had to take a chance.

"Lieutenant Sandheim," I said in a stern voice. "Report."

The gambit seemed to work. Everett didn't salute—I was clearly not a superior officer—but he straightened up as if he were at attention and stuck his chin out. He was a good soldier.

"The last thing I remember clearly is seeing you at the Stud Muffin and asking for help," he said.

So much for simple. I would have to go with that. "I'm told you'd heard the voices of two ghosts," I said. "Do you know who they were?"

Everett closed his eyes; it was obvious he needed to concentrate hard, and his emotional state was not helping. "I remember saying it," he answered. "But my mind was not right. I was not rational."

"Just saying you heard ghosts is not a sign that you weren't rational," I told him, as gently as I could. "I see ghosts, and I hear them." I didn't mention that he was one of the ghosts I saw and heard.

Everett got the message, though. He opened his eyes and looked at me. "Is this the way I'm always going to be?" he asked. "I'll spend eternity in a gas station men's room?"

I wasn't sure how the afterlife worked—even the ghosts I knew had no idea—but I tried to reassure the poor guy. "Don't worry," I said. "After a while, you'll be able to travel outside. But please, tell me about the ghosts you heard."

That, of course, is when my phone rang. And honestly, it was simply a reflex that made me take it out of my pocket and look at the incoming number, having every intention of ignoring the call so I could talk to Everett.

But the call was coming from Helen Boffice.

"I'm really sorry," I said to Everett. "I really have to take this call." Never did it sound lamer.

"What have you been doing?" Helen demanded before I could say a word. "Are you any closer to proving who killed Joyce Kinsler?"

Everett reacted to her question, staring at me a moment, then shaking his head. He must have been able to hear her from where he was situated.

"I don't think you're the one who should be asking questions," I responded. "I'm wondering why you moved out of your house today."

"You're faster than I thought," Helen answered. "I might have underestimated you."

"How about coming clean?" I suggested. "It's either you or your husband who killed Joyce. Nobody else had a motive except you two. Which one of you killed her?"

"We didn't kill Joyce Kinsler," Helen answered with a cold laugh. "You can believe that."

"How many people are dead?" Everett asked. "Did one of these people . . ." His voice trailed off. I shook my head; no, Helen and Dave didn't kill him.

"Why should I believe you?" I asked. "Convince me."

There was some jostling on Helen's side of the phone and then another voice came on. A man's voice. Dave Boffice's voice.

"She's telling the truth," he said. "We didn't kill Joyce. Joyce . . . well, Joyce had no quarrel with either of us. That's true."

Everett's eyes widened enormously at the sound of Dave's voice, and before I could say anything, he was pointing at the phone. "That's the voice," he said, agitated.

I put my phone on mute and said to Everett, "What do you mean? You recognize Dave Boffice's voice?"

"I know that voice; there's no way I could ever forget it. But I never knew anybody named Dave Boffice." Everett started to pace in midair the way Paul does with a perplexing problem. Only Everett didn't have a goatee to stroke, and in his case it was more of a march.

"Okay, so you don't know Dave," I allowed him. "Whose voice do you think it is?"

Over the phone, Dave was shouting, "Hello? Hello?"

"That's my son, Randy," Everett said, his voice a gasp. "But he died in a motorcycle crash years ago."

Twenty-seven

I was going to have a huge amount of information to relay to Paul when I got home, but right now, I had to act to keep Dave and Helen (or Randy and Helen) from hanging up and vanishing into the night. I took the mute button off the phone without taking my eyes off of Everett. "I'm still here," I told Dave.

"Who's there with you?" he demanded. "You're taking too long to answer. Is that cop Sprayne there listening in?"

"No, he's not here. There's not a living soul in the room besides me." That was accurate.

"Well, you can't stand there and accuse me—"

"How do you know I'm standing?" It threw him for a second.

I looked at Everett to confirm; he nodded. And in a flash I decided on a course of action that I was certain was going to make Paul either elated or, if it were possible for a ghost, suicidal.

"Tell you what—I'm going to be having a little gathering tomorrow night at my guesthouse," I said. "Helen can tell you where that is, and you're both invited."

"If you think you can simply invite us and then have the police show up, you're mistaken." That was nowhere near what I had in mind.

"No police. Believe me, I won't call Sprayne because I want you to be there. The only cop in town I would call refuses to set foot in my house." I looked at Everett again, then at the bathroom door, wondering if Kerin was listening in. "I am going to tell everyone there exactly who killed Joyce Kinsler. And there's another murder that's involved— you might want to hear about that, too."

There was a long pause on Dave's end of the line. Then Helen's voice cut in. "Another murder?" She sounded shaky.

"Oh, yeah. Didn't Dave tell you? Somebody killed his dad. See you tomorrow. Around eight." I disconnected the call and resolved not to answer again if (If? Ha!) they called back.

Did Helen know Dave was really Randy? Did she know about Everett's murder? Did she know about Everett? All good questions. I'd have to ask Paul.

"Do you know what you're doing?" Everett asked me.

"How much do you remember about what happened to you?" I countered. Mostly because I was fairly sure I *didn't* know what I was doing.

"Nothing about what . . . about that. Ghost Lady, what *did* happen to me?"

"I'll explain it all to you in a little while," I answered (mentally adding "as soon as I know"). "But first we have to make plans. I have to invite a lot more people to my house tomorrow night. I'm not going to be in a room with those two by myself, especially since I don't know which one to be afraid of."

"And me? What are my orders, Ghost Lady?" Everett pulled himself up to full height, which almost brought his head to the ceiling. He was making himself stronger by drawing from his military experience, probably the time in his life he felt most in charge of his actions.

"First thing, you have to stop calling me Ghost Lady," I said. "My name is Alison. And we have to figure out if there's a way to get you out of this bathroom."

"How are we going to do that?" he asked.

"I'll consult with the experts."

"I can't teach him how to get out of the bathroom," Maxie complained. "I can't even teach *him*," she pointed at Paul, "so how would I be able to teach the homeless guy?"

Paul might've been less than tickled about the way he was being brought into the conversation, but his Sherlock Holmes sense was too engaged for him to take offense. He looked positively thrilled.

We were meeting in Melissa's room, along with Melissa and Mom. Maxie had brought a box of crackers, some cheese and a couple of glasses with water for Liss and wine for Mom. Anything for Liss and Mom. I'd have gotten a surly glance and a snarl of "Why not do it yourself?"

Mom reported that Dad was at Josh's store and would be by later.

I'd seen to the guests, who were in a high state of anticipation over tomorrow night's performance. Okay, Cybill was in a high state of anticipation. The others were talking about it as if it were an odd obligation, although I'd told them explicitly that they didn't have to attend. But all of them had indicated they'd be part of the festivities.

So had Jeannie and Tony (and Oliver); Phyllis, who saw it as an interesting crime story; Marv, because I'd asked him to; and Josh, who had said it was progress that I'd called to ask. That was promising. Sort of.

I'd also invited Katrina Holm, who wanted to see Joyce Kinsler's killer brought to justice, and Brenda Leskanik, who had been a little more problematic because she said she wanted to put her life with Everett behind her and saw no reason to enter that mind space again. But I needed Brenda to be there, especially if Dave Boffice really was her supposedly deceased son, Randy. The problem was, Brenda saw no reason to show up, and I didn't want to spill the beans about her son unnecessarily. I couldn't be sure about Randy and didn't want to raise her hopes only to dash them again. I decided to go visit Brenda again the next day to convince her in person.

Kerin Murphy had agreed to come with her entire posse. When we'd talked about it in the car on the way back from the Fuel Pit, she'd seemed eerily eager to attend, which made me think she expected something humiliating to occur. To me. Kerin wouldn't show up if she thought anyone else was going to be humiliated; that wouldn't have any entertainment value.

"I'm just asking you to try," I told Maxie. "We'll go over there tomorrow, and you can talk to Everett. You don't even have to go in—he can stick his head up through the roof. I got him to try it after he realized he's a ghost. He can do it, but he can't move beyond that. If it doesn't work, fine, but it would be a big help to have him here."

"You sure I don't have to go inside?" Maxie demanded.

"I promise."

She didn't say she would do it, but she pulled out the laptop and started typing again. As far as I was concerned, that was as good as agreeing.

I had not called Detective Sprayne with an invitation, because Dave and Helen would recognize him and flee as soon as they saw he was there. I trusted McElone but knew she wouldn't set foot inside the house if she could avoid it. I'd call her later and figure out a way she could be nearby, but not on site.

"Let me see if I understand this plan," Paul said, trying once again to organize this ragtag group into what he preferred to view as a wildly efficient detective agency. "You're going to let Cybill do her ceremony to keep evil spirits away from the house, and then tell the suspects that you know who killed both Joyce and Everett. What are you going to say?"

"I'm not going to have to say anything," I told him boldly, although I felt the opposite of bold. "They're going to say it all. Because you two and my dad—and Everett if he can show up—are going to scare the truth out of them. And I'm not worried about Cybill, because I don't believe she can do any of what she says she can do. I'm only letting her put on the show because I didn't want her bad-mouthing me to Senior Plus Tours."

Paul waited a moment, clearly expecting there to be more to what I was saying. But it was Melissa who broke the silence. "Is that it?" she asked.

Everybody's a critic. "Why?" I asked. "Do you have a better idea?"

She pondered for a moment. "Not really."

"Hang on," Maxie said. "I just figured out Joyce Kinsler's password, and I think I can get some more information."

We all stared at Maxie and waited. I'd never seen her look so focused. "You really should get a new laptop," she said without looking up.

"Get me a chunk of Helen's millions and we'll talk," I answered. Then I thought about it and added, "You know I was kidding, right?"

She didn't respond to that but said, "Paul." He rose up to look. "See here? And here?"

"What?" I asked. "I can't stand on a ladder to look. What?"

"It looks like there were large deposits and then withdrawals made to and from Joyce Kinsler's account. Four . . . no, five times in the past few months," Paul said.

Maxie couldn't let him take the credit. "I found the records. It looks like right around the time Joyce wanted to qualify for a mortgage on the town house, and then when she decided to buy a car, tens of thousands of dollars showed up in her account, and it's not from the direct deposit she got from her company instead of a paycheck."

"Where did the money come from?" Melissa asked.

"That's a good question," Maxie answered, talking over Paul. "It looks like they were made in cash deposits. Not traceable."

"Can you check the most likely source?" Paul asked. "I think we all know where the money came from."

Maxie looked unsure. "Helen's money was in a lot of places," she said. "I'll have to do some looking."

"Do," Paul said. Maxie stuffed the laptop inside her trench coat and rose up through the ceiling.

I looked at Paul. He said, "That's a real lead, but we still don't know how or why, or if it relates to whether Randy Sandheim became Dave Boffice. We don't know how the murderer got into the men's room and then out, with the door locked from the inside. The window measurements you gave me are inconclusive; I really wish you'd tried to squeeze through. A small percentage of people might be able to get through. We don't know what happened to the knife that was used to kill Everett. We don't know how someone forced Joyce Kinsler to hang herself, or hanged her, and we don't know why they would. We don't know why all the photographs are missing from Joyce's town house. And we don't know who left the threatening messages painted on this house, or if those are related to the murders."

"That's a long list of what we don't know this late in the game," I said. "What can we do? Everyone associated with both murders will be here tomorrow night."

"Do Dave and Helen know about the reputation of this guesthouse?" Paul asked me.

I shook my head. "Helen wasn't one of the Senior Plus tourists even before she rented a room to not stay in it," I told him. "I didn't get the impression she was hanging around town talking to people about the place; she just wanted a private investigator to follow her husband around and a sneaky way to pay for it."

"That is interesting," Paul said. "We can assume now that the reason she told you she wanted you to do that was a lie. So why did she *really* want a report on Dave's movements, and why not just write a check? And why give all that money to the woman she thought was her husband's lover?"

"Maybe you should ask his mother-in-law, the one he visited that day you were following him," Melissa said to me.

Paul's eyebrows raised. "You know, I'd forgotten about that," he said. I had, too, but I just patted Melissa on the head affectionately and she smiled. "It looks like tomorrow is going to be a very busy day."

Twenty-eight

It took a little doing, but after I'd seen to the guests and the morning spook show (including a ghost duet on guitar and frying pan), I convinced Maxie to meet Everett on the roof of the men's room structure at the Fuel Pit. (She hadn't been able to hack into Helen Boffice's bank accounts yet and was pessimistic about her chances after working on it all night—in short, she needed the break.) I had Marv fill up my Volvo while we were there, to give him a plausible excuse for my being at the station—New Jersey and Oregon are the only states where it's illegal to pump your own gas—and he lobbied to fix the latch on my wagon, but I demurred since I couldn't afford to leave the car there for the rest of the day. I had places to go.

While he was filling the car, a question occurred to me.

"Marv," I asked, "where's the trap for your sewer line?"

Marv, who probably had not been expecting that question, thought for a moment. "Around back," he said. "Behind the trees. Why?"

I ignored the question. "Have you had any backups lately? Since Everett died?"

"Funny you ask that, Alison. We had a sewer backup about three days later." Marv squinted at me as if I were a bright midday sun. "What are you getting at?"

I did some quick calculations. "What happened with the sewer?"

"I had Mickey Cochrane come up and clean it out," he said. "It wasn't too bad, and it didn't back up into the restrooms, so we didn't have to shut down or anything. Alison—"

"Mickey didn't find anything special blocking the line?"

Marv shook his head. "He said it was just the usual buildup. Why?"

"I think Mickey might've missed something, Marv," I told him. "I'd get Mickey to come out before you get another backup and clean out the trap."

"What do you think he's going to find there?" Marv asked.

I didn't want to plant ideas in his mind. "Just have him do it, and if he finds something special, you have him call Lieutenant McElone before he does anything else, okay?"

Marv was clearly baffled but agreed, and was indeed on the phone to the local sewer expert and rooter before I headed back to the scene of the ghost training.

Maxie was quite happy with her assignment by the time I left. Not having to go into the restroom itself, coupled with her first clear view of Everett cleaned up and in uniform, combined to warm her to the job, and she was trying her best to explain outside movement ("You just have to *think* your way outside") to him when I announced I was leaving and got no response from either ghost. I was no longer relevant in this setting.

My first stop, then, was to see Detective Lieutenant Anita McElone.

"It's too early in the day on a Sunday to see you," she

said, reiterating remarks she'd made when I'd called to ask if she'd be in. "I was going to go to church, so this had better be really good because God doesn't like it when I blow him off for silly stuff."

"Well, hopefully you won't have to make any excuses," I answered. "How about this: Dave Boffice is really Everett Sandheim's dead son, Randy."

Now you would think that such news would elicit a reaction from an investigating detective. You'd be wrong. McElone just looked at me. "And how do you know this?" she asked.

"I have an excellent source," I said, which was true. Everett should know what his own son sounded like.

"Is it the kind of source I could bring into court and have testify in front of a judge?" McElone said, and I got the impression she knew what my answer would be.

"Um . . . no." I wasn't even sure Everett could get out of the Fuel Pit men's room, and even if he could make it to court, the odds were slim that the judge, the jury, the prosecutor, the defense attorney or pretty much anyone else in the courtroom would be able to see or hear him.

McElone's voice dropped half an octave in resigned disappointment. "You gonna tell me you heard this from a ghost?" she asked.

She'd opened the door, so I walked through. "Everett," I said, nodding.

"Oh, good," McElone answered. "So he can tell you who killed him, too."

"He, um, doesn't remember," I was forced to say.

"Convenient." McElone sat down at her desk and started hitting computer keys. "Might as well check on the possibility, anyway." She took a pair of half-glasses from her top desk drawer without looking and put them on to better assess the screen. It made her look like a very burly librarian. "The dates are close enough," she said. "Randy was reported missing, but no body was ever found. His Harley was found at Sea Haven by Officer Daniel Boyle just over seven years ago, in a ravine off a higher elevation of Route 36."

"Could he have just walked away?" I asked.

"It's possible, but an injured guy walking down the main street of a beach resort would probably draw a little attention." She clacked a few more keys. "Still, the first records of David Boffice seem to appear less than three months later, when he showed up in bank records opening an account in cash and showing what could have been a fake driver's license as ID."

"Then so far Everett's story bears out," I said to myself.

McElone gave me a sour look. "Yeah. The dead guy only you can see has real credibility here. I should be run out of the police department just for listening to this stuff."

"And yet, here you are." I told her about the gathering I was organizing for the guesthouse tonight because it seemed the thing to do, though it only served to annoy McElone.

"You're bringing in some suspects on a murder that I'm investigating just on your own authority?" McElone snarled. "Were you planning to tell the local police about this little shindig of yours?"

"I'm telling you now," I pointed out. "I didn't think you'd want to come over, since my house scares you."

McElone looked around to see if anyone had heard me say that; luckily for her the Sunday morning crowd at the Harbor Haven Police Department was sparse, and no one was nearby. "Keep your voice down, okay?" she scolded. "I'm a professional. If my job brings me to a place that . . . isn't my favorite, I'll cope with it. Now, what time is this goofy party of yours supposed to start?"

I gave her the details and headed to my car. With the police presence in place, it was time for me to beef up the list of witnesses and suspects.

Next up was driving to Brenda Leskanik's house. She'd

agreed to see me today only because I hadn't let her off the phone until she would; Brenda was too straight a shooter to hang up on the woman investigating a murder, even if it was of the man who had abandoned her and their young son.

"I don't see the point," she was saying now, bringing me an iced coffee from her kitchen and setting it down in the cup holder of the massive recliner she'd directed me to in her living room. "I've done all I can to put that life behind me. Randy's gone, and Everett's gone now, too. What's to be gained?"

I couldn't tell her that Everett was now officially haunting a gas station bathroom or that Randy was possibly not as dead as she might have thought. But I could say, "You can gain a sense of justice. Maybe you can gain some peace. This bothers you enough that you want to stay away; doesn't that tell you something in and of itself?"

The iced coffee was really good, and after the morning I had experienced so far, the caffeine was more than welcome. Brenda looked skeptical, which is to say that she looked like most New Jerseyans, and said, "I don't know about that, Alison. Pain is a warning system. If something hurts, you're meant to stay away from it."

"The way you didn't mention Randy had been involved in something criminal, because that was too painful?" Paul had suggested I throw that out. He didn't know, but he believed that one motive for changing your identity is that authorities are after you.

Brenda evaded my gaze. "How did you know about that?" she asked. You could always count on Paul.

"It just made sense."

"He was dealing drugs and might have been high when he went off the road," Brenda said, still not looking at me. "There were warrants out for his arrest."

Things were starting to fall into place. I needed Brenda there tonight. "You're in a lot of pain, Brenda," I said truthfully. "Face it. Deal with it. Make it go away."

"I have been dealing with it," she argued. "It's better not to confront it. You don't pick at a scab; you let it cover over and get tough. You don't go after it."

"Unless going toward it can help ease the pain," I countered. I'd been rehearsing since we'd agreed I could come and talk to her, so I'd had that one more or less ready.

"There's no guarantee it will," Brenda said, sitting down across from me in an armchair with slightly worn material on the armrests. "What can I do that could help?"

"You can point out anyone you recognize," I answered, feeling guilty that I wasn't cushioning her for the shock I assumed was coming to her. "You can be there to tell me if I'm going wrong. I didn't know Everett before he had his difficulties; you did. That's very valuable to me."

Brenda's mouth twitched. I decided to press a little. "If you had sustained a wound in the service, but you had to go back to get someone who had been left behind, would you decide the pain was too strong, or would you ignore it and help a fallen soldier?"

She looked almost angry, her nose crinkling a bit, and for a moment I thought she was going to take a swing at me. "You hit a nerve," she said.

"I really need you there," I told her, "and I've found that being nice isn't always the most effective tactic."

"I noticed that." Brenda shifted in her chair and took a sip of iced coffee that she probably didn't even want just to buy herself a moment. I gave her another by taking a sip of mine, which I definitely wanted. "Okay, I'll be there tonight," she said. "But I'm not making any promises."

"Neither am I," I answered.

It was an impulse to visit Margaret O'Toole, Helen Boffice's mother, but I had my reasons. Really. It was possible she could shed some light on the history of Helen's first marriage and her subsequent fortune, which she appeared to not be spending. Also, she might have some insight into Helen and Dave's sincerely odd marriage and its resemblance to a really high-spirited poker game between two ultra-competitive riverboat gamblers.

But mostly, it was because my daughter had suggested it, and that girl is always a couple of blocks ahead of me. When she grows up, the world had best watch out for her.

The problem was, when I arrived at Margaret's house, she wasn't there. The workmen were still working on the back of her roof, and after a few moments of waiting by the front door, I walked around back and approached one who was picking up unused shingles and piling them for removal.

He looked at me questioningly for a moment, then asked if he could help me. I said he could, if he knew where Margaret O'Toole might be.

"Who's Margaret O'Toole?" he asked.

"The woman who owns this house," I said after a moment. "Your customer."

"Oh, we've never seen her," he said. "She hasn't been back here since the storm. Went to stay with her sister in Ohio or somewhere. I don't know if she'll come back after we fix the house up, or if she'll just try to sell it." He shook his head. "Good luck with that."

"But I saw her here a few days ago," I protested. "She must be overseeing the work, no?"

"Oh no," the guy answered. "Her daughter was here for a while, but she hasn't been around for a couple of days."

An alarm went off in my head, but I didn't know why. "Her daughter?" This question-on-question thing could be useful in more than social situations.

"Yeah. Helen. She's paying for the work, I'm pretty sure. You want me to check?"

Yes. I wanted him to check.

While he did, I took a look inside the house through the glass doors on the rear deck. I didn't go inside, but it was clear from where I was standing that the place was over-crowded with furniture. There were too many chairs in the living room and extra seats in the dining room that didn't match the table or breakfront. It was like a furniture ware-house had sent its excess to Margaret O'Toole's house.

And on one wall in the living room, not nestled in a corner where you'd expect, was a very large antique grand-father clock.

I couldn't prove it, but it sure seemed like Helen Boffice had moved a lot of her possessions into her mother's house.

Just what I needed. More unanswered questions.

Twenty-nine

"Helen's first husband Bryan Darnell died five years ago in March," Maxie reported. I'd picked her up at the Fuel Pit— she reported that Everett was "making some progress" but could not yet move freely outside the men's room structure—and brought her back to the guesthouse with new marching orders to research on my decrepit MacBook. "He was running in the park and keeled over. Fifty-eight years old." I cut her off before she could say how old she thought that was.

"Was there a medical examiner's report?" Paul, his feet sunk into the game-room floor, wasn't stroking his goatee, but I was willing to bet he wanted to.

Maxie nodded. "Yeah, because he died in a public place. The doctors found evidence of buildup in three arteries. He must have eaten like a lion."

"So we can assume that Bryan was not murdered," Paul said. "What did he do for a living?"

Maxie scrolled through whatever information she had

accessed. "Owned a small pharmaceutical company, do you believe it? Sold it to a much bigger one a year before he died. That's where Helen's inheritance came from."

"I don't understand," Melissa said. She was sitting on a barstool next to the covered pool table, eating a salad she'd made herself (per her grandmother's carefully written instructions) for lunch. "If Mrs. Boffice's mother isn't in the house, who did you see with Mr. Boffice at lunch?"

"That is an excellent question," I told her. Then, as I often do when I'm asked an excellent question, I looked at Paul for the answer. Because I didn't have a clue.

"I think there's a very good chance it was *Helen* Boffice," he said. "If you're right that Helen had moved out of the house with Dave and was staying in her mother's house, I think that's an indication that we are very close to solving this case."

Melissa and I both stared at him and said in unison: "We *are*?"

"Yes. You've gotten some very good information, and the pieces are beginning to fall into place." Paul paced a little. It's weird to see when you don't have a view of his feet; he sort of looks like one of those tin figures that used to be in the shooting galleries at the Seaside Heights board-walk, moving back and forth with no visible propulsion.

"Okay," I said. "How?"

He stopped moving and looked at me. "I don't know yet," he said. "But it'll come together soon, I'm sure."

That was helpful.

"How could that be Helen?" I asked him. "I've *seen* Helen. That woman had gray hair and was taller and older than Helen. In short, that wasn't Helen."

"Maybe," Paul said. There's no point in talking to him when he gets like that.

But, of course, I was going to try. "What can I say at the thing tonight?" I asked him. "All I've got is more questions."

"This was your idea," Maxie said. "Wing it." You can always count on Maxie. *I* can't, but you can.

I ignored her and looked at Paul, who looked back. "What?" he said.

"I'm asking what I have to go with tonight," I repeated. "I've built up everyone's expectations, I've got all these people showing up, now I have to deliver. What should I say?"

"I have to go with Maxie on this," Paul answered. "I didn't advise you to set this evening up to be the revelation; I would have been much more comfortable just continuing the investigation."

"So you're telling me it's my fault?" That couldn't be what he was saying.

"Essentially, yes. That's what I'm saying," Paul answered.

"Paul . . ."

Melissa looked over at me; sometimes I can tell when she's trying me on for a role model. She didn't know how she would handle this situation, so she wanted to see what I would do. So I managed not to scream, which I considered a true victory.

"We'll help you as much as we can," Paul said. "It can't hurt to have all the suspects in the room at the same time. And we'll follow through on your plan to startle them into talking. Maybe you'll get lucky."

"So I have essentially no options left," I said, thinking aloud.

"That's about the size of it," Paul said. "But I think you should ask Joyce's friend Katrina Holm to e-mail you any photos she might have of the two of them together."

Katrina had not been home when I called, but I'd left her a voice mail and hoped she'd get back to me before the evening's festivities would begin. That hope was starting to wane when Josh arrived. He was there early because he knew I wanted to talk, and everyone—even Maxie!—backed off to offer us some privacy. And I was desperately trying to formulate words that would inform without repelling. Was that so much to ask?

"Okay, you've lured me out here. What's the big secret?"

Josh looked at me with a combination of amusement and what I chose to see as impatience but was probably worry. He'd come by after dinner, which had been pizza that night because Mom wasn't cooking. In a few minutes, Cybill's ceremony—which she'd been preparing since the moment it had been mentioned—would begin, and there was no telling what deep insanity would ensue. I'd insisted she give me a full description of the spell she thought she was going to cast to protect my house, but she'd been unfocused about it, saying that it would "seal the premises from the advances of evil spirits, goblins, the undead, those who would cause mischief and those who would damage the aura of the family within."

"Yeah, but what are you going to *do*?" I'd asked.

"I will be peaceful," she had said, as if that answered anything.

I looked at Josh. "It's not a big secret," I said. "Okay, maybe it is a big secret, but it's not something I especially wanted to keep from you. I wanted you to know, but I was afraid it would scare you off, that you'd think you shouldn't have to deal with a woman as clearly unhinged and disturbed as I am."

"You're procrastinating," he said. We were watching the ocean from the hill in my backyard. The sand comes up closer to the house now, reminding us of the storm, but the dune closest to us had probably prevented flooding and kept my guesthouse in business. Josh put his forearms on my shoulders.

"I'm explaining," I insisted, trying to get lost in his eyes but remembering that I still had to open up my particular can of crazy and let it spill out all over him. "I don't want you to think that it was reluctance on my part."

"Alison," Josh said, "I've known you since the fourth

grade. Granted, there was a twenty-year gap when we never saw each other, but there's very little you can say that will make me think you're any crazier than the girl who used to come into the paint store and mix up the cans on the shelves because you thought people would buy blue when they wanted gray and get a lovely surprise."

"It was a good plan," I said, extending my lower lip.

"Assuming no one could read the labels," he agreed. "Now. Stop stalling. Let's hear it before your in-home reenactment of *The Exorcist*, which I really don't want to miss. Right now, no more explanation about your motives. What do you need to tell me?"

And I just couldn't do it.

I wanted to; I tried to. The words *There are two ghosts in my house, and they're real* were right there in my frontal lobe. I just couldn't force them out of my mouth. "I'm not sure I want to have any more children," I said. Technically, it was true; I hadn't given any thought at all to the idea of having another baby, especially since Josh and I weren't within driving distance of that conversation. But it seemed like the kind of thing I might be holding back in order to avoid driving him away. Sort of.

"I really don't think that's what this is about."

Damn. He actually knew me well; this was the price one pays. My mind, racing, didn't clear the words before they exited through my mouth: "Um . . . I'm still stuck on what to do with the game room?"

Josh let out a long breath. "And I so wanted to see that exorcism," he said.

"What does that mean?" But I knew what it meant. And I wasn't happy about it.

"It means, call me when you really want to have this talk," Josh answered, removing his arms from my shoulders and turning back toward the driveway, where his car was waiting. "I'll be happy to hear from you then."

I called his name a few times, but he kept on walking.

* * *

"The ceremony is about to begin," Cybill said, and she swirled into the game room looking solemn and ecstatic at the same time.

There was quite a crowd assembled to watch: Tom and Libby Hill had come down first, expressing a desire to get "good seats," and they had indeed taken two of the chairs I'd put out and situated themselves almost in the exact center of the room.

Harry and Beth Rosen had arrived home from dinner just after Jeannie and Tony had shown up with Oliver, who looked embarrassed in the sailor suit Jeannie had put him in, and with good reason. Jeannie grinned at me, secure in her belief that I was Mistress in the Art of Deceiving Guests into believing my house was haunted, and stayed at the back of the room, playing with Oliver near one of the bookcases.

At some point, Marv Winderbrook arrived and went over to the side of the room, by the windows, looking confused. I could empathize.

Melissa, Mom, Paul and Maxie had all entered at once from the kitchen, although the rest of the assemblage could see only Liss and Mom. I looked around for Dad, whom I had told to be in the house on the extremely unlikely chance that Cybill could actually do what she'd said she could, but he was nowhere to be seen. I'd have to sidle over to Mom at some point and find out if he actually was on the premises. If not, I'd feel compelled to shut Cybill down, and I had no cover excuse to use for that purpose.

Maxie had reported it was unlikely Everett would be able to achieve mobility soon enough to get here, and while Paul had tried to summon Matthew Kinsler, he had not yet received an answer. I wasn't sure whether he could leave a ghost voice-mail message.

Lieutenant McElone had indeed arrived, dressed in

plainclothes (as she usually was on the job anyway) and in her personal car to divert suspicion. But she stayed out on the porch, apparently operating under the mistaken assumption that the ghosts couldn't go outside. She looked nervous enough to take up smoking but so far was restraining herself. At the moment, she was instead appraising the "note" left by my mysterious graffiti artist (whom I still suspected was Cybill) and moving her tongue back and forth on her front teeth.

Phyllis Coates, looking for a good feature story even if I couldn't unmask Everett's killer, had arrived with her notebook and informed me she'd take down as much of what was said as possible. Great. Having a friend who runs a newspaper isn't always an asset, but I'd invited her, fool that I am.

Brenda Leskanik had not yet arrived. Maybe my powers of persuasion were not what I had imagined them to be. Or maybe Brenda had more to hide than simply some scarred-over pain involving her dead ex-husband and her possibly-less-dead son.

Katrina Holm arrived a few minutes before the appointed hour. She looked tired, her eyes were a little puffy, and she clearly had to steel herself before walking into the room. But once inside, she showed no hesitance and said hello to me. She introduced herself to Mom, Melissa and a few of the others, though not to Cybill (who at that time was "clearing her mind" on one side of the room, a state achieved, apparently, by putting her fingers to her temples).

I was about to make my way to Katrina to ask if she'd brought a photograph when the guests of honor, Helen and Dave Boffice, drove up at the last minute in a very sleek-looking but nondescript car that had probably cost more than my entire budget for on-site renovations this year, a far cry from the plain old Toyota Dave had been driving when I was following him. After a few moments, they tentatively came inside. Helen, in an incongruous hoodie and dark sunglasses that covered most of her face, looked like Lindsay Lohan out on yet another perp walk; Dave's eyes were hooded and he assessed the room carefully. They stood as conspicuously as people can stand when trying not to be noticed, on the opposite side of the room from Jeannie and Oliver, near the French doors to the backyard, probably as a contingency plan in case I had cleverly brought in undercover police officers who looked like middle-aged tourists, a jolly mother, a contractor inspecting the crown moldings, an eleven-year-old girl, her grandmother and a baby. Little did they know the only undercover cop on the property was afraid to walk inside.

As they passed me on the way in, Dave Boffice mumbled in my direction, "I have a gun."

I wanted, immediately, to get Melissa out of the room. I thought to say, "Nice way to prove your innocence, Dave," but he was already past me and taking up his station at the far end of the den.

Before I could get to Mom and Liss, however, Cybill was beginning her spiel.

"I'll need candlelight only," she said. Before anyone could respond, she reached over and hit the light switch, and the game room went completely dark. I could hear a couple of the guests pull in sharp breaths, but almost immediately, a match ignited in Cybill's hand, and she lit three candles I had placed on the covered pool table. She was a good showman—she had total control of the room instantly.

I was trying desperately to think about the task at hand, about making a statement about the murders and getting Paul and Maxie to outdo themselves, if I could just get them to understand what it meant to me, if they would simply get it through their transparent heads that this was my house and my life and they were getting to be more of an impediment than a help.

It's possible I was also thinking a little bit about Josh at that moment and letting my feelings get the better of me. It's possible. I'm not saying for sure.

"This house is infested," Cybill began. Swell. Now she would have my guests thinking about bedbugs in their rooms. Cybill was turning out to be an even greater threat to my business than I had anticipated, and the storm had already done enough. "There are undead spirits that have penetrated this house and endangered it." That was simply inaccurate: Paul and Maxie weren't undead; they were dead. That's the opposite of undead, isn't it? Did that mean I was undead?

I shouldn't have let Josh walk away. I should have blurted it out. Even if he thought I was crazy, that would be better than his thinking that I didn't trust him. Dad had been right. Maybe I should call him.

"Tonight we will find the source of this infestation," Cybill went on. "We will root out the cracks in the foundation and seal them. We will rid ourselves of this plague and cleanse this house of its infection."

As she spoke, Kerin Murphy and four or five of her interchangeable minions arrived at the game-room entrance. Kerin folded her arms like Mr. Clean when he encountered a grime outbreak, looked smug—her go-to expression—and gestured for her posse to fan out and man the perimeter, which they did. I wasn't sure what Kerin had in mind, but I could be reasonably sure I wasn't going to be crazy about it.

At least one killer in the room, and I was worried about the cast of *Mean Girls: The Previous Generation*.

Maybe I could text Josh about the ghosts and he'd come back. Was that the kind of thing you could text someone? It seemed crass, somehow.

This was Paul and Maxie's fault, I decided. Mostly Maxie. If they hadn't been in this house when I'd bought it, so much of my current difficulty simply wouldn't have happened. I wouldn't have a PI license, certainly, and would not be involved in the investigation of two murders. Suspected killers—at least one holding firearms—would not be in the room.

Of course, I also wouldn't have found Dad again or probably wouldn't have reconnected with Josh after all these years, but those incidentals didn't occur to me at just that moment. It's funny how thoughts are influenced by circumstances, isn't it?

Maybe *funny* isn't the word.

Cybill lit some incense sticks and placed them in a vase I'd given her (one that I didn't much care about) to put in the center of a card table she'd asked me to set up in the middle of the room. "This scent will repel the spirits in the house," she said. I couldn't say it was doing much for me, either, but Paul and Maxie, watching with some fascination, didn't seem especially repelled. Except that Maxie started to wrinkle her nose. Paul leaned over and whispered something to her; she nodded in agreement then looked at me. Unhappily.

Cybill struck a dramatic pose: One arm bent at the elbow and drawn back, the other aimed at the ceiling as she craned her neck upward, like she was about to shoot an arrow into the sky. "This is a safe house!" she hollered. I noticed Libby Hill wince at the volume. With the candlelight in the room and the echo from the high ceiling, it did indeed create an eerie feeling. "We will tolerate no more interference from these evil beings!" She began to twirl slowly. "You are not welcome here! Be gone!"

I'd actually gotten my phone out to text Josh to come back so we could talk honestly. I had typed "sorry" and hit the Send button when my mind caught what had just been said. Wait! This didn't sound like a spell that would keep new ghosts out!

"Cybill!" I said, breaking the mood and making everyone look at me (Melissa stared, alarmed by the tone the presentation had taken). "This is not what you promised!"

I looked up. Paul and Maxie looked positively sickly; their usual transparent pallor slightly tinged with green it seemed from where I was standing. Paul looked at me and weakly murmured, "Do something."

"The house must be cleansed," Cybill insisted. "The presence of these spirits is in opposition to all living beings who enter. They must be cast out."

"Stop! Now!" I advanced on her and walked through the crowd, ignoring her astonished expression. "I've been very clear about this—I don't want you to get rid of the ghosts in this house!"

Cybill turned and smiled at me and dropped her voice. "It's okay," she said, sotto voce. "You don't have to put on a brave face for your business. This way, I can rid your house of these evil demons and you appear to be against it."

"I *am* against it!"

Cybill nodded tolerantly at me. "Very good," she whispered.

Kerin Murphy stood forward among her crowd, with the most irritating smug grin I could imagine—and I'm pretty imaginative. She folded her arms and spoke loudly enough for everyone in the game room to hear.

Clearly, this was the moment she'd been waiting for.

"You see?" she said to the crowd, most of which looked perplexed. "She *is* the ghost lady!" Was that it? Kerin's plan all along, to out me as a true believer and regain her stature in the community? It was sort of clever, in a really vile way.

I saw Libby turn to Tom and mouth, "Who's that?"

"Not now, Kerin," I said. I was too annoyed and, yes, panicking about losing the ghosts in my house—where was Dad?—to have time for her nonsense.

"No! Not this time! You've been denying and denying and making me look like a fool because you insisted the ghost thing was just for business, but I know you believe! You made *me* look like the crazy one. *You're* the crazy one, Alison!"

Tom and Libby Hill looked fascinated, but the Rosens, in the opposite corner, seemed more unnerved; they were looking toward the hallway as if trying to figure an escape route. Dave Boffice leaned over and said something to Helen, who put her hand to her mouth to stifle a giggle. Lovely. The suspects were finding me amusing.

Cybill simply went back to chanting. "I cast out these spirits. I cast out these spirits. I cast out these spirits . . ."

Paul's eyes widened and he actually seemed to double over in pain.

"No!" I shouted at Cybill. "Stop *now*! You're hurting my friends!" Before Kerin, who looked positively jubilant, could bray her victory to the heavens, I turned toward her. "Fine! You want me to say it? There are two ghosts in this house, their names are Paul and Maxie, and they've never done you or anyone else an ounce of harm. They've become my friends, they watch my daughter, and they help me with my business. So what exactly is your problem, lady?"

Phyllis was in the corner, furiously taking notes. The feature article in the next *Chronicle* was a sure thing whether I liked it or not, so I decided to like it.

"You want me to say it?" I shouted to Kerin. "You want me to claim the title? Fine! I *am* the ghost lady!"

Paul grinned and straightened up. Maxie, next to him, was still doubled over, but it was with laughter.

"Oh, that was priceless!" she managed to cough out between guffaws. "I loved it!"

"What?" I was so confused I could barely move. There was a murderer, maybe two, in the room, and I was losing track of my purpose here. I really had to focus.

"It's about time," Paul said with satisfaction. "Do you feel better? I feel better."

I looked at Cybill, who had stopped chanting and was watching Paul with a grin. "I think we did it," she said to him with a wink.

"Did what?" I asked. I can be pretty dense sometimes.

"Who are you talking to?" Jeannie asked. I chose to let that go by. She'd rationalize it later.

"Your spirit friends wanted to be acknowledged," Cybill explained. "They felt you were ashamed of them, and they had a need for you to take responsibility."

"You mean you two . . . you three . . . you were all in on it the whole time?" Okay, *very* dense.

"I'm sorry, Alison," Paul said. "But the point had to be made." I made a mental note to kill him later, then realized someone had beaten me to it.

"I'm confused," Katrina Holm said. "Is this about Joyce's murder?" Helen Boffice's head turned and she sat down, but I couldn't see her face to get a reaction.

My attention was then diverted to the game-room entrance, where Josh Kaplan stood, looking a little wary. I wasn't sure when he'd gotten there.

I had three priorities: getting Melissa out of the room, getting a picture from Katrina, and getting revenge on my resident ghosts and Cybill.

"So you see!" Kerin wasn't off her soapbox yet. "She admits it! She likes living with these daemons!"

I stopped dead in my tracks. "Daemons?" I said out loud. "It was you! You defaced my property!"

Busted. Kerin's eyes widened, and she tried to find a way out. "What are you talking about?" she asked.

"Oh no you don't," I told her, advancing. "You painted those crazy slogans on my house."

"It was just a little graffiti," she tried. "I tagged your house . . . a little."

"It was thousands of dollars' worth of damage, and I will be suing you." Okay, so that was an exaggeration, but she didn't know that.

"I did it to get even." Kerin had clearly decided to be offensive in her defense.

Enough was enough. I glanced at the Boffices, just to be sure they weren't going to bolt, then advanced on Kerin.

"Get even for *what*? I was never trying to do anything to you, Kerin. You weren't a significant enough presence in my life for me to think about how my friends were affecting you. So please tell me, why exactly are you so hell-bent on revenge? Because I found out about your little fling, and your husband still hasn't forgiven you? Because you're not the big cheese in the PTSO anymore?"

"You destroyed my life!" she spat.

"No, I didn't."

"You made sure that article ran in the newspaper!" Kerin countered.

"No, that was me," Phyllis chipped in, not looking up from her notebook.

"It was her fault!" Kerin said, but her posse was looking less convinced than before.

"Did I cheat on your husband?" I asked.

"You . . ." Kerin just trailed off. But her hands were unmistakably taking on a resemblance to talons, and that couldn't be good.

She ran at me, but Maxie had seen that coming and picked up a tray I'd brought in to serve drinks. She held it up at the last second, and Kerin ran face-first into it. It wasn't hard enough to do any serious damage, but I'd bet Kerin might need a consultation with a cosmetic surgeon about a deviated septum in the next few days.

"Now, *that* was a good trick," Tom Hill said.

"Thank you," I said to Maxie.

"What are friends for?"

This threatened to go on indefinitely, but there was a gasp from the entrance. Brenda Leskanik stood there, her face as white as a sheet. She looked like she'd just seen a ghost. And she was one of the few who hadn't.

"Randy!" she shouted. Everyone in the room turned to look at her. Except Dave Boffice, who was directly opposite his mother and appeared to be completely stunned.

Standing next to him, Helen Boffice stared at Brenda,

took off her dark sunglasses—which had seemed preten-
tious to me to begin with—and stared.

From across the room came another wheeze of shock, the
sound of someone who had been punched in the gut. I
turned to look in the direction of the sound and saw Katrina
Holm looking like she'd just seen . . . you get the idea. But
this time it was literal.

"Joyce?" she breathed.

Helen trembled and looked at Katrina. She made a low
sound in her throat.

"That's Joyce Kinsler," Katrina said to no one in
particular.

Thirty

I wish I'd had time for my mind to soak up all that information. That Dave Boffice was really Randy Sandheim was no surprise. And I'd suspected, once Paul had asked for a photograph of Joyce Kinsler, that she might not have been the woman I'd discovered in the kitchen of Joyce's home. But the idea that Helen *was* Joyce, I'll admit, threw me a little, and I wasn't alone—everyone in the room was stunned and motionless. Okay, some of them were just confused, but the ones with context were stunned and motionless.

Then I looked at Helen's right hand, and saw the finger she couldn't straighten out, and I realized that every time I'd seen her, she'd covered that hand with the other. To hide the finger that Matthew Kinsler had told me his daughter had caught in a car window at a young age and cried all night about.

Holy mackerel.

But I couldn't even say anything in time: Dave/Randy, who, as advertised, had brought a gun with him, produced it from inside his jacket. He pointed it at me, then at Katrina, then at Brenda, then, for no particular reason, at Josh. He didn't seem able to decide who he might want to shoot should the urge arise.

From the back of the room, I heard a small protest as Mom hustled Melissa out and toward the front door, no doubt to tell McElone, who was outside, what had happened. Dave (and that's what we'll call him for the sake of sanity) didn't seem to care; he let them walk out with no protest. On his part. Melissa was last heard arguing that she could defuse the situation all by herself, to no avail.

Katrina took a step forward. "I don't understand," she said to Helen, aka Joyce. "Why did you pretend you were dead?"

"Because she didn't want anyone to know that the woman hanging in Joyce's house was Helen Boffice," I said. Okay, Paul said it, but only a select few could hear him, so I reiterated it. Now I understood why there were no pictures in Joyce Kinsler's house after the murder—the killer(s) didn't want anyone who entered to know that the woman who died was not Joyce. And even Matthew hadn't seen the remains—the dead woman was already in a body bag when he had arrived at Joyce's house. Now if only McElone could summon up the courage to come inside the "freaky" house . . .

I didn't have to wait long. Standing in the game-room doorway, police-issued firearm held in front of her, Lieutenant Anita McElone held her gun on Dave and said, "Don't do anything stupid. I'm a police officer."

Dave looked at me and appeared more peeved than anything else. "I said not to bring any cops," he snarled.

"Yeah, like I always listen to murderers," I answered.

"I don't understand," Harry Rosen said to Beth. "Is this part of the show?" She looked contemplative but didn't answer.

"I can grab the gun," Maxie offered, but I shook my head; it was too risky.

"We're not murderers." Joyce seemed to want the spotlight. "It was a question of circumstance."

"You killed you own father and your own wife, Dave," I said, ignoring whoever she was. "How could you do that?"

Dave looked at McElone, and his eyes got meaner. "You don't want to do anything rash, Officer," he said.

"Lieutenant," she corrected him. I didn't see how that helped.

With Helen being Joyce, it started to make sense. I looked up at Paul but spoke to Dave. "You married Helen for her money, didn't you, Dave? After you changed your name and got some fake ID, you married her for her money. But she wasn't spending it."

"Don't say anything," Joyce warned Dave. I noticed that Paul's eyes were closed tight; my guess was he was on the Ghosternet, probably trying to contact Matthew Kinsler or Helen Boffice.

So I went on: "You lived with Helen for more than five years, trying to figure out a way to get at her millions."

"Who's Helen?" Libby Hill had her hand raised to ask the question.

I didn't answer her. "But then you met Joyce, and the two of you hit on a scheme."

"Do I have to shoot you to shut you up?" Dave asked. I didn't think he was waiting for an answer.

McElone passed the Rosens, who accommodated her by taking a step back, and still had her gun drawn, very close to Dave now. I figured I could distract him long enough for McElone to disarm him.

Paul's eyes were open again. "I think you've got it, Alison," he said.

So I kept going. "You knew about creating a new identity; you'd done it before. All you had to do was get Joyce some of Helen's ID, and as Helen's husband, you had the access. Then you could skim off the money you wanted. Helen had so much, it probably took her months to notice."

From out of nowhere, I felt Josh standing next to me, his shoulder just a little in front, so he could move quickly if there was shooting in the room.

And I felt really bad about not telling him there were ghosts in the house.

Joyce smiled a very unattractive smile. "You're guessing," she said. "You have no proof."

"Not really." McElone could cover Dave, but I was afraid Joyce might have a weapon, too. I had to keep talking. "There were withdrawals made from Helen's bank accounts"—it was true I couldn't prove that yet, but I bet McElone and the cops could—"and deposits for tens of thousands into yours, Joyce. Why would Helen give you that kind of money? Why would you show up at my door and pretend to be Helen? Actually, now that I think of it, why *did* you want me to follow Dave?"

Tony appeared on my other side, and I wondered if Dave could even see me clearly with all the square feet of people trying to help. I was getting tired of being protected.

Libby Hill took her husband's arm, smiling, as if they were watching a really cool movie. I decided not to point out that the gun was real and probably loaded, even if it wasn't exactly aimed with accuracy at the moment.

Jeannie, somewhere behind me, was carrying Oliver out of the room. Probably to change his diaper, but it was just as well; she didn't seem especially scared, either.

Phyllis leaned in a little closer to hear so she could quote Dave and me later. Her hearing isn't what it used to be. And you thought her eyes were bad.

Sure enough, Joyce produced a gun of her own from her pocket and pointed it at me. "That's it!" she shouted. McElone, forced to choose one to aim at, stuck with Dave, to whom she was closest. Another couple of steps, and she'd be able to touch him. Dave, looking out of the corner of his eye at her, probably knew that he was not going to do well if he turned to train the gun on McElone.

"You knew Dave was going to see Helen during his lunch hours, didn't you?" I said, trying to provoke a response that, hopefully, would not be bullet-ridden. "And you couldn't follow him yourself, because he'd recognize your car. Were you trying to patch things up, Dave?"

Dave looked furious, and probably would have fired if McElone hadn't been close enough to put the muzzle of her gun on the back of his neck. "Don't," she said. Dave's jaw clenched a few times, but he lowered his gun. McElone took it from him carefully.

"Randy," Brenda Leskanik moaned from across the room. "Why?"

"For the money," I told her.

"No. Why did you change your name? Pretend to be dead? Why didn't you let me know where you were?" She stared at her son and looked as sad as I've ever seen a woman look. "Why?"

"What are you doing here?" Dave groaned.

Brenda didn't get a chance to answer because Joyce took a step toward me, still about ten feet away, and Tony and Josh closed ranks. I could barely see her over all that man.

"I'm walking out of this room," she said. "And nobody's going to do anything about it, right?" She didn't look at McElone, but it was clear to whom she was speaking.

At that moment, Matthew Kinsler floated down through the ceiling, took in the scene, and gasped at the sight of his daughter. "Joyce!" he said. "Joycie, you're alive."

Melissa tried to look around the entrance to the game room, and I saw Mom pull her back into the hallway.

"Yes, she is," Cybill told Matthew. "But she's claiming to be Helen Boffice."

"Who?" Matthew asked. "Oh. The wife."

Joyce looked sharply at Cybill. "Who are you talking to?" she demanded.

"Thanks a heap, Cybill," I said.

"I'm losing track of who can see whom," Cybill answered.

Matthew's face darkened as he watched the scene and heard his daughter's voice. "What happened to you, Joycie?" he wondered aloud.

"It's your father," I told her. "He's here, and he's worried about you."

"I should have known better than to get involved in this ghosty stuff," McElone said. "Somebody killed Everett Sandheim and Helen Boffice." She looked at Joyce. "And I'm starting to suspect someone here who's actually *alive*."

"Don't look at me," Marv said. "I didn't kill anybody."

Suddenly, I knew why Marv was there. "You got the report from the sewer guy, didn't you?" I asked him.

"Yeah. You were right—Mickey came by and took a look. Sure enough, he found something."

"Don't say it yet," I suggested. "Let's see who can guess." I turned toward Joyce. "What do you think might have shown up in the sewer line behind the Fuel Pit?" I asked her.

Finally, her voice: "How on earth would I know?"

"Because you put it there. You stabbed Everett eighty-six times, and then you made sure that the weapon disappeared, didn't you?" I made a point of watching Joyce's face closely as I said it.

She smiled, ever so slightly.

"I did nothing of the sort," she said.

"But you did. On the advice of a friend, I measured the window at the Fuel Pit's men's room." I gave Paul a quick glance, and he nodded. "Randy here couldn't have made it out that way, even if he walked inside with Everett leading him. Brenda couldn't have possibly done it. But you, with that little slim frame, you would have fit."

The smile evaporated. "I don't know what you're talking about," Joyce said.

I ignored her protest. "The door was locked from the inside. The window was the only way out, and you were the only one whose hips would make it out that little window. I have a witness who saw Everett talking to a woman just before he went off and died. And after he was stabbed eighty-eight times with a small blade, that knife disappeared. Until it surfaced in Marv's sewer line. There's an easy way to dispose of a small weapon in a bathroom, isn't there? But even a tiny penknife can stop up a sewer line, Joyce. Didn't you know that?"

"I did not stab Everett eighty-eight times," she insisted.

"No? How many, then?" That was McElone.

"You did it, Joyce," I said. Josh stood close again, seeming to sense that there would be danger. "You killed Everett first—why, because he knew your husband, Dave, was really his son, Randy?" Joyce remained silent, and she hadn't even been read her rights yet. "But Helen must have found out what you were doing, because she moved out of the house with Dave and went back to her mother's place and was repairing the storm damage. But then Dave started going over there. Why, Dave? Because if you reconciled, you could have access to her money? That hadn't worked before."

Dave looked up with an odd smile on his face, a cold one. McElone was securing zip strips to his hands, which were gun-free and behind his back. "I signed a prenup," he said. "I couldn't get a dime of her money if we got divorced."

Matthew looked at me sadly. If he'd been alive, he would have had tears in his eyes. "Did she really do it?" he asked. "Why?"

"A good question," I responded, having given up all pretense. Tom Hill looked up where he expected I'd been looking, and instead of making eye contact with Matthew, he looked directly at Maxie without knowing it. Which was just as well. Maxie's current T-shirt read simply, "What?"

But her style of wearing it might have made Tom's wife, Libby, slightly anxious.

"Do you see this?" Kerin Murphy preached to her invited crowd, who were looking downright confused. "She talks to people who aren't there! Just like Everett did! She's just as crazy as he was!"

And then it all made sense.

I ignored Kerin, since that was what annoyed her most, and looked at Joyce. "That was it. Everett recognized his son. Brenda didn't know Randy was alive, did you, Brenda?"

Brenda's neck tensed, but she shook her head.

"Randy wasn't expecting to run into his father, but he did," I continued. "And Everett started talking about it. Dave was worried that if anyone believed his father, he could be exposed. He knew Everett was spending too much time in the Fuel Pit restroom and that there were security cameras at the door, but not in the back. He was too big, so he sent you, Joyce. With a little knife that could be easily disposed of."

"There's no proof," Joyce reiterated. She couldn't get too close to me. She was small enough that Josh or Tony might have been able to wrestle the gun out of her hand. But it would have been dangerous in such a crowded room.

"There is. Brenda knows her son. And Randy had warrants out on him for distributing narcotics. He knew people who could get fake IDs, so he could appropriate an identity if he needed one. He needed one."

"That's right," McElone told me. "I checked the records on David Boffice. He died when he was four days old. You look a lot older than that, sir," she said to Randy. "You went off a cliff with your Harley, and everybody thought you were dead."

"I *was* dead," Dave said over Joyce's protests to be quiet. "I got revived by a hiker who knew CPR. When I woke up in the hospital as a John Doe, I realized I could get the warrants off my tail if I cleaned up and stopped dealing. I never wanted to be Randy Sandheim anyway. That guy was a loser."

Brenda looked at the floor and bit her lower lip.

"I went into rehab and got clean. I'd seen the headstone for this little baby when I was working at the cemetery, so I got some ID from a guy I knew, took the name and started reading books about finance."

"Will you shut *up*?" Joyce insisted. "They can't *prove* anything."

"It's enough," McElone told her. "Put down the gun and you can avoid any further charges. But I'm warning you, I am the best shot on the police range."

"You don't want to fire your gun in a room full of civilians, *Lieutenant*," Joyce sneered. "You're just going to have to let me leave."

McElone stopped in her tracks. She tried to get an angle, but Joyce was small and standing too close to Phyllis and Marv for a clean shot. Interestingly, Phyllis didn't look up from the notes she was taking but stepped back anyway. Marv looked positively absorbed in the drama, not realizing he was part of it. He stayed put.

The guests looked thrilled.

"Now just back away," Joyce told her. "You don't want anyone to get hurt."

"Oh, Joycie," Matthew Kinsler said. He backed up to the ceiling in sorrow and seemed incapable of any voluntary movement.

McElone didn't answer, but her eyes got angry as she took two steps back away from Randy and Joyce.

"Let's go, David," Joyce said. Apparently she'd signed on for that name and was sticking with it.

Maybe I could slow her down. "Forty-seven times, Joyce. You stabbed Everett forty-seven times. Why so many?"

"It was a small knife," McElone suggested, seeing what I was trying to do. "Maybe he wouldn't have died with only a couple. And Everett wasn't in mental shape to hold off the attack. He went into that men's room before he started bleeding a lot, and she followed him in, just stabbing away with that little penknife. Why didn't you bring your gun or a bigger weapon, Joyce? Because you couldn't get rid of those as easy as the penknife?"

"It's a nice theory, Lieutenant," Joyce said. "I bet you can't prove it."

I saw Paul gesture to Maxie, who moved toward the covered pool table to look for a cue. She moved the drop cloth I was using for a cover without disturbing the candles that were still burning there.

But Joyce was on top of the situation. "I start shooting if anything weird happens," she said, looking directly at me. "I don't want any of your magician tricks." Paul held up a hand and Maxie dropped the cloth.

"They're not tricks," I answered. "The ghosts are real."

"I don't care."

I felt Josh close ranks in front of me, and I nudged him a little. This wasn't going the way I'd planned—well, the way I'd planned to plan—and it was really starting to annoy me.

"Well, I do," I told Joyce. "I've had it with you. You think you can just move anybody out of your way when things don't go perfectly for you? Sorry, but life ain't like that."

Joyce and David were almost at the door as the crowd parted to let them out. After the stress of the past week, I felt outside the scene. I'd forsaken my deceased friends, alienated the best guy I'd met in years, and paid short shrift to my guests in an attempt to bring this woman to justice, and here she was about to escape through my door, the one with the strange writing from Kerin Murphy just past its jamb.

"Why did you hire me?" I demanded. "You killed Everett, and you were going to kill Helen. Why did you want me to follow your boyfriend around?"

Joyce's eyes narrowed. "Because he couldn't be trusted.

Because he was trying to patch things up with his wife. I needed to know where he was, and I couldn't watch him. Once she was dead, I figured you could find enough evidence that I wasn't the one who killed her. Now back off."

"You don't get to walk away," I said.

Joyce let some air out of her mouth in a sound of amusement and disgust. "Yes, I do," she said. "Sometimes people actually do get away with murder." And she turned to leave.

"That's it?" Beth Rosen called out. "The bad guy wins? What kind of mystery theater is this?"

"Yeah," Tom Hill chimed in. "It's not a very satisfying ending. I mean, this woman is way overplaying her role. Nobody's that evil."

Joyce Kinsler's face took on a frightening expression, one that I still see in anxiety dreams to this day. She sneered at Tom and said, "You don't think so?" And she pointed the gun directly at me. "Watch this."

I don't know where it came from. I don't know what motivated me. Some circuit breaker in my head must have blown. But I can tell you that I wasn't the least bit afraid. I wasn't worried about what would happen to me. I felt like the room had slowed down, that there was all the time in the world to do what I needed to do. And I started to walk toward Joyce.

"You don't get to win," I said.

"Alison," Paul warned. "Don't."

Josh tried to grab my arm, but I was on a mission and shook it loose. I must have been moving faster than I was aware of at the time. Tony also sort of dived in my direction, but I was already out of his reach.

All I saw was Joyce and the gun she had pointed at my chest.

"Stop," she said. But she didn't have time to say anything more.

I socked her square on the jaw with a balled-up fist and a week's worth of rage. Before she could pull the trigger on her gun, she had dropped it. McElone ran across the room to pick it up off the floor.

But I wasn't done. I wailed on Joyce for a good half-minute—no, a *great* half-minute—before Josh managed to grab hold of my shoulders and pull me back. "Easy, champ," he said. "Save something for your next bout."

Joyce, on the floor, wasn't unconscious, but I'm willing to bet she wished she was.

The guests broke out in applause.

McElone, taking no chances, cuffed a semi-alert Joyce and a stunned-but-still-uncomprehending Randy, and led them out of the room, muttering something about "this freaky house."

I don't remember much else. The adrenaline rush must have faded because suddenly I was crying and Melissa was hugging me. Paul and Maxie, looking astonished, were hovering over my head. Matthew Kinsler, badly surprised, rose up through the ceiling and out of sight.

Mom knelt next to me—I was in one of the chairs, I think—and asked if I wanted some soup. I think I might have said I did.

Phyllis wrote in her notebook, said something about the story of the year, and began interviewing Cybill.

I looked up for Josh. He was standing next to me, as unobtrusive as ever, but smiling with what appeared to be relief. I held out a hand to him, and he took it and didn't let go.

Kerin Murphy looked at my still-clenched fist, said a quick good-bye and beckoned to her posse. None of them moved. I'd never seen anyone slink out of a room before, but Kerin certainly did do that. (I never got the $3,000, which figured.) The women from her entourage stuck around for a few minutes, then left without a word. It might have had something to do with Maxie swinging the pool cue she took from under the drop cloth over their heads.

Tom and Libby grinned joyously as they left, shaking

my hand, saying what a good show it had been and how much they'd enjoyed their last night at the guesthouse.

That was the moment my father appeared from the basement, looked around at the painted paneled walls and said, "I've got it! A fitness room!"

Thirty-one

It took some time to process all that had happened. McElone took Randy and Joyce back to the police station and sent some uniformed officers to question the remainder of the guests and attendees, especially about the confessions they'd heard. We were up late, although the officers did make a point of questioning Melissa first—she'd been out of the room for much of the drama anyway—so that she could go to bed after completing an art project I had assigned her. More on that later.

Phyllis Coates was considerably more thorough than the cops in her questioning but promised she would follow up with me and Mom before the *Chronicle* came out on Thursday. The guests were leaving the next day, so she had to get all the information she could from them immediately. She talked to anyone the cops weren't questioning.

Matthew Kinsler eventually came back down through the roof, sadly thanked Paul, Maxie and me for our efforts, and left, saying he'd follow Joyce through her coming ordeal. He never directly addressed his daughter's crimes but shook his head a lot while he was talking. I felt awful for him, but there was nothing I could do to help.

By contrast, Brenda Leskanik said she'd check in with the Harbor Haven police in a few days to keep track of her son. She said she didn't think Randy wanted to see her, hadn't much reacted to her presence, and somehow didn't seem like the Randy she knew. She seemed less sad than rocked; she'd thought her son was dead, and then she found out he'd simply decided not to be her son anymore.

I was glad to have Melissa. Of course, I always have been.

Cybill, basking in the glow of her new celebrity, commiserated for a while with her coconspirators, Maxie and Paul, at the swell prank they'd played on me. In light of things, and since Maxie and Paul were already dead, I decided to be a good sport about it. But I did scold them pretty adamantly about their timing. Then Cybill went off to talk to a reporter from News 12 New Jersey, who had just driven up in an unobtrusive blue van with a satellite dish on its roof.

The guests, fully convinced this was the best ghost show they'd seen all week (Libby Hill actually tried to tip me "for the ghosts," with a wink), thanked me roundly for the entertainment, commented on how realistically the actors playing the policemen were questioning them, and eventually went up to their rooms to rest and pack to go home the next day.

Sprayne showed up within minutes of McElone's call to him. We didn't really say anything to each other, he looked Josh up and down, and went about his business. There wasn't much else to do.

McElone finished up her work, looked around the front room, shuddered, and left.

Initially, Mom refused to leave, but we gave up on the soup (I didn't have anything in the house that would make a soup base, but I did have some instant chocolate pudding), and eventually she saw that I was all right. She also saw some of the looks Josh and I were exchanging and said she'd call me in the morning. Dad said he'd hitch a ride with her and be back the next day whether Mom dropped by or not.

I'd considered his fitness-room idea and thought it was good, but I didn't give it the absolute okay until I cleared it with Maxie, who approved. Dad smiled and followed Mom out of the house.

Of course, Paul and Maxie weren't going anywhere. So even when Josh and I were left "alone," we had two ghosts kibitzing over our heads. It was going to make things a little more awkward, and they were already awkward enough.

I led Josh out onto the porch, hoping at least Paul would take the hint and stay in the house, but no such luck. I'd have to play this scene out before an audience.

We admired Melissa's completed art project, which covered the spooky graffiti Kerin had left on the wall to my house, something I fully intended to see McElone about in the morning. If I could press charges against Kerin Murphy, it would be a good start to the day. The least I could do was sue her for $3,000.

The project Melissa had completed was a sign on poster board, in bright green and blue letters (any house with an eleven-year-old has poster board on hand at all times). It boldly read, "HAUNTED GUESTHOUSE."

"I like it," Josh said. "It'll bring in the tourists when word spreads beyond Harbor Haven."

"I have to talk to you," I blurted out. "I've been trying to work up the courage for weeks."

Josh turned and looked at me. I expected his face to be concerned, but it was a touch amused, as if he'd been waiting for this moment. Of course, I knew that this was the same expression he got on his face when he was tense. So I read nothing into it. "Tell me," he urged.

"Here it comes," Maxie said. Thanks a heap, Maxie.

The words came out fast, almost as if they were one long word. "The ghosts are real and their names are Paul and Maxie and they live here in the house and they've become friends of mine," I said in one breath. Before Josh could interject, I went on. "I understand if you think I'm crazy and you don't want to see me anymore, but I don't want to lie to you about it and that's what's true. The ghosts are real."

He took a step back to assess me, but it wasn't the step back I'd anticipated, one that would indicate horror or disgust. In fact, his face didn't change expression at all—there was still that look of slight amusement.

"There, now," Josh said finally. "Was that so hard?"

I must have blinked a couple of times because while I was trying to decide what to say, Josh laughed. "Wow," he said. "You really thought I didn't know?"

"You knew there were ghosts here?" I managed to choke out.

He did a half-grin with the left side of his mouth and shook his head, but in an "oh Alison, you nut" way, not a negative one. "I didn't *know*," he said. "But I knew you believed, and that was good enough for me."

I felt all the tension wash out of me. It was replaced mostly by guilt. "You trusted me, but I didn't trust you enough."

"Oh, you're being too hard on yourself," Josh said. He took a moment to think. "Well, maybe not."

I punched him on the arm. My knuckles hurt from wailing on Joyce.

Josh looked up at Paul, who nodded. "Come on," he said to Maxie. "We need to go inside."

"No, we don't." She saw Paul's look. "Oh, man . . ." And they were gone.

I turned my complete attention to Josh. "Why didn't you say something?" I asked.

"Why didn't you?"

"Because I figured you'd think I was insane."

He looked thoughtful. "Until you told me, I couldn't be sure you trusted me. After your ex-husband and a couple of the other guys you've told me about . . ." His voice trailed off.

Josh was right: I'd built walls because of The Swine and after. "But you're different," I said.

"I needed you to see that."

I turned to face him full-on. "I see it," I said. "What do you see?"

He kissed me. And that was good.

When it ended, I said very quietly, "I'm going to talk to Mom about watching Melissa tomorrow night. I don't have any guests the next day."

Josh's face showed interest. "Really!"

"Yeah. I think it's time I saw your place, don't you?"

He kissed me again. And it was better than good.

"I don't remember much," Everett Sandheim said.

Maxie and I found Everett at the gas pumps of the Fuel Pit. He'd been able to make it out of the men's room, but not much farther yet. Still, he thanked Maxie for the instruction and said he hoped to do better than that soon, "maybe get to the road and start wandering around a little."

After I'd said good-bye to my guests—each of whom had expressed their pleasure in the stay (especially the "murder mystery ghost show" the night before) and promised to report back to Senior Plus Tours about their experience—I'd driven Melissa to Mom's for the day and a sleepover. Maxie had hitched a ride and I hadn't objected, particularly since this stop to see Everett was on the agenda.

McElone reported that Joyce Kinsler had refused to speak after being arrested and had retained an attorney who had advised her against doing so. Randy Sandheim, on the other hand, had been singing like Adele all night long in an effort to get a deal from the county prosecutor.

They were still piecing together the forensics of Helen's death, but it appeared her neck was broken before she was hanged, to make it look like suicide. Either way, forensic experts did not believe Joyce could have managed the feat herself, so Randy—who could easily have at least assisted in the murder before going back to his office and letting me see him "discover the body"—was still a major suspect. McElone told me a deal for Randy would probably not include immunity. And getting Joyce to roll over on Randy was just as possible; she had expressed some interest in letting investigators know all the things *he* had done wrong, McElone told me.

According to the lieutenant, Randy had pretty much sealed Joyce's fate already. "She'll go away for a long time," she guessed.

It was hard to know which one of them finally had the upper hand.

"You don't remember about Joyce Kinsler?" I asked Everett now. We'd given him a very sketchy recap of the past evening's events.

"I really don't have that time clear yet," Everett answered. "I suppose it might have been Joyce who stabbed me. I wasn't in the best shape mentally the past couple of years. I don't know what I'll get back and what I won't." He shook his head in disbelief. "Randy."

"The police said he got out of the accident with his motorcycle, healed and detoxed as a John Doe, then took on the name David Boffice on leaving rehab," I reported.

Maxie, eager to take credit for her online research, added, "He met Helen Boffice after she had the millions, figured he could live well with a wife like that, and married her after about six months," she told Everett. "But Helen was smart. She insisted on a prenup. Randy hung in there, living well but not like a millionaire, until he met Joyce Kinsler. It looks like she'd come from a series of bad relationships, and she'd decided that anything she needed to do for four million dollars, she'd do."

Everett took what for a living person would be a deep breath. He didn't let it out, because there was no air involved in the process. "I don't know," he said. "I let that boy down at the worst time, I guess. What happened afterward is partly my fault."

"You had an illness," Maxie said, with more compassion than I would have expected. "You can't blame yourself for that."

"He was my son," Everett said soberly. "I should have done more."

"I'm sorry I didn't do more for you when I could have," I told him sincerely.

"Don't let it worry you, Ghost Lady," Everett said, then caught himself. "I'm sorry. Alison."

I waved a hand. "Ghost Lady is fine," I told him.

I had one more stop to make.

Maxie stayed in the car when I drove around the back of the Fuel Pit and parked near the dune where the homeless had set up their community. The beach was probably closer to the street now than before the storm, but they were sheltered from the main road by a row of trees and some garbage cans.

It took a few minutes to locate Cathy Genna, who emerged from the trees as if from a fog, a little at a time. I was struck again by how ethereal she was, how she almost floated off the ground. She was a calm soul, I supposed; there was no hurry or tension in her movement or her voice.

"You came back," she said. It was a statement of fact, nothing else.

"I promised I would when I found out what happened to Everett," I reminded her.

"And you have found out." Again, not a question.

But I answered as if it were. "Yes. Do you want to know the whole story?"

Cathy smiled sadly. "No," she said. "The circumstances don't really matter. Do you know if Everett is at peace?"

I wanted to tell her that Everett was less than three hundred yards away, but there would be no point in confusing the issue. "I don't know about peace," I said. "But he appears to have cleared his mind, and he accepts what happened to him."

Cathy picked up a beer bottle from the sand. "It's a shame what people do to the beach, don't you think? Even with all they're doing to fix it again." She examined the bottle. "You can't even get a deposit back for this one." She moved to the nearest trash can, almost full, and dropped the bottle inside. "Too bad they don't have a recycling bin here." She turned again to look at me. "What about you? Are you satisfied with what you found out?"

I hadn't considered that. "I don't know," I told her. "Everett's still dead. Does it matter if we found out how it happened?"

Cathy smiled. "You're learning," she said.

"We never did find out about the other ghost," I told her. "Everett said he heard Randy and another ghost. A woman. I wonder who that was."

Cathy nodded. "Me, too," she said.

And vanished.